MEASURING UP

WRITTEN AND ILLUSTRATED BY
JANET M. DANN

DANNWORKS

Friday Harbor, WA

Measuring Up

Published by DannWorks
Friday Harbor, WA

First Edition

Illustrations by Janet. M. Dann

Cover photo ID62595978 © Rachel Hopper
www.dreamstime.com

Cover design & interior layout by W. Bruce Conway

ISBN: 978-1-7334951-2-7

Library of Congress information will be provided by publisher upon request.

Printed in the United States of America by KDP, an Amazon company

Dedication

This book is dedicated to Marie Skuffeeda, my friend and consultant regarding all things horse related. Marie is a nationally recognized equestrienne, and knows horsemanship from ranching to fox hunting. She is the inspiration for the character, Flora Doyle. I have been very fortunate to have her input both technically, and in hearing her talk in a personal way about the human-horse relationship which is as natural as that between human and dog.

Acknowledgements

My husband, Tsolo, graciously didn't complain about my attention being focused on my laptop and Wyoming, or my distant look which signaled I wasn't exactly present. His support is essential, and I thank him for it.

My go-to person for all things horse, ranch, rodeo and the 1930s was Marie Skuffeeda, friend and equestrienne, also with some personal knowledge of the *Dirty 30s*.

Marie and I have lunch together weekly, and she never seemed to tire of me greeting her with questions such as, "Say, Marie, where would a cowboy carry a flask?" or "How would a con artist cheat in a horse race, and what could you do about it? Tell me about Quarter Horses; How does a horse show anger?" and on and on. Marie's knowledge, and love of horses infuses this book. I am ever thankful and may have just a few more questions...

Lynn Carlson provided me with a list of possible names for Wyoming cowboys of the 30s. He was another source of rodeo information, his background being from Utah.

Betty Moyer comes from a family of Montana ranchers, and also offered information and stories of how it was.

Cameron Weaver is another friend who was generous with name suggestions, and other helpful input. He has read the first three books in the series, and been very encouraging about the fourth.

Mark Hopkins was generous with suggestions and observations.

Andrea Rose eagerly read the manuscript, and is one of my sources about all things Jewish involving the Epstein family characters. I'm very appreciative of her encouragement, and assistance.

My sister-in-law, Huda Shaver, kindly read the manuscript, and offered valuable insights in fleshing out parts to give more background from the previous books, for those who have not read them. She was also very supportive.

Billie Hobbs edited this volume, and did a dandy job. I thank her for her knowledge and efficiency.

I also thank W. Bruce Conway for his expertise, in self-print books, and support and encouragement.

Description of Characters

THE DACIAS – JOSIF and IZABELLA – Parents of MARIE, age fifteen, married to AUGUST WAGNER, twenty-one. Their other children are: ROSE ,thirteen; CAROLINE, eleven; and MICHAEL-JOSEPH, eight. UNCLE JON is JOSIF'S father's brother and AUNT MAGDA is JON'S wife. THE DACIAS immigrated to South Dakota in 1929 from a share-cropped home in Oklaho-ma, as described in Fate be Damned.

THE WAGNERS – Neighbors of the DACIAS. MRS. GER-TRUDE WAGNER, was recently wid-owed. Her husband, GERHARD, died over the winter. FRITZ, twenty-four and AUGUST, twenty-one were orphaned in 1918 when their parents died of the Spanish Flu Epidemic. GERHARD, and GER-TRUDE, also known as GRANDMA and GRANDPA WAG-NER raised them.

THE EPSTEINS – New Yorkers DAVID, and REBECCA, parents of DEBORAH, 9 and DANIEL, 8. MRS. IDA EPSTEIN, DAVID'S mother, and friend of Irina who helped with her rescue from the Iron Guard in Long Dance Home, set in 1932. The Epstein children spent the summer of 1933 with the DACIAS while their parents were away. During this time, MICHAEL-JOSEPH DACIA, and DANIEL EPSTEIN were kidnapped by Chicago gangsters. This, and other attempts by the gangsters to exact vengeance are described in Debts and Vengeance.

THE ARIOSTOS: – Neighbors of the DACIAS and WAG-NERS, ARNOLD and GINA were mar-ried in Debts and Ven-geance. GINA used to be part of the Italian mob, but fell in love with ARNOLD, and helped capture the gangsters. EVA-LINA is GINA'S mother from Italy, who speaks no English.

MR. BOWMAN – Another neighbor of good repute who was chosen by AUGUST to judge the race.

THE DOYLES – FINLEY, father of FLORA twenty-two, FRED twenty-one, and FRANK twenty. FLORA is getting married to FRITZ on the Fourth of July after the rodeo. FLORA was first introduced in *Debts and Vengeance*. The DOYLES live in Wyoming in the Black Hills.

THE DELANEYS – FLOYD and TRIXIE are back-up vocal artists preying on AUGUST WAGNER.

CHANCE CONROY, LEFTY WILLIS, and TREY WILLETTE – con artists working with FLOYD DELANEY.

SLIM STANTON – foreman of the DOYLE'S Lucky D Ranch.

HANK and PETE – ranch hands.

WADE WILCOX – Cowboy FLORA dated once.

LOUISE LA VOI – Leather-worker with her family, and friend of FLORA.

MOOSE JOHNSON – A cowboy the same size as FRITZ.

TIM and TOM OLSON – Cousins who become friends with MICHAEL-JOSEPH, and DANIEL. Their fathers run the Double O Ranch.

VELMA – Local telephone operator.

CCC – THE CIVILIAN CONSERVATION CORPS, begun by FDR in 1933, was one of the earliest of the New Deal programs. It was a voluntary public work relief program that operated from 1932 to 1942 for unmarried, unemployed men between ages 18 and 25. A portion of their pay was automatically sent home to their families. The CCC fought fires, and reforested, as well as built many rustic visitor centers at national parks, and monuments. They also worked at flood prevention. They lived in camps and had strict rules of behavior, and hygiene.

ONE DOLLAR BILL – A one dollar bill in 1934 is equal in value to eighteen dollars and seventy-four cents in 2018.

Table of Contents

Synopsis of Fate Be Damned

Fate be damned was the attitude Romanian immigrant, JOSIF DACIA, took when he left Romania with his wife, IZABELLA, two children, ALEXANDER and MARIE, and his AUNT MAGDA and UNCLE JON for a life of hope and opportunity in America. In Romania, many believe that one's fate is determined and cannot be changed. Others take the future in their own hands, and fight to determine their own fate, strong and fixed on the American dream, who will let nothing stop them. JOSIF DACIA is one of those.

From Ellis Island, the DACIA family migrated west until becoming sharecroppers in Oklahoma. When their farm blew away in the *Dust Bowl*, the DACIAS drove north with their team of beloved plow horses, PETER and PAUL, looking for a farm to rent or even buy in South Dakota. Along the way JOSIF resists all offers of help, which he deems charity, and angrily pushes north.

In the town of Centerford in southeastern South Dakota, the DACIAS find a farm, and because of their driving passion to own land, sign a mortgage for a one-hundred-sixty-acre farm with a total price of $3,200, and monthly payments of one hundred twenty-eight dollars, plus any principle they could afford. Josif sets a personal goal of two hundred dollars per month, hoping to pay for the land in his lifetime to hand down to his eldest son, twelve-year-old ALEXANDER.

In farm country your neighbors are part of your life;

you can try to ignore them, but they share boundaries with you, as well as the weather. Like a spider's web, one strand cannot be disturbed without impacting all the others. Most of the neighbors of the DACIAS were hardworking farmers trying to make a living against the increasing odds of drought and a struggling economy. Then there was the neighbor who was looking for big, easy, money through bootlegging disguised as farming.

The WAGNERS were the honest farmers. GRAND-PA and GRANDMA WAGNER were raising their grand-sons, sixteen-year-old AUGUST and twenty-year-old FRITZ – solid, raucous boys who loved to fight anyone and play pitch with the neighbors.

The LAMBS were the family with an uncle and brother from Chicago who were associated with the mob – CLARENCE, aka C.D., and VINCE. The Centerford farm was owned by VERNE LAMB and his wife, BELLE. VERNE and his son, JULIUS, are bigoted and furious that the DACIAS are renting neighboring land that once be-longed to BELLE's family but had to be sold for back taxes.

C.D. has arranged for a huge still to be brought to VERNE'S farm. He destroys VERNE'S current small still and takes over the farm. VERNE and VINCE are broth-ers, but there is no love lost between them. VERNE is furious with VINCE and C.D. but has no choice except to go along. BELLE is dying of cancer, JULIUS is still in school, and VERNE needs a supplemental income besides farming.

ALEXANDER and JULIUS attend the local one-room schoolhouse together. There, JULIUS torments AL-EXANDER and ends up knocking him down and kicking him in the ribs until he becomes unconscious. ALEXAN-DER has broken ribs and is taken to the hospital in Sioux Falls when he develops pneumonia.

C.D. appears to be a fumbling, mild-mannered old man, but he is a conniving and evil person who soon becomes known to the DACIAS as a *strigoi*, a vampire-like creature in intent. A *strigoi* sucks the life and vitality from living things, not by sucking blood, but by evil acts and lies. After death, they can become literal bloodsuckers. Garlic and crucifixes are the trusted *strigoi* deterrents.

C.D. kills two gangsters who accompanied the still to the LAMB farm, and has VINCE and VERNE bury them in the silage pit behind the barn. Unseen by the others, C.D. also hides a lock-box of money and jewels in the pit. This is loot which he stole from incarcerated Chicago mob boss, PRIMO MORETTI, before leaving Chicago.

C.D. also kills the local sheriff, framing the DACIAS, and plots to have the DACIAS burned out. The DACIA men are arrested, ALEXANDER dies in the hospital, and VERNE and C.D. kill each other back on the LAMB farm. VINCE and JULIUS, who are drunk and have been sent out to do more violence, set up their own death when a can of gasoline in the back seat tips over, and they cause an explosion when they light their cigarettes.

When the truth is discovered about who killed the sheriff, the DACIAS are released. The WAGNERS and other neighbors who have come to the aid of the DACIAS participate in ALEXANDER'S funeral. After the forty-day mourning period, a feast is held by the DACIAS for the neighbors, and people of many ethnicities attend. It is during this time of community support and comfort that the DACIAS realize they belong, and indeed have become Americans.

Synopsis of Long Dance Home

In the spring of 1932, the DACIAS receive a letter from their niece, IRINA, the last of their family still in Romania. The letter states that she is marked for death by members of the Iron Guard and must defect from Romania when her dance troupe – she is the lead female dancer – tours the U.S. in August. She hopes that her family will be able to meet her in New York when the troupe performs at Carnegie Hall, but if not, she will attempt by herself to make her way to Centerford, South Dakota where the DACIAS have a farm..

Getting to Carnegie Hall becomes a challenge for both IRINA'S aunt and uncle, IZABELLA and JOSIF DACIA, as well as herself, as the Iron Guard tries to kill her before the tour leaves. IRINA flees through the Transylvanian Alps, pursued by DEBEN, fellow dancer and devotee of the principles of the Iron Guard. IRINA is captured but seen by other dancers before DEBEN can kill her, thus ensuring that she lives to go on the tour.

On board *The Atlantia*, IRINA is befriended by IDA EPSTEIN, a New York philanthropist who recognizes IRINA'S situation and takes steps to help. MRS. EPSTEIN'S son, DAVID, is a journalist for *The New York Times*, and MRS. EPSTEIN has the ship's photographer take many photos of IRINA for publication in the *Times*, so that her face becomes as well known to New Yorkers as the Statue of Liberty, and she would have many friends when the troupe performs and she defects.

JOSIF and his family vainly try to raise enough money to buy a car to drive to New York and are about to give up when their neighbors, brothers FRITZ and AUGUST WAGNER, come up with a solution. They buy a Hudson Super Six without an engine and take the DACIAS to the local gravel pit where their cousin once jumped out of a similar car before it plunged to the bottom of the pit in a race. FRITZ, JOSIF, and seven-year-old MICHAEL-JO-SEPH DACIA lower themselves into the pit and remove the still-intact engine from the wreck, later transferring it to the engineless Hudson the WAGNERS had bought for ten dollars.

Getting a car, however, was only half of the problem for the DACIAS. A cross-country trip would require money that the DACIAS need to survive the year and pay the mortgage. As much as he wanted to help his niece, JOSIF would never risk losing his land. The family desperately searched for options.

At this point Italian and Greek gangsters, who had been playing cat and mouse with each other, have a positive impact on the DACIAS and their neighbors. The Italian mob, represented by PRIMO MORETTI, and the Greek mob, led by ZEKE VOLAKIS, have an encounter at the neighboring farm now owned by ARNOLD ARIOSTO, brother of BELLE LAMB, who died in 1929 of cancer. BELLE's husband, VERNE, and his family: UNCLE CLARENCE, aka C.D. Lamb; brother, VINCE; and son, JULIUS, all died in *Fate Be Damned* while trying to harm the DACIAS.

In *Fate Be Damned*, mob-connected C.D. hides money and jewels stolen from PRIMO MORETTI while he was in jail, as well as buries PRIMO MORETTI'S brother in the silage pit behind the barn on the then LAMB farm. The Greeks heard about the money and jewels, and now both gangs are looking for the treasure on the now ARIOSTO farm.

By a series of coincidences, the sheriff and his deputy, as well as JOSIF DACIA and his UNCLE JON, GRANDPA, FRITZ and AUGUST WAGNER, and ARNOLD

ARIOSTO are all at the ARIOSTO farm when the rival Greeks and Italians are there, and are forced to hide deep in the ARIOSTO barn together. When this fiery situation erupts out of the barn and into the open, a huge fight begins which results in the capture and incarceration of both gangs.

Italian gun moll, GINA CAMPANELLA, and ARNOLD ARIOSTO are immediately attracted to each other, and ARNOLD helps GINA flee the barn before the shooting begins. In the farmhouse, GINA calls the police, resulting in her getting off lightly.

GINA and ARNOLD become engaged.

In the nick of time for IRINA, the sheriff shows up at the DACIA farm with reward money for capture of the gangsters and the return of stolen property; enough to make the trip to New York and help with home expenses.

JOSIF and IZABELLA decide to be the ones to go after IRINA, leaving the farm and children in the care of UNCLE JON and AUNT MAGDA. However, they soon realize that they need someone to help with reading maps in English, street signs, etc., as well as with fighting in case of an encounter with Iron Guard thugs. The person chosen is neighbor, nineteen-year-old AUGUST WAGNER, well-known for his size, strength, and love of fighting.

While on the drive to New York, AUGUST composes a song on his new guitar about the fight with the gangsters. He names it *The Dakota Six* for the six local farmers who bested the gangsters, thus earning the gangsters' everlasting hatred.

The DACIAS and AUGUST make it to New York and rescue IRINA with the help of the EPSTEINS. All go to the EPSTEIN'S brownstone where they meet DAVID'S wife, REBECCA, and their two children, seven-year-old DANIEL and eight-year-old DEBORAH.

While with the EPSTEINS, IRINA requests asylum, and AUGUST records an album featuring *The Dakota Six*, which is an instant hit with New Yorkers who have taken both IRINA and AUGUST into their hearts. The DA-CIAS spend some of their reward money on books and a radio, JOSIF now feeling pride and a sense of accomplishment in achieving the American dream.

MRS. EPSTEIN invites her friend, IRINA, to stay with her in New York to look for work as a dancer, but IRI-NA decides to first live with her family in South Dakota.

The group returns to their farms, and the DACIAS discover that FRITZ and other neighbors have enlarged the DACIA'S house to make room for IRINA.

There is a huge neighborhood picnic at the DACIAS the next night, and AUGUST sings a new composition about IRINA'S flight, ending in: *her heart is here now, IRI-NA'S found home.*

Synopsis of Debts and Vengeance

Although adopting many American attitudes, JOSIF DACIA still labors under feelings of obligation to the EP-STEINS who were instrumental in rescuing their niece, IRINA, from the Iron Guard the year before in 1932. DA-VID EPSTEIN, journalist for *The New York Times*, also sent the DACIAS a lifetime subscription to the Sunday edition of the *Times*, providing a wonderful educational tool for the whole family.

Thus, JOSIF is more than happy to welcome the care of the two Epstein children, nine-year-old DEBORAH and eight-year-old DANIEL, for the summer while the adult EPSTEINS go to Germany to try to get REBECCA'S parents to leave and move back to New York with them before Hitler gains any more power.

MRS. EPSTEIN travels with the two children to Sioux Falls, South Dakota by train, where they are met by JOSIF and IRINA and taken to the farm in Centerford. There, DANIEL EPSTEIN and MICHAEL-JOSEPH DACIA realize that they are one day apart in age, very close in size and intelligence, and both play the clarinet, although one is outgoing and the other reserved. They are not at all convinced that they'll be friends.

ROSE DACIA, eleven, and CAROLINE DACIA, nine, immediately take DEBORAH EPSTEIN under their wings and orient her to farm life, including the privy and flour sack dresses, common farm attire during *the Depression*. DEBORAH sees her coming summer with petulant resignation.

DANIEL and MICHAEL-JOSEPH play clarinets to-gether and are taught to smoke by AUGUST WAGNER out behind the WAGNER barn after dinner. New experi-ences for the EPSTEIN children are having to share a bed and the terror of a prairie thunderstorm exploding with blinding light and pounding over the house at night.

The good things DEBORAH discovers are the giant and gentle plow horses, PETER and PAUL, especially Paul, and soon the love and support of the entire DACIA family.

While the DACIA and EPSTEIN children are getting to know each other, PRIMO MORETTI and ZEKE VOLAKIS are in Leavenworth Penitentiary seething in rage over the playing of AUGUST WAGNER'S song, The Dakota Six, which has recently been on the radio. The song, which has gangsters being beaten by farmers, prompts listeners to make pig calls, even in the pen.

PRIMO and ZEKE want vengeance on everyone mentioned in the song, but most especially on AUGUST WAGNER. They divide up their plans for vengeance between their two gangs on the outside.

AUGUST is kidnapped and taken to the Greek stronghold where he will be forced to write and sing a new song in which the gangsters are the heroes and the Dakota Six die. The song will be recorded, and radio stations *encouraged* to play it.

After AUGUST has disappeared, MICHAEL-JOSEPH talks DANIEL into running away late one night to Sioux Falls where they will hop a train to California, find AUGUST, drink some orange juice, and come right back with him.

MICHAEL-JOSEPH'S plan is foiled, however, by two Italian mobsters who've been assigned the destruction of the DACIA family by kidnapping their only son. The unexpected inclusion of DANIEL in the kidnapping makes the boys very valuable and promises elevated status in the family for their captors.

MICHAEL-JOSEPH and DANIEL are taken to a secluded shack where they are tied to their chairs. A ransom note is put in the DACIA mailbox. The two boys torment the mobsters with things only eight-year-old boys would think of, including smoking a cigarette after a large meal of hard boiled eggs, baloney, canned corn, and orange crush, resulting in MICHAEL-JOSEPH upchucking on a drunk mobster. The only option, if he wanted ransom money, was for the mobster to not kill the boys, although he could keep on drinking, hopefully to the point of passing out.

Screeching clarinets alerted Peter and Paul to the boys' whereabouts; the wagon they pulled contained the DACIA girls, DEBORAH and IRINA. Both MARIE and IRINA were armed. In an act of courage, DEBORAH ran from hiding, pounded on the shack door, and demanded that the door be opened. When the drunk gangster emerged, he was captured, as was the drunk gangster who returned from Centerford after being pumped for information by GINA, who plied him with more whiskey.

AUGUST and the boys were saved. The boys had been rescued by girls. PRIMO and ZEKE were humiliated and furious. They were beginning to be seen as vulnerable; and in Leavenworth Penitentiary, that can be as good as dead.

PRIMO calls the Capo di Tutti Capi, LUCKY de-LUCA, in Chicago who agrees to arrange and carry out PRIMO'S vengeance for the reputation of the mob. Arrangements are made to have AUGUST, IRINA, and any DACIAS who would like to come, go on a two-week road show through South Dakota, Wyoming, Montana, and North Dakota before returning to Sioux Falls. The pay will be generous, impossible to refuse in such hard times.

AUGUST, fourteen-year-old MARIE DACIA, UN-CLE JON and AUNT MAGDA, as well as IRINA all are to go on the tour. AUGUST and MARIE have been showing interest in each other, and this trip is also seen as a chaperoned opportunity for them to see if they like each other well enough to marry. AUGUST will sing, and the DACIAS and IRINA will dance to and play Romanian music. IRINA and AUGUST both have name recognition from the events described in *Long Dance Home* and attract good crowds.

The vengeful part of the road show tour will be that AUGUST will be involved in numerous bare-knuckle boxing matches along the way. These matches will be against professionals who will take a toll on AUGUST, then a dive after two rounds, until in Fargo where AUGUST meets up with giant VESUVIO DEMONADO who will go longer than two rounds then pummel AUGUST to death by blocking him in a corner with his huge mass.

The women will be taken to Chicago and sold into prostitution. The other WAGNERS will be shot, and the DACIAS and ARIOSTOS burned-out on ARNOLD'S and GINA'S wedding night.

Happily, AUGUST, who has been training under the guidance of other road show performers, is able to prevail over VESUVIO, and all escape. LUCKY de LUCA washes his hands of PRIMO, and both PRIMO and ZEKE are killed in prison. With the death of PRIMO, all contracts are called off.

Side plots of the HENRY REEVES Road Show include the purchase of two Appaloosa horses by AUGUST with the assistance of FLORA DOYLE, who with her family from Wyoming, both ranch and race horses at local fairs. AUGUST bought the first horse, SKY, for MARIE to ride to school, and BILL for himself. When AUGUST tries to give MARIE the horse, JOSIF punches him in the face, telling him that such an expensive gift is only given in marriage arrangements. After a private talk with MA-

RIE, AUGUST proposes. MARIE accepts, and a wedding is planned for shortly after MARIE turns fifteen in the spring.

The DOYLES truck the horses to the South Dakota farm and spend a few days there. During this time, FRITZ and FLORA become attracted to each other and promise to write.

During the summer MICHAEL-JOSEPH and DAN-IEL have become fast friends and taken nicknames. DAN-IEL is Captain Nemo, and MICHAEL-JOSEPH is Tarzan. Parting is difficult for all the children, but the EPSTEIN children vow to persuade their parents to let them return, maybe even come with them. They promise to write letters to each other every week.

When MRS. EPSTEIN returns to the DACIAS, IRI-NA decides to return to New York with her, now ready to look for work and more training as a dancer.

The book ends with letters to and from JOSIF and DAVID about the kidnapping, with DAVID absolving the DACIAS of all blame. The children's letters discuss the readiness of their parents to travel west to the farm, and IRINA'S letter to her family back in South Dakota sums up the story by quoting MRS. EPSTEIN: *Where there is understanding, there is love, and with love, there are neither debts nor vengeance.*

DEVILS TOWER, WYO.

* * *

CHAPTER ONE
The Letters

On Saturday, June 23, 1934, Mrs. Epstein returned to South Dakota by train. Fritz Wagner picked her up at the Sioux Falls Depot and drove her to the Wagner farm where she had stayed the year before while accompanying the Epstein children to and from New York City and the Dacia farm.

This year, she carried four letters with her from her son and grandchildren, which she delivered to their recipients. The first was from her son, David Epstein, to Josif Dacia.

Dear Josif,

I hope this letter finds you well and set for company. We leave tomorrow, Friday, ready or not. The level of excitement around here is tremendous. Deborah and Daniel have been packed for weeks. Rebecca and I are also quite excited to see you both again, as well as your farm and South Dakota. The trip to Wyoming for Fritz's wedding will be icing on the cake!

Just a reminder that the Times is covering the cost of the trip for all of us. I'll be taking a lot of photos and writing articles along the way. This is a great opportunity for the paper, and it couldn't happen without you and Fritz.

The paper has thought of everything, sending us with three tents, sleeping bags, and cooking gear for all ten of us. We sent Mother on the train yesterday with the cooking gear, tents, and most of the sleeping bags.

Since you are reading this, she's already there, and Fritz has picked her up. She's looking forward to a relaxing time on the farm with Mrs. Wagner and your Aunt Magda while everyone's away. Personally, I'm looking forward to spending some time in the country fishing, swimming, smelling the clean air...

Just between you and me, I've been practicing roping, using a western lariat. Will Rogers is a frequent visitor at the Times, and we've become quite friendly. When he heard that we'd be going to Wyoming, he gave me some advice. He said I should learn how to ride if I had any expectation of getting out alive. He also suggested that I learn how to rope in a hurry. So, I've taken riding lessons in Central Park, and have been going up to the roof to practice roping. I've gotten quite good and have even mastered a few tricks Will showed me.

I haven't made a fuss about this in front of Rebecca, as she's a bit nervous about going into such rough territory. I've been assuring her that we will be going through some of America's most beautiful country. That we'll be educating both our children and ourselves. She'll do almost anything to that end. She's also determined to be with them for this adventure to keep them safe. So, with varying expectations, here we come.

We plan to arrive in four to five days and will call when we get close. Looking forward to this vacation with you and the Wagners.

See you soon,
David Epstein

* * *

The second letter was from her granddaughter, nine-year-old Deborah, to the Dacia girls, Rose and Caroline.

Dear Rose and Caroline,

I'm so excited! We're leaving tomorrow. I've been packed for a while, although Mama keeps taking me shopping at Wanamaker's. We now both have very pretty Western outfits, with hats and boots and scarves. My suitcase is full. So is Mama's. I think our clothes won't really fit in, but I don't want to upset her. I think she feels that if she looks nice, she won't have to do dirty things. If you have room in your suitcases would you stick in some of your old clothes for me? I want to do some dirty things like riding horses and whatever else they do on a ranch.

I guess I can't ask you any questions to answer. I wish it was time for bed already, although I may not sleep. I'll go find something to do until then.
I'll see you all soon!
    Bye,
    Deborah

* * *

The third letter was from Daniel to Michael-Joseph Dacia.

"*Ahoy Tarzan,*

Tomorrow's the day! We plan to leave by 7:00AM and have breakfast in New Jersey. This will be such fun. I'm glad we got our parents to agree to this trip. And we get to go to Wyoming. That's the Wild West! I wonder if we'll get to wear holsters and carry pistols? Will we get our own horse to ride? Will there be buffalo and Indians?

Do you think anyone else will play a clarinet? You're still bringing yours, right? I'm bringing mine.

Good and bad news here. Mama went shopping for Western clothing for us to wear. I already feel embarrassed, and we're not even there yet. Almost everything she got for us has sequins and fringe; I have a lot of embroidered bucking horses on mine, and Papa's have buffalo, stars, or someone riding a bull. My cowboy boots are red. Papa's are gold. Almost everything Mama and Deborah have matches. A lot of it is pink, or silver. Everything is very colorful.

Would you bring some of your clothes for me to wear? I think we might stand out if we wear what Mama bought.

Maybe your father could bring some extra work clothes too. I really don't think Mama understands what's involved in running a farm, or I'm pretty sure, a ranch. She's being very brave though and talking about how pretty it will be in the country.

So, the only hurdle left for the Epstein Wild West Expedition is packing the car. The Times is sending us with three tents, ten sleeping bags, and a huge camping cook-set. There was no way to do it until Grandma decided to skip the drive out there and take the train. We were able to send the cook-set and a bunch of sleeping bags with her. Now we have a space as big as Grandma we can fill with our stuff. It's still going to be tight. Papa is bringing a camera from the paper but has decided to write articles by hand instead of bringing a typewriter.

We, of course, all have our Brownies. I'm going to have more photos with this year's report about how we spent our summer vacations. I know mine will be the best again this year.

Papa says we won't camp out until we meet up with you and Fritz. We'll be staying in hotels along the way. Mama's happy about that.

Well, Tarzan, I guess I should sign off now. Early to bed for our big trip tomorrow.

Oh, I forgot to tell you. Papa's got a rope and is practicing with it on the roof. He doesn't know I saw him. Do you know how to lasso? Maybe we can learn when we get to Wyoming.

Signing off,
Captain Nemo

* * *

The last letter was from Irina to her Romanian family in South Dakota.

Hello Uncle Josif, Aunt Izabella, and the whole family,

Everyone is very excited about the trip, and I know you'll all have lot of fun together. I wish I was to come along, but I now have new job and no time off.

I've been promoted at the dance school I was both teaching and studying at. I'm now one of the lead ballerinas and we're all preparing for big performance in fall. I'm so happy with all the training I've gotten, and my new opportunities. As you know, I'm still staying with the Epsteins, so Rebeca's parents and I will hold the fort down while everyone's away. (How do you like the new saying I learned?)

Give my regards to all the Wagners, and my love to all of you, Irina.

CHAPTER TWO
South Dakota Preparations

The drive from Manhattan to Centerford, South Dakota took four days. The Epsteins hadn't ventured far from New York before, and everything was new. They noted the change in countryside from densely wooded hills with streams, ponds, and rivers to gradually flattening land, much of it being farmed, with many of the crops dried and withered in the fields. It was hot and dry, and there was little relief from the sun in the cloudless sky.

The Epsteins' satin clothing was stuck to their skin, and even with the windows down, the breeze didn't penetrate the thick fabric. Those by a window tried to position their arms to allow the air to flow up their sleeves. Rebecca's thick black hair stuck to her neck, and her heavy waves barely stirred in the breeze.

Their flashy Wanamaker western outfits were seeming more out of place the farther west they went from Manhattan, but Rebecca still felt that it was always better to be over- rather than underdressed. To her it was a sign of respect to dress nicely while traveling or visiting. She didn't see any disparity between their clothing and that of the locals. In her mind it was all western clothing; hers was just of a higher quality.

The Epstein's Model 18 Ford turned into the Dacia's driveway mid-afternoon on Monday, the 25th. It had barely stopped before the back doors sprung open, and Daniel and Deborah ran to greet their friends. David got out and opened the door for Rebecca.

The Dacias stared in awe. Rebecca was wearing a pink cowgirl shirt with white fringe and pink rhinestone stars. She wore loose-legged, pale blue, flowing pants, reminiscent of Katherine Hepburn. Her low boots had a cowboy motif and she wore a blue scarf tied jauntily at her neck. Her dark hair highlighted her high cheekbones and dark brown eyes. Her look was friendly, although a bit reserved. A pink cowgirl hat stayed on the seat.

David was of medium build with a broad face like his mother's, friendly inquisitive eyes, and brown wavy hair. He was sporting a gold shirt with green fringe and sequined embroidered bull riders. He was wearing pressed blue jeans and gold boots. His gold cowboy hat also stayed on the seat.

The children were wearing clothes matching their parents. Their looks also matched. Daniel had dark wavy hair like his mother's, and Deborah's matched her father's brown, but cut in a cute bob.

Izabella moved into action to prevent any awkwardness. "Rebecca and David, it's so good to see you both again!" She looked at the children running toward the pasture where the horses were grazing. "I guess we'll see Daniel and Deborah when they get back from the horses."

"Pardon their manners," David said, shaking hands with Josif. "They've been so excited about coming back, they can hardly contain themselves."

Josif introduced the Epsteins to Uncle Jon and Aunt Magda, the equivalent of grandparents to the Dacia children. Uncle Jon was Josif's father's younger brother and Magda was Uncle Jon's wife. Jon was wiry, as was Josif; both men wore thick mustaches.

Magda had become stout in her fifties, but still was striking in looks. She kept her greying brown hair under a flowered kerchief, and saw her role as protector of the family, especially the children.

Jon wore a cap over thinning grey hair and looked at the world with eyes always on the verge of smiling. He would do whatever it took to keep the family going and was always there for Josif in his demanding role as patriarch.

Josif's eyes were sharp and alert. He felt responsibility for everything that occurred to his family and farm. He was always vigilant and insistent on social propriety.

"We are glad to meet parents of Daniel and Deborah," Uncle Jon said. "Are wonderful children."

Aunt Magda agreed. "Were brave and helpful when were here; you must be very proud of them."

"Yes," Rebecca said. "They've become so confident and willing to try new things. I'm afraid they've exceeded me in courage. I've only known city life; all this is very new to me. I'm not sure what to expect in Wyoming. It's even farther west than here."

Izabella put her arm around Rebecca's waist. "You will get used to things too. It is rougher out here, but also very pretty. You and I will meet Wyoming together; everything will be fine."

Although having had five children, Izabella still had a good figure. She wasn't slim anymore, but her maturity gave her the look of her much-deserved stability and competence.

Josif and Izabella were similar in size to the Epsteins, although about six years older. Both couples had a son born in 1925; both could easily trace their immigrant roots. When the Dacias had come to New York in 1932 to rescue Irina and stayed with the Epsteins, they had become friends.

The following year, both families had their only sons

kidnapped by Chicago gangsters. Josif and David had spoken on the phone and through letters about the ordeal. Josif would always feel responsible no matter how much David tried to convince him that it was the gangsters who had failed his family, not him or Michael-Joseph.

Rebecca had been devastated by the kidnapping in spite of reassurances via a *New York Times* article and the realization that she had spoken to her children on the phone before leaving on their emergency trip, and that had been after they'd been rescued. The children had sounded relaxed and happy, and since they didn't tell them about the kidnapping, not afraid and in need of their presence.

This experience had not only bonded the relationship between the Dacia and Epstein children, it also bonded the relationship between the adults of the two families.

The group ambled toward the pasture, and Josif pointed out the different buildings. "I recognize them all," David said. "I've studied the photos the kids brought back so many times."

Rebecca and David noticed the new smells. Prominent was the smell of horse, both animals, and of their droppings. There were also pungent smells identifying pigs, cows, and chickens. Flies were everywhere. The ground was rough and dusty except in spots where animals had passed, and these were best avoided.

"And there are the horses that my children love," Rebecca said, watching Deborah hugging Paul's strong neck while he nuzzled her hair. She tried to stay focused on the heartwarming scene rather than the smells.

"Come here, Mama," Deborah called to Rebecca. "Come meet Paul."

As the adults approached, Deborah and Daniel finally remembered their manners, running to greet Josif, Izabella, Uncle Jon, and Aunt Magda. Josif and Uncle Jon shook hands with Daniel and kissed Deborah on the forehead. Izabella and Aunt Magda hugged both.

"We're so glad to be back," Deborah said.

"Yeah," Daniel added. "Thanks for letting us come and stay again. We're happy Mama and Papa are here to see and do everything we did."

"Well, maybe not everything, Captain Nemo," Michael-Joseph said.

"No," Daniel agreed. "Certainly not everything."

Michael-Joseph and Daniel were almost identical in size. Daniel's hair was a little darker and wavier, Michael-Joseph's eyes a little more wandering in search of adventure. Both blood brothers and friends for life since being kidnapped together the year before by the mob from Chicago's South Side.

Josif patted Daniel on the shoulder and turned to David and Rebecca. "Now we introduce you to other members of family. These are our partners. We would not survive without them. This is Peter on left and Paul on right. They are very gentle."

Rebecca looked lovingly at Deborah and tentatively put her hand on Paul's cheek. He held stock-still. His cheek was soft and warm.

"Look in his eyes, Mama," Deborah directed her mother.

Rebecca obeyed and saw that Paul had been watching her, his big brown eyes soft and gentle. Rebecca smiled and stroked Paul's neck, her fear evaporating. "He is very nice, dear," she said to Deborah. "I can see how he would be your friend."

"He was my best friend when Daniel was kidnapped," Deborah said. "He and Peter found the boys when they heard their clarinets." She hugged Paul and rested her head on his neck.

"I thank these horses with all my heart," Rebecca said, holding back tears.

11

"Yes, we are so grateful to you and all the horses for what you have done for our family," David said, shaking Josif's hand again.

"Can we ride the horses?" Daniel asked.

"Of course," Josif replied. "But maybe later. Let me tell you what we have planned." All eyes turned to Josif. "Tonight, we go to Wagners for dinner." The children exchanged excited glances. "Marie and August be there, and Arnold, Gina, and Evalina, Gina's mother from Italy. She has decided to stay with Gina and Arnold to help raise the baby, due in middle of September. So, she is new neighbor," he explained to the Epsteins.

"Your mother is already there, David, and women been cooking all day. August and Marie will ride Bill and Sky over." Deborah quietly clapped her hands and beamed.

"Tomorrow we have picnic at Goose Lake and eat fried fish and leftovers. We take wagon and Peter and Paul; Marie and August will bring their horses too. Will be fishing, swimming, riding, and baseball." Josif beamed at the group as the children erupted in joy. David looked triumphant. Izabella assured Rebecca that there would be plenty of time for sitting at a picnic table by the lake drinking coffee.

Josif raised his voice and spoke again. "Day after picnic we leave for Wyoming." More shouting and cheering. "Is cold lemonade inside. We leave for Wagners in two hours; stay clean until then."

The children scattered and the Dacias ushered David and Rebecca into the house. Josif called the Wagners and David spoke to Mrs. Epstein. Josif mentioned that they must have had a dusty drive and got out a decanter of *tuica*. Izabella got out crystal goblets and Aunt Magda put out a plate of boiled eggs, bread and cheese.

Josif poured and all raised a glass. "To wonderful adventure together!" Josif toasted, and all took a sip.

David's eyes widened; Rebecca's watered. "To furthering our educations and seeing more of America!" David toasted, and all took another sip.

"To get four pies made, Aunt Magda and I stop now," Izabella said, laughing. "You like to join us while we make rhubarb pies and men talk?" she asked Rebecca.

When the women had closed the kitchen door, David brought up a topic which had been weighing heavily on him. "You know, Josif and Jon," he said quietly, "Rebecca isn't the only one who's a bit nervous about spending time with a bunch of rowdy cowboys. When you're from New York City, you can expect a bit of ribbing. Especially wearing outfits like these. I hope it doesn't get any worse than that."

"I know what you mean," Josif said. "For a long time around here, we were *Bohunks*. It wasn't until we start playing at weddings that people learn our names. Finally, we make friends. Before that we not sure if we can live here. You remember what we tell you about how our first son Alexander die?"

"Yes, Irina told us the details. We're so sorry that happened to you."

"At first I thought that I cannot escape my fate. That bad luck would follow me for trying. But my son is buried in this country. We have paid for our land with his blood. My daughter is married to our neighbor, and there is no place we belong more than here. You and I must be strong in Wyoming. We must do our best and be men of honor. No man can do more than that."

"Josif, I couldn't agree with you more, on a philosophical basis that is. But I've gotten advice from someone who knows, and there are two other things we have to do."

"What you mention in your letter?"

"Yes. We have to be able to ride and rope."

"Oh boy, you mean like in rodeo?" Uncle Jon asked David.

"We don't have to be rodeo good, but we should be able to ride without falling off, and to throw a rope over something. A moving something is best."

"You say in letter that you practice roping on roof in New York, and ride horse in Central Park. How was that?"

"Well, in New York they ride English style with a different saddle than they use out West. They stand up and down in the saddle and I did a lot of bouncing. The saddles don't have saddle horns, so there's nothing to hold onto. With the roping I did better."

"What did you rope on roof?" Uncle Jon asked, taking another sip of *tuica*.

"Mostly vent pipes, and a chair and coat rack. The pigeons were too small and fast, and the rats too cagey."

"I can ride pretty good," Josif said. "But I never learn this roping. After I get your letter, I buy special rope for roping. I will bring tonight and to picnic tomorrow. You and I and boys can practice. You can also practice riding on Bill or Sky. If you can sit in chair, you can ride these horses. They are very easy."

In the kitchen the women were discussing the various challenges they would be facing. Aunt Magda and Izabella were working at calming Rebecca as if she were a skittish cow about to give birth.

"Just try to relax," Aunt Magda advised. "Let things happen at their own pace. Just try to do what everyone else is doing. Don't try to have things the way you know them. Let them show you their ways."

"Yes, we will do what the other women do," Izabella added. "And I know one thing we can do that they don't know."

"What's that?" Rebecca asked.

"We can cook and bake food that they never try before. Delicious food like chicken *tocana*, Italian wedding soup, stuffed cabbage rolls, grilled minced meat balls, and *mamaliga* with cheese and sour cream. I'm bringing a few spices and ingredients that Flora might not have in her pantry. Is there anything special you like to bring? We'll be going through Sioux Falls where we can shop."

"That's a good idea, Izabella. I can do wonderful things with chicken, and maybe make some Chinese food. I bet they've never had that."

"Neither have I, but I was thinking of delicious sandwiches we had in New York. Were called Reubens, I think."

"Yes, of course. And cheesecake, blintzes, and strudels!"

"Is good thing Fritz is taking truck," Aunt Magda commented.

Dinner at the Wagners involved a lot of horseback riding. Sky and Bill were in constant motion. Both Deborah and Daniel brought their horses to a gallop, riding bareback. Rebecca refused to ride but promised she would at the picnic. David and Josif rode off down the road together, while Daniel and Michael-Joseph watched.

"I was afraid this would happen, Tarzan," Daniel said. "My father's trying to become a cowboy overnight. He wants to fit in, so he doesn't make a fool of himself. He's afraid he'll be seen as the New York Jew city slicker. I felt like that when I first got here."

"Well, that didn't last long," Michael-Joseph said. "You sure weren't a city slicker when you were here, and neither was Deborah. My papa will help him, and so will Fritz and Flora. We'll look out for him too. He'll be okay."

* * *

Deborah, Caroline, and Rose, ages nine, ten, and twelve, sat together on a log at the edge of the Wagner's grove. Deborah wore her dark brown hair in a short bob and the Romanian girls had their lighter brown hair in braids. "You've got extra clothes for me, right?" Deborah asked.

"Yup," Rose answered. "Outdoor clothes, and not our worst stuff either."

"Thanks. I might wear this outfit while we're traveling to keep my mother happy. But when we get there, I want regular clothes."

"That would be a good idea," Rose said. "They'll make terrible fun of you if you go wearing that."

"I wish I could convince my mother of that," Deborah said. "She loves pretty clothes and can't think of any time when you shouldn't wear them."

"Well, wear them on the day we're supposed to arrive, then say you don't want your good clothes to get dirty, and quickly get into ours."

"Do you think there'll be kids our age there?" Caroline asked.

"You mean, do we think there'll be boys our age there," Rose corrected, and they all laughed. "I think there'll be lots of kids, and that means lots of boys," she said knowingly.

"And I bet we get to ride horses every day," Deborah added.

"Just don't expect them all to be sweet like Sky and Bill," Caroline said.

Bill and Sky were Appaloosa horses, originally bred by the Nez Perce Indians as reliable trail horses. This breed was known as bombproof, unspookable, easy to handle, gentle, and smart. Perfect horses for kids to ride to school. August had bought them during horse races at the Pioneer Days Fair in Billings, Montana, one for Marie to ride to school, and one for himself.

* * *

Over fried chicken and mashed potatoes, August made an announcement. "Whaddaya know? I just got a five-day singin' job at the Corn Palace in Mitchell. There'll be a buncha singers and it'll be on the radio."

Marie looked proud but uncertain. She and August were newlyweds, only being married several months, and she was barely fifteen. Romanian customs encouraged marriage shortly after a girl came of childbearing age, especially if she were being asked to date.

An established man marrying a younger woman was seen as ideal for the future of their family. Twenty-one-year-old August and Marie had expressed a serious interest in each other, and Josif had made it clear to August to either marry Marie or stop seeing her.

As August's older brother, Fritz, would inherit the family farm, August had to make his own way. His involvement in Irina's rescue from the Iron Guard when she defected two years before while performing at Carnegie Hall had made him a hero in New York. His song, *The Dakota Six*, had given him national fame. Now he was trying to make a living through farming and performing.

"I start on Tuesday, so I'll be there when you folks come through," August said.

"We just hope it's a better job than the one you got at the World's Fair in Chicago," Marie added. Marie was not quite full-grown although she was mature-looking. She was about five foot four but promised to put on a few more inches. She was developing the look of calm competence of her mother. Her large brown eyes, soft brown hair, and delicate features had first attracted August when they'd met five years previously. He also sensed she had the level head he sometimes seemed to lack.

The Epsteins looked at Marie quizzically.

August ran his hand through his short brown hair, hung his head, and avoided eye contact.

"A supposed friend of Herman B. Henty from WNAX in Vermillion called August and offered him a job singing at the Fair outside one of the pavilions. He gave him a fifty-dollar advance and promised him twenty-five dollars a day for a week. He told us what hotel to stay in and where to eat. Then when it was time to get paid, he deducted the cost of the room and food from August's pay, and August only got ten dollars a day." She stared at August.

"It was supposed to be our honeymoon," Marie continued, "but August spent all his time singing in front of a peep show, and I spent a lot of time at the Midget Village or going through exhibits by myself." Marie's frustration and disappointment were evident.

"Peep shows?" Rebecca asked, looking horrified. "What are peep shows doing at the World's Fair? We thought we might stop at the Fair on the way home. Maybe it isn't suitable."

"Most of the Fair is fine," August said. "It's just around Sally Rand's fan dance show. There's a lotta shows you can't exactly call art, like Sally Rand's. A lotta those shows aren't for kids."

"Yes," Marie added. "Most of the Fair is fascinating. Everything is so modern. They have premature babies in incubators on display. Nurses take care of them, and you can watch through a window."

"In the automotive buildin' you can watch a Ford car bein' made from beginnin' to end while you watch from a walk around the edge," August said, perking up some.

"You can even buy a car you just watched bein' built."

"You can take a cable car called the Sky Ride from Northerly Island to the shore for forty cents, or you can take the elevator up to the top of one of the towers for a huge view for another forty cents," Marie said. "It's amazing."

"Goodyear had its blimp, and the Germans had their Zeppelin," August added. "You can get a ride, but it costs three dollars each, so we didn't go.

"There're villages from all over the world, even a village of Indians from Florida, and a man who wrestles an alligator," he added.

There's a strange statue of a huge robot pushing a man and woman forward," Marie said. "The man and woman look kind of afraid. I guess it's supposed to represent the theme of the fair: *Science Finds, Technology Applies, Man Conforms.*"

"Somethin' I never thought I'd see was two beer gardens. You could sit right out in public and have a beer," August said.

"Not if you're not twenty-one," Marie mentioned. "Then you have to go to an exhibit by yourself."

"It's worth seein', that's fer sure," August said.

"Yes, it's like a county fair with the attractions and rides, but it really is a fair of the world. Plus, like its name, *Century of Progress*, it's full of new inventions. And it was so crowded," Marie said, looking at August. "It's easy to get separated there for hours."

August hung his head again.

"Well, this time I got a real agent," August said, changing the subject. "Bert Hanson was personally recommended by Herman Henty. That other fella was a liar. He got ahold a my phone number somehow and had only met Herman Henty once. He wasn't any friend a his."

"And this Bert Hanson wants a ten per cent cut,"

SCIENCE ADVANCING MANKIND
HALL OF SCIENCE
1933 WORLD'S FAIR

Marie complained. "He wanted it even before August got paid."

"That isn't too unreasonable, or unusual," David said. "A theatrical agent will ask that much, especially if your performance is on the radio. You should get a spike in record sales from that exposure."

Marie looked somewhat mollified, and August raised his head a little.

"Regarding that first job where the supposed friend called you, the way around that is to have a written contract," David explained. "Have every detail written out, make sure all your questions are answered in writing, and everybody signs and dates the document."

August perked up. "Ol' Bert did send me a contract to sign. It seemed okay. I get a hundred dollars for five days singin', and the room and food were included. He even sent me back a copy he'd signed." August looked triumphant.

"That sounds better," Marie said. "I hate it when people try to trick you and steal your money."

"You cannot stay in your house alone, Marie," Aunt Magda stated. "I will live with you while August is away. Congratulations on job, August."

"We were gonna ask you if you would," August said. "I don't like the idea of Marie bein' alone at night, and we've got that extra bedroom."

"And I can give Magda a ride to and from the Dacias if she wants to come home to feed Jon for lunch," Gina said. "Riding in a car is soothing in my condition. I'd love having an excuse to do as much of it as possible."

"You have my permission," Jon said. "You could even drive over with Magda around breakfast time."

"With Josif, Fritz, and August away, I'll be available to help out wherever needed," Arnold offered.

With you and Jon around, things should be fine. But Mr. Bowman and the Sorgenstroms are also close by," Josif reminded Marie. "Call for help if you have any problems."

* * *

Between supper and dessert, August approached the boys. "Meet me out behind the barn in about five minutes," he whispered. "There's somethin' I wanna show you fellas."

The boys were waiting when August emerged from the back door of the barn. "What's up, August?" Michael-Joseph asked.

"Well, you boys are goin' out to Wyomin'."

Daniel had a feeling in his stomach that reminded him of his first cigarette.

"Yeah," they both said.

"Well, there's prob'ly gonna be a lotta kids there for the weddin' and rodeo."

"Prob'ly."

"You're both about nine now?"

"We'll be nine in August."

"Well, I think it'd be a good idea for you fellas ta know how ta fight."

Daniel couldn't tell if he felt sick due to relief or fear. He decided it would be good to learn to fight. He certainly hoped he wouldn't have to.

"I'm gonna show you boys a jab," August said, while crouching and bringing his fists up. "You can win most fights with a good jab. Just remember three things. The first is a drill. The second is the snap of a wet towel, and the third is the kick of a mule. Your fist should twist like a drill, be fast as a snapped towel, and hard as a mule kick." August demonstrated lightly into the boys' hands. "Practice this a lot into pillows that you hold for each other. Get good at it with both hands."

The boys each punched August's huge outstretched palm. August was about six foot two, solid and well-muscled. He was large boned and had pleasing features, although he carried a scar on his right cheekbone from his time as captive of the Greek mob at their headquarters in Sioux City. He had learned boxing techniques while on the Henry Reeves Road Show, when he was tricked into repeated boxing matches against professional boxers. The mob-backed plot had been to soften August up for the kill by a monster of a boxer, Vesuvio Demonado, who had orders to kill August in a well-publicized fight in Fargo at the end of the road show. This act of mob vengeance had also failed.

"You need to be able to hit about ten times as hard, and much faster. And don't be standin' around waitin' for the other fella to make a move. When you're fightin', you wanna take the fight to him; get the upper hand as soon as possible. And a coupla other things. Jump around on your toes. Don't just stand there. Duck and weave. Fake 'im out. Don't just hit him once. When he's stunned, get in another good one. The fight'll be over in no time."

"Where's the best place to hit someone?" Michael-Joseph asked.

"Well, in the chin works good, but it hurts your hands. Go for the gut, hard and fast, and a lot."

"Wow," Daniel said. "Anything else we should know?"

"Yeah, here's a dandy. When you're ridin' in the car and can't be punchin' pillows, you can pretend practice. Practice in your mind. Practice until you're throwin' knockouts; see it and feel it without movin'."

"Gee, August, does that really work?" Daniel asked.

"You bet it does. When I was in all those fights the mob set up, I didn't have time to practice. So, I did pretend fightin'. I'd remember fights I'd been in and refight them in my mind, only better. I practiced my jabs for hours. Oh, and one other thing. Push-ups. You boys gotta do as many push-ups as you can squeeze into a day. When you make a muscle, it should be as big as an orange. Show me your muscles."

The boys grimaced and squeezed up the biggest biceps they could. August felt the results.

"Well, right now you got muscles about the size of a coupla fried eggs. You fellas need a lotta work."

August got on the ground and demonstrated a push-up. "Now you two try."

Michael-Joseph and Daniel got on the ground and did a few push-ups. "Well, the first four or five aren't so bad," Daniel said.

August shook his head. "You fellas need to be able to do a hundred at a time."

Daniel collapsed on his face. "Come on, Captain Nemo," Michael-Joseph said, doing a few more. "How's your summer vacation report gonna look if it's only about all the different times you got beat up?"

After the dessert of the Dacias's rhubarb pies and fresh coffee, everyone's attention turned to roping. Fritz had already figured out his fiancée would expect that a man could rope, especially her new husband. He'd been throwing a rope at everything on the farm that moved for months.

Josif had a rope; David had three. "One for each of us. I figured we're all in this together," he said. The two extra ropes were given to Daniel and Michael-Joseph.

The boys looked at each other in amazement. They each had a rope. Cowboy self-images raced through their heads.

Fritz and David demonstrated the basics. Everyone found something to rope, played out their ropes, and circled the loops overhead. When they let go, they learned the first lesson in judging how far a length of rope goes and how wide the loop needs to be. Practice went on until dusk and it was time for everyone to head for home.

"We come by around ten o'clock tomorrow morning," Josif said as everyone prepared to leave. "We will drive team and wagon and carry extra supplies."

Deborah and Daniel kissed their parents good night and headed out to the Dacia's car. Gina, Evalina, and Arnold also left, and Mrs. Wagner took the Epsteins upstairs to show them their rooms. August and Marie rode home on Bill and Sky, and all was right with the world.

CHAPTER THREE
The Good Life

With persistent urging and gentle pulling, Deborah and Daniel got their mother to the wagon. Uncle Jon placed a turned-over bucket next to the front wheel, and David gave her a hand up. Rebecca had no choice but to ride in the wagon, as everyone else was. Deborah led her to a seat on the bench at the rear of the wagon. Blankets and towels padded the seat, and Aunt Magda and Izabella joined her. Others sat on a bale of straw or stood holding on to the wagon's sideboards.

Uncle Jon drove, and as the wagon pulled out the long driveway, began singing *She'll be Comin' 'Round the Mountain*. Everyone knew the words and joined in, and Rebecca didn't have time to fret.

Fritz drove the Wagner's Pontiac with his grandmother and Mrs. Epstein, and Arnold, Gina, and Evalina came in their car. They were joined along the way by August and Marie riding up on Bill and Sky.

The cars passed the wagon, and August and Marie rode after them calling that they'd get things set up.

By noon a fire was crackling in the pit, and a coffee pot was on the edge of the grate beginning to perk. The horses were grazing, food was appearing on the picnic table, and the men were untangling fishing lines. Michael-Joseph and Daniel were sent into the grove by the lake to get worms.

Deborah ran up to her mother and hugged her. "Isn't it beautiful here at Goose Lake?" she asked. Without waiting for a response, she continued, "This is where I caught so many fish. More than anyone else. Then we went swimming and played baseball. We can do all that again, but today will be even better. Today we also get to ride Bill and Sky! Don't worry, Mama. They're very easy to ride."

David was in seventh heaven. It was a beautiful, sunny day at a deep blue lake in South Dakota. Redwinged blackbirds were trilling from the cattails and meadowlarks warbling from the tall prairie grasses. When August handed him a fishing pole his life felt complete. When August handed him the can of worms, he froze with uncertainty.

David was a pacifist and had considered becoming a vegetarian. Concerns for the health of his growing children prevented him from imposing this diet on his family. Still, it was hard for him to kill anything, even a worm. August was watching him, and soon others did too.

"Heck, David," August said. "Just grab one and stick a hook through it. It won't bite."

"It's what you have to do to catch a fish, Papa," Daniel said. Then having an inspiration, he appealed to his father's scientific interests. "It's part of the natural food chain, Papa. You're just speeding things up a little."

"David," Rebecca said, "all this fuss about a worm?"

David couldn't see asking one of the men or Michael-Joseph to bait his hook. He gritted his teeth and slid the hook through the worm, silently apologizing to it the whole time. It was with guilty relief that he dropped his hook and worm into the water.

Uncle Jon gave Rebecca a fishing pole with its baited hook already in the water and out of sight, as he had done for Deborah the summer before. Others lined up along the dock with their lines in the water. Soon bobbers bobbed, then bullheads, yellow perch, and crappies were pulled out of the lake and put in a bucket of water. All the Epsteins had caught a fish and were elated. Rebecca seemed almost giddy. "I never thought I'd catch a fish," she said. "Wait 'til I tell my friends in New York. They won't believe it."

"I know what you mean, Mama," Deborah replied.

* * *

David had caught a yellow perch. He was both proud and horrified. He was the cause of this fish's death. He watched its mouth futilely opening and closing. Blood oozed from where the hook had been removed, tearing its flesh, its gills searching for air. David apologized silently to the fish and thanked it for its life. He hoped it would die quickly, without further pain.

He recognized his hypocrisy as a meat eater and acknowledged his debt, thanking those who killed animals for him, trying not to dwell on the fear and pain he imagined the animals experienced before death.

David's dark thoughts were interrupted by the girls yelling that it was time to ride the horses.

The children rested their fishing poles against a tree and ran to Bill and Sky. Both horses were wearing western saddles with broad stirrups and saddle horns. It was Rebecca's time to ride a horse. She dreaded this part but was eager to get it over with. Petting a horse was one thing but getting on one something else.

Sky and Bill were tall horses with unmistakable black and white markings. Sky's head and forequarters were black, although his head had a light blaze. The rest of his body was white with black spots. His hooves were striped.

Marie stood at Sky's head while David guided Rebecca's left foot into the stirrup. Rebecca still had her right foot on a small stool Izabella had brought along. She stood on her left foot and fell on her stomach across the saddle. She clutched Sky's mane in her left hand and the saddle horn in her right. With David guiding her foot, she slid her right leg over the saddle and sat up. Marie handed her the reins, which she grasped with her left hand, letting go of Sky's mane.

Izabella mounted Bill and started him at a slow walk. Sky walked along next to him. "These horses are very best to ride, Rebecca. They are not afraid of noises or anything. You could carry cup of water on one of these horses running and it would not spill."

Rebecca relaxed a bit as she realized she was safe. She sat up straighter and loosened her grip on the saddle horn. She tried to hold the reins as Izabella was. "Why are these horses so special?" she asked.

"These are Appaloosas," Izabella explained. They are Indian horses and trained to be stable and reliable. Sky and Bill were both racehorses that August bought at a fair in Montana. First, he won by betting on Flora's horse, then he bet on a horse Flora recommended.

"Sky ended up being a bride price from August to us, which we gave to Marie. We were very pleased that August followed the Romanian customs about marriage. It was the only way Josif would allow August to give Marie such a gift.

"You've seen the pictures of your children riding these horses galloping." Izabella smiled at Rebecca. "Flora is the one who taught them to ride. When we get to Wyoming, she may be able to help you too."

Rebecca looked dubious. "I was hoping this would be all of my riding," she said.

"You have taken the first big step, Rebecca. Is possible you and your family will visit again. Your children love to ride. Would be good for you to learn too."

"This isn't too bad," she said. "But it's still a long way down, and I'm not really the adventuresome type." The two horses continued to walk. Rebecca began to enjoy the feeling of smooth movement and power under her. She looked around her and saw a meadowlark on a post. When it sang, she softened her shoulders.

She moved her feet in the stirrups and experimented standing on them, lifting herself off the saddle.

"Just sit in relaxed way," Izabella said. "Let the horse move you and you just go with it. Is very relaxing."

Rebecca did as she was told. She began to feel a part of Sky's movements and to enjoy the connection. She appreciated the view from her elevated position.

Rebecca imagined what it would feel like to be on a horse running at full gallop. The thought made her grab the saddle horn. Then she briefly indulged her imagination and saw herself flying across the prairie on a galloping horse, her black hair loose and flowing. She imagined the speed and power. It was overwhelming.

"Deborah and Daniel both galloped these horses," she said. "I see why they changed."

The two women continued their ride. Rebecca gradually gained confidence, letting go of the saddle horn.

Izabella grinned. "If we don't come back soon, they'll come after us on Peter and Paul. Everyone is back there with cameras. Let's head back."

Rebecca laughed and turned Sky around, following Izabella's movements.

Deborah squealed with glee when she saw her mother. She was riding Sky, a huge smile on her face. Everyone cheered. Daniel got a picture with his Brownie, and David with his Speed Graphic.

* * *

Swimming and roping happened at the same time. David began with a cannonball into the lake, followed by

BROWNIE CAMERA

Daniel and Michael-Joseph. The girls joined hands and followed. The water was cold, but they soon got used to it and raced each other swimming around the dock.

Josif and Fritz roped stumps, car fenders, and even each other. They were soon joined by the swimmers who had changed in the woods. Mrs. Epstein sat in David's car edgeways on the back seat with the door open, where she could see everyone. She had asked David to teach her how to use the Speed Graphic, and now she took a few pictures.

Aunt Magda and Uncle Jon cleaned the fish at the water's edge. Arnold got the huge frying pan and bucket of lard from his car. He heaved the frying pan onto the grate. Grandma Wagner threw several large scoops of lard into the pan while Gina and Evalina seasoned and floured the fish filets.

Rebecca eyed the bucket of lard. She and David had decided they wouldn't try to enforce Jewish kosher laws on hosts who might not have options. Izabella joined her at the picnic table. "Is kind of you to eat pork while you are with us. I know that is not your way."

"It would be impossible to ask that of non-Jews who don't know our beliefs. We don't want to put extra strain on anyone or set ourselves apart."

"You are doing very well with that. It seems you are much braver than you thought."

"I guess I am! I didn't want to disappoint Deborah. She's made big changes and benefitted from them. I was beginning to realize I was teaching her to be afraid. So now I must follow her example if I want to keep up with her." Both women laughed.

"And now Marie is married. I'm sure she can tame August and keep him in line. She seems like a level-headed girl."

"Yes, she is. And Wagners gave them farm as wedding present. Is only two miles away. When they have children, they'll be close by."

"And Fritz is bringing Flora back to live on the farm with his grandmother. That's how it is with us and David's mother. It's nice to have a grandmother in the house."

"We were sorry to hear about Grandpa Wagner's passing last winter," Rebecca added. "What happened?"

"He died in his sleep."

"That's best."

"Yes."

"Is Grandma Wagner managing okay?"

"Yes, with Fritz there the farm runs fine. With August on his own farm, it is now very quiet at the Wagners. Mrs. Epstein will enjoy the peacefulness of the country there."

Leftovers from the dinner the night before were brought to the table. Loaves of the morning's bread and tender fried fish filets were passed around. Lemonade, coffee, and *tuica* were poured, and a chocolate-frosted sheet cake served.

When shadows lengthened, Deborah and Daniel felt contented. Their parents had experienced the joys of a picnic at Goose Lake, as they had the year before. Everything was going well. Their mother had ridden a horse and liked it; their father as well. Tomorrow they would leave for Wyoming and make new memories together. Everything would be wonderful.

CHAPTER FOUR
At the Corn Palace

The next morning Fritz drove his truck into the Dacia yard at 8:00 AM. Uncle Jon and Josif had all the luggage lined up on the porch. Fritz stepped out of the cab and climbed onto the back of the truck. Boxes and suitcases were handed up to Fritz who placed them in the truck bed. The truck already held the Epsteins and Fritz's luggage, as well as the three tents, ten sleeping bags, and a cook-set for ten. Fritz had included his saddle, which prompted Josif to add his.

Aunt Magda rushed out with a box of food and Uncle Jon carried out a heavy box wrapped in a thick blanket. Pieces of burlap wrapped around six quarts of *tuica* protected them from breakage. Grandma Wagner had also contributed a box of food.

When everything was in, Fritz threw a huge canvas tarp over the load, tying it down with his rope. "You know, those Wyomin' fellas won't have brand new, stiff yellow ropes. I've been tryin' to soften mine up. I even drug it behind the truck a coupla times." He looked at Josif and David and glanced at the boys. "I figure leavin' it in the sun and wind oughta help age it some. If you guys wanna tie your ropes up here, go ahead."

Daniel and Michael-Joseph climbed onto the truck and tied their ropes onto the load. Josif and David threw theirs up for the boys to secure as well.

Marie rode up on Sky. She told everyone that August had left around 6:00. He was riding his Indian Motorcycle with a sidecar. He expected to easily cover the one hundred five miles to the Corn Palace by 8:00. Performances would be going on all day, and August would try to find them between his acts.

Marie handed a bag to Izabella. "Some food for the trip," she said.

The sound of Arnold and Gina Ariosto's Ford announced their arrival. Evelina was with them. They greeted everyone and Gina gave Izabella a bag. "In case you get hungry along the way," she explained.

Gina and Arnold had been married the previous August. In his late twenties, Arnold was a tan-skinned, blue-eyed, hardworking man with the muscles to prove it. His red-highlighted, brown, curly hair framed a face with a strong aquiline nose and high cheekbones.

Gina was considered the beauty of the neighborhood. Of medium height, with light olive skin, a very curvy figure, perfect features, and shoulder-length black hair, Gina was now pregnant, due in mid-September.

Gina's mother, Evelina, still held much of the family beauty, although she was now in her early fifties.

* * *

Michael-Joseph and Daniel said good bye to those staying behind and got in the cab with Fritz. Izabella and Josif also said good bye. Aunt Magda and Uncle Jon reassured them that they would look after Marie while August was away.

Remaining small items were put in the car. With waves and shouted good byes, the truck and car pulled out of the driveway and headed to the Wagners. There, everyone said good bye to Mrs. Epstein and Grandma Wagner, and the boys joined the Epstein car.

The three vehicles left with Fritz leading in his truck. There were now five ropes tied over the tarp.

* * *

The caravan arrived in Sioux Falls and found a large grocery store. Rebecca was disappointed not to find supplies for Chinese food. "How many do you think we'll be cooking for?" she asked Fritz in the store.

"Well, we're bringing ten; there's four in Flora's family, plus they got a foreman and a coupla hands. Then there'll prob'ly be a lotta neighbors. Since we're gettin' married on the Fourth of July and Flora's family is puttin' on a rodeo, it'll be the biggest thing around. It's gonna be a wingding of a party!"

"Of course, all women will bring food," Izabella assured her. "Lots of food. Women here very good about that. If they are like women in South Dakota, there will be very many casseroles and lots of fried chicken. Also, vegetable dishes made from last fall's canning, sausages, sauerkraut, cookies, pies, and cakes."

"It'll probably go on for days, Mama," Daniel said.

"Yeah," Michael-Joseph added. "If a cowboy wedding's anything like an Italian wedding, it could take five days to end."

So it will be a big celebration like a Jewish wedding," Rebecca mused. She was quiet for a moment, then doubled the amounts of supplies on her list.

"It's on the *Times*," David said. "All of you, get whatever you need. We want to do this right and help the Doyles, not impose on them."

Two fifty-pound bags of flour, one hundred pounds of beans, two hundred pounds of potatoes, fifty of coffee, fifty of sugar, twenty of butter, five of salt, yeast, and a tub of lard were set aside. In the canned goods section, two cases each of canned peaches and apples were selected, as well as one of canned pineapple. Luckily the store carried cream cheese, and Rebecca put all they had in her cart.

The storekeeper approached Rebecca, pointing out all the delicacies he carried. "We have nuts of all kinds, dried apricots, and even dates, olive oil, olives, Baker's chocolate, canned salmon even. Very exotic items."

"I guess I better go make room in the truck," Fritz said, and ambled out to the parking lot.

When the shopping party returned to the truck, they found all the truck's contents on the pavement. "I thought we might as well sort this out now," Fritz said. "We'd have to shift stuff around to make room for all those groceries anyhow."

The group decided to put the food and saddles in first. Clothes and camping gear would be placed in easy reach by the tailgate. To keep the dairy products cold and the butter from melting, a large enameled mixing bowl had been purchased and filled with ice. It was placed on the box of perishables and everything wrapped in blankets. The sacks of potatoes were stacked all around to keep everything in place.

By the time the truck was repacked and the tarp reapplied, five ropes tying things down didn't look so unusual.

The group proceeded to Mitchell and found the Corn Palace. Placards announced a *Jamboree of Country Music*. August's name was prominently featured; he would next be performing at 2:00PM. The group found rooms at the nearby King Korn Hotel and checked in, then found a restaurant for lunch.

* * *

David purchased their tickets and they found seats close together. David identified himself as a reporter for the *New York Times* who would be doing a story about the Palace. He was given permission to take photos from throughout the theater and behind stage. August Wagner's friends and family were moved to better seats.

David was directed to the actors' entrance and with his press badge, got backstage. Hearing August's voice practicing a song, he followed it. The sound of a woman talking stopped him. "Shit, August, why don't you loosen up a little? Your precious *Marie Sweet Marie* ain't here now," she said, mocking the song August had written for Marie the year before.

"Trixie, I'm not here to loosen up a little. I'm here to make money and not embarrass myself by not practicin'," August said. "Why don't you go pester your husband, Floyd? You remember him, don'tcha?"

"Floyd doesn't care. He likes 'em young, and I like 'em big like you. We could trade off."

August stopped playing and looked Trixie in the eyes. "Trixie, if you were a man, I'd knock you flat and then some. Get away from me and don't talk like that around me again."

David walked around the curtain at this point and greeted August. Trixie looked David up and down appraisingly and stood up. "Think it over, big boy," she said to August, and sauntered off.

David's eyes were wide. "Who was that?" he asked.

"That piece a work was Trixie, one a the backup singers. Her husband, Floyd, is just as bad."

"One of the challenges of being a star, I guess," David said.

"You got that right. It ain't all fun and glory. There's a lotta bloodsuckers floatin' around."

"Well, we're all here and sitting in the front. Being friends and family with a star gives us privileges. I'm moving around taking photos for the *Times*. I hope my flash doesn't bother you when you're performing."

"Naw, I'm pretty used to that."

"I guess this show will be going out over several radio stations and is being recorded. That will be great publicity. Also, when I get back to New York, I'll be writing a series of articles with photos. You'll be in at least one with a photo. New Yorkers still feel they discovered you and that you belong to them, just like Irina. You've got a lot of fans."

"I sure know that. If it weren't for New Yorkers, I might never've cut a record. Because of them I have a way to make money besides farmin'. I still wanna farm but need money to get things started. I don't wanna begin my life with Marie with our family in debt."

* * *

David got some more backstage shots, then found a spot with a good view of the stage. Trixie Delaney and her husband, Floyd, were backup singers for solo artists. A record company was recording the *Jamboree* and felt that having at least three voices enhanced the songs.

* * *

As it turned out, August would be the exception on the last day when he sang a new song to Marie.

* * *

David had to work to get a photo of August without Trixie in the shot. She frequently stood too close to August and smiled at him instead of Floyd. At these times Floyd seemed pleased, backing up to leave the image of Trixie singing with August as a duo. August tried not to show his disgust, or to push Trixie away with his elbow. He smiled when he sang, but there was clearly no joy.

The entire Wyoming party was getting fed up with Trixie and Floyd. Izabella and Rebecca were ready to go up on stage and slap Trixie. Josif had plans for Floyd, as did Fritz. The girls were exchanging angry glances of disbelief and the boys were mentally practicing their jabs at Floyd.

When the group met with August for supper, the Delaneys were a main topic of conversation. "I've sure got some choice words for that pair," Fritz stated. "And somethin' special for that Floyd," he said, making a huge fist.

"You be careful of them," Josif said to August. "Is clear they are trouble."

"That Trixie tramp is trying to hurt our Marie," Izabella said, not hiding her anger.

"She can't even sing that good," Rose said, and the girls agreed.

"Want me and Daniel to rough Floyd up for ya, August?" Michael-Joseph asked.

August smiled. "Thanks for the offer, boys, but Floyd's one guy I'd like to take care of myself." Everyone smiled in appreciation of the image.

* * *

August was staying at the Prairie Gold Hotel, the same one used by Henry Reeves and his road show the year before. "It's not the same bein' here without Jon, Magda, Irina, and Marie," August lamented. "That turned out to be fun, lookin' back on it. This ain't."

"We'll get to the ranch on Sunday," Fritz said. "Grandma has the Doyle's phone number. Call us when you get home."

"I sure will. I don't expect any trouble from them Delaneys, but you never know. As long as Magda and

Gina are lookin' after Marie, I feel better."

"Yes," Josif said. "Either one of them would be like facing a Turk, especially if the children are involved."

Everyone stood up to go. "I got one more show tonight, then hit the hay," August said. "I hope you all enjoy your Wyomin' vacation. And Fritz, I'll see you next when you've got your better half in tow. Have a nice weddin'."

CHAPTER FIVE
Camping in the Badlands

The wedding party ate breakfast in the hotel cafeteria and checked out by nine. They found a store which sold ice and refreshed the ice in the bowl over the dairy products.

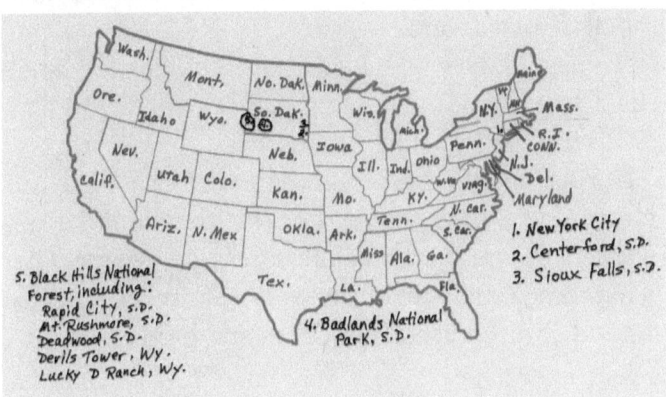

The drive took five hours over a dusty road with unexpected potholes and washboard ruts. Miles and miles of dry fields with stunted crops and scattered white farmhouses under a pale blue sky were the only scenery. It was too hot to keep the windows closed and dust drifted into the cars, covering everything.

The towns were small with few services, so the drivers filled up whenever gas was available. Rebecca tried to wash off the dust whenever possible, but some stations only had outhouses. These she avoided entirely. One station had a picnic table with benches under a cottonwood tree, and it was put to use.

The Wagner and Dacia boxes of food were hauled out and placed on the table. Mrs. Wagner's contained three jars of sauerkraut, two dozen hard-boiled eggs, baloney sandwiches wrapped in wax paper, salted beef in a jar, two loaves of crusty bread, and four dozen sugar cookies. A few old forks and plates were included.

The Dacia box had large pieces of wrapped *mamaliga*, white cheese, canned stuffed grape leaves, fried pork fat, a large jar of pickled eggs, and a bag of cookies. The bags from Marie and Gina each contained four dozen cookies and a dozen hard-boiled eggs. Gina's also included a large chunk of Genoa salami.

"I guess Daniel and I will have cookies for lunch," Michael-Joseph said.

"Us too," Rose said for the girls.

During lunch they realized what was left from lunch would be their supper. Luckily, they found a small convenience store shortly before entering the park. There, they purchased the bulk of the store's entire stock: cans of beans and chili, soda crackers, pop, and hard candy.

* * *

The group arrived at the Badlands campground around four. The Badlands had appeared without warning. They were made of mountains, buttes, and valleys, but they were below ground level. They looked formidable. One entered them by going down.

The campground was in a broad, flat area, surrounded by low mountains made of rough, rounded volcanic stone. It was rustic with several outhouses and water spigots. Camping areas were roughly outlined with stones around the perimeters. There was a picnic table with benches at each site. The ground was hard and covered with a thin layer of loose gravel.

The men parked the vehicles and unloaded the truck. The three tents were distributed: one for the women, one for the men, and one for Fritz who might need his own when he brought his new wife home.

Josif gave the boys the job of putting up the tents. "Have you ever done this before?" Daniel asked Michael-Joseph.

"Nope, and I may not now. There's so much tent, it's hard to know where to start," he replied.

The boys spread everything out for one of the tents, walking over it with dirty shoes, and looked at the assembly instructions. They studied the steps, and understanding the process, gave it a try.

The only problem was putting the rope through the tent so that the floor was on the side. The boys quickly corrected this error. They pulled the rope taut over the poles with the notched tops and pounded in stakes to keep tension on the ropes.

The girls pounded in the side stakes and then pulled the side cords taut, tying them to the stakes. The tent now ballooned out at the sides and the flaps were impossible to close completely.

It sagged a bit in the middle but was standing. The boys soon got the other two tents up. David took a picture.

* * *

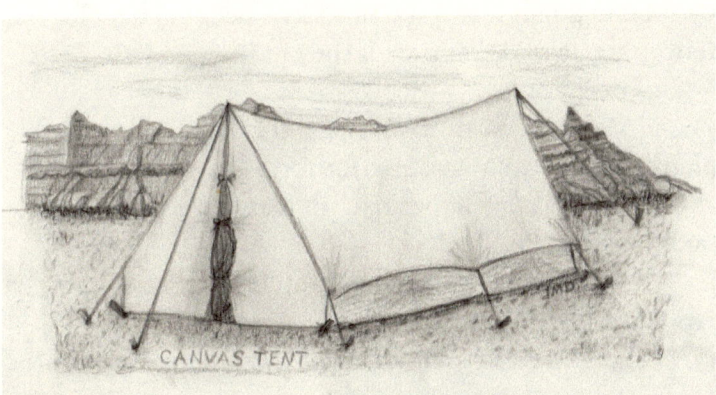

CANVAS TENT

Izabella and Rebecca opened the cookset. It was huge. Its label called it *super family size*. It contained ten plates and sets of silverware, two sizes of pots, a frying pan, two large spoons, and a spatula. A coffee pot, Coleman gas stove, tablecloth, napkins, and matches were also in the box.

"David, come light this," Rebecca called, indicating the stove.

Izabella grabbed the coffee pot and their coffee and sugar. She filled the pot at a nearby spigot and returned it to the stove that David was attempting to light. "Soon we have hot coffee," she said.

Josif grabbed a mason jar of *tuica* from the box. "First, we wash dust down."

Fritz rummaged around under the seat of his truck and produced a quart of whiskey. "I've got some dust washer, too, but we can start with yours."

David finally got the stove to light and joined Josif and Fritz.

The men passed the bottle a few times, then got their ropes.

The boys climbed up onto the truck bed and threw down the ten sleeping bags. Izabella and Rebecca studied the floor of the tent. It looked small for five, about five by six and a half feet. "We need five sleeping bags for our tent, Izabella said. Let's see if they fit."

They didn't.

"Maybe it work if we open the bags and make big blanket for bottom and one for top. Then we have three at one end and two at other, with feet in middle," Izabella said.

"I don't suppose we have much choice," Rebecca replied.

The tents had six-foot head room along the center,

tapering to one foot at the edges. At least that was how it was designed. In reality, the rope sagged, and headroom was only five feet.

The women brought in their suitcases, as well as the girls'. This covered the floor of the tent. It was decided to stack them outside at the edge of the tent.

Sweaters and jackets were pulled from the suitcases and folded into pillows for everyone.

"It looks uncomfortable," Rebecca noted.

"Yes," Izabella agreed. "I can't think of anything to put down for padding; the blankets are around the ice bowl."

"There isn't enough room to sleep in the cars."

"It may be cold tonight; I'm going to sleep in my clothes. I may put on more," Izabella said.

"That will help with the padding. Let's make our pillows out of shirts and keep the sweaters and jackets to wear," Rebecca suggested. "I'll keep one outfit for Deborah and me in the suitcase to look nice when we get to the Doyles."

"Good idea. And if we have to camp again, maybe we can find soft grasses for padding. They would smell sweet and fresh."

* * *

The women opened the suitcases and made a pile of clothing for everyone to wear during the night. They also refashioned the pillows. Then they went to the men's tent and did the same for them. Fritz was left to his own devices.

* * *

The scenery around the campground was spectacular. Low buttes and pointed peaks shone in the late afternoon light. Their multicolored bands of rose and tan stone glowed warmly. Scattered low grasses grew in places receiving the most shade. Prairie could be seen in the distance. David stopped roping practice and took more pictures. "I've never seen anything like this," he mused. "It's fantastic."

The women got out the food and heated up the beans and chili. Izabella got out some *mamaliga,* fried pork rinds, white cheese, and pop. Cookies were for dessert. Another round of *tuica* finished off the meal.

While there was still some light, the men looked at the map. "I've got reservations for all of us at the State Game Lodge in Custer State Park tomorrow," David said. "We can head to Rapid City in the morning and get more ice and anything else we need. We'll see Mt. Rushmore and Custer Park tomorrow and stay at the lodge.

"The next night we'll be in Wyoming. I hope we can find a place to camp along the Belle Fourche River after we explore Devils Tower. Does everyone like that plan?"

"I like any plan," Josif said. "All this country is new to us. I like wherever we go."

"I love the idea of the lodge, a restaurant, and a soft bed," Rebecca said. "The country is nice too. I hear that the Black Hills will be prettier than the flat land we saw today. And Devils Tower is supposed to be fascinating. I'm sure it will be lovely along that river too."

"Yes, I am happy with the plan," Izabella said. "Everything is new and beautiful. I am very happy to be here."

"I'm good too, David," Fritz added. "I'm comin' to get married. That's the main thing I care about."

"We like it too," the children agreed.

"Then the next day after camping on the river, we get to the ranch?" Michael-Joseph asked.

"Yes," Josif replied. "The next day we go to Doyle ranch, have rodeo, and get ready for wedding."

CHAPTER SIX
Sightseeing and Comfort

No one slept well during the night in the women's tent. The girls had put too much tension on the side ropes, and the tent flaps didn't meet when tied. There were large gaps. It was cold and the ground was hard. There were small stones and a few larger ones. Feet with layers of socks struggled with each other for room. Giggles and occasional hard kicks and under-cover thrashing didn't help.

Will this never end? Rebecca wondered as she turned over again onto a familiar pointed rock. She longed for the lodge they were heading to.

Izabella had curled into a ball with a shirt over her head. She was trying to count backwards from one hundred in English.

In several hours the effects of the beans, chili, and hard-boiled eggs were sensed. "Whoever's doing that, stop right now," Rebecca said sternly.

There was a pause, then Izabella said, "I'm trying, but it does no good."

The girls broke out in hoots of laughter at that comment. Rebecca tried to maintain her decorum, but when she got up to open the tent flaps all the way, a quiet *phoot* revealed she was also part of the problem. There was a moment of silence, then a sound of something like choking. Rebecca began laughing and couldn't stop. The others joined in.

* * *

In the men's tent, the boys weren't helping either. Daniel turned over about every twenty seconds, accompanied by an exasperated sigh.

Michael-Joseph incessantly squirmed in place trying to relocate the stones under him.

Josif and David tried not to imitate their sons, but they couldn't lie still either.

"Would be good to sweep ground under tent next time," Josif said tersely into the darkness.

David wondered what it would take to placate Rebecca after this, as he again rolled onto his side.

Soon the effects of their recent diet were noticed in the tent.

"Cut that out," Josif said in a no-nonsense tone.

Michael-Joseph and Daniel tried to muffle their laughter in their sleeping bags, with no luck. "This is just something else from our last trip out here that we're sharing," Daniel said. "It helped to save our lives."

Well, it might kill us tonight," David said.

Suspicious sounds were heard from the men. "Papa!" both boys said in unison, and the snorts and laughter began in the men's tent.

* * *

Other than being aware of the noises from the other two tents, Fritz was able to find a fairly smooth location and doze.

* * *

With the first light of day, the bleary-eyed campers emerged from their tents. They were disheveled and tired. David lit the stove and Izabella made coffee. Cookies were distributed. When the warm rays of the sun penetrated the valleys, everyone warmed up. Cups of steaming coffee and cookies helped. Layers of clothing were removed and repacked.

The boys were given the job of taking down the tents and packing them. They were seemingly much bigger now and wouldn't fit in their carrying sacks. The boys tied them with ropes and stacked them next to the reassembled cook-set and suitcases behind the truck.

With the goal of Rapid City for a hot meal and comfortable chairs, the group was soon repacked and headed out.

* * *

They left the park along a road that ran through miles of prairie grassland. David stopped the group to take photos and wandered up a slope through tall grasses for a better view.

As he topped the rise, he found himself twenty yards from a small herd of bison. David froze in place. He slowly inserted a new two-shot film holder into his camera. He took a picture, removed the holder, flipped it over, and composed another picture.

Before he took the shot, one of the bison turned to look squarely at him. It lightly pawed the ground. David decided against another photo. He slowly backed down the slope, being careful not to fall.

The bison lowered its massive shaggy head. Its small eyes were fixed on David. "Everyone get in the cars and be ready to go," he called out to the others without turning

AMERICAN BISON BADLANDS NATIONAL PARK

his head. The bison took a few quick steps forward. David heard car doors slam behind him.

David still had his hand in his pocket. He removed it with a flash bulb between his fingers and popped it into his camera. He continued to back up. "Is everyone ready?" he called.

"Yes," everyone called back.

David stole a quick look over his shoulder. He was about ten feet from the driver's side of his car. The bison continued to advance. "Get ready!" he yelled and took a picture. The flashbulb went off with a blinding light. The bison stumbled, then stopped in its tracks and shook its head.

David bolted for the car and got in the driver's seat. As he was starting the engine, Fritz pulled his truck between the bison and the Epstein car. David put the car in gear and headed out of the park. The Dacias and Fritz followed closely behind. When the boys looked out the rear window of the Epstein car, the bison was standing in the same place, still shaking its head.

"That was close, Mr. Epstein," Michael-Joseph said. "You were great!"

"I got a picture of you, Papa," Daniel added.

"I almost had a heart attack, David," Rebecca said with her hand on her heart.

"I got two great pictures," David said.

"And mine," Daniel reminded him.

"Yes, that might be one I keep on my desk at the *Times*," David said, smiling at Daniel in the rearview mirror.

* * *

The group arrived in Rapid City in about an hour and found a café. The travelers cleaned up in the restroom and ordered hearty breakfasts of eggs, ham, fried potatoes, toast, milk and coffee.

David noticed that an employee hurried into the restrooms after everyone had finished cleaning up. When he came out, he stared at the two families and mouthed *they're okay* to his boss. He also noticed that his family was the subject of much interest. Some customers were smirking, and others chuckled and shook their heads.

Daniel and Deborah hid behind menus; Rebecca seemed oblivious.

As the adults finished their coffee, David and Joseph looked at the map. "I was thinking we could drive around the wildlife loop in Custer Park, as well as seeing Mt. Rushmore," David said. But today, everyone seems a bit road weary. I think we should do a little less. I got some excellent photos of those bison, and I bet we'll see wildlife wherever we go. So, I suggest that we just go to Mt. Rushmore and then to the State Game Lodge today. We can take baths, organize our belongings, and be rested for our entry into Wyoming tomorrow."

Hearty yeses greeted the suggestion.

David went to the counter and paid the bill. The café was able to refresh their ice supply, and the caravan headed out for Mt. Rushmore.

* * *

The drive was through spectacular country of tree-lined, steep, winding roads. The granite spires of the Needles and distant views resulted in many stops for photo taking. There were hairpin turns, rock tunnels, and massive, wooden, curved spans of bridges recently constructed.

Along the way they saw mountain goats, bighorn

sheep, a small group of elk disappearing into the trees, and a white-tailed deer.

Mt. Rushmore was in its beginning stages. Work was finished on George Washington's head, and the group learned that it would be dedicated that Wednesday, the Fourth of July. Thomas Jefferson would be the next carving.

Washington's head was huge, and his features could be clearly seen from the visitor viewing area. An informational sign said that the heads would be sixty feet tall.

"What an achievement!" David said, while taking photos.

Everyone stood and stared.

GEORGE WASHINGTON ON MT. RUSHMORE
JULY 4, 1934

* * *

More wildlife was seen along the Peter Norbeck Scenic Byway to the State Game Lodge. It was cooler than in the Badlands, and as David had already taken many photos, the drive was easy.

* * *

The State Game Lodge had been built in 1922 and served as the summer Whitehouse for Calvin Coolidge in 1927. Custer State Park had recently been dedicated, and the state was eager to attract tourists.

The lodge was large, grand, made of wood planks, and set against dark ponderosa pines. It was three stories tall and rested on a high stone foundation. It had a somewhat rambling shape, giving it many corner rooms with windows. A few burros approached the cars looking for food, and bison wandered freely around the grounds.

The group got checked in and shown to their rooms. There were five reserved rooms at the end of a hallway. Each couple would have a room, as well as Fritz, the girls, and the boys.

Rebecca was eager for a hot bath, but it was decided to have lunch first. The dining room was elegant with white tablecloths and full place settings. Buffalo burgers with French fries were ordered all around. Neapolitan ice cream was served for dessert.

The Dacia children had never eaten in a place such as this. They stared at the furnishings and other customers. They felt awkward, a bit uncertain, and underdressed. They could see that their parents weren't relaxed either. The Epsteins seemed right at home. The food was delicious, but the Dacias were glad to return to their rooms. The girls and women were looking forward to hot baths.

"I'm sure ready for a bath too. But its only 2:00, and I'm kinda interested in that Wildlife Loop," Fritz said.

"The desk clerk said it was a one to two-hour drive around the loop, depending on how fast you drive," David added.

"The women will be bathing, so we should stay out of way," Josif said.

"We wanna go too," Michael-Joseph blurted out.

"We can all fit in my car," David said.

* * *

The men said good bye to the women, bought some beverages for the road, grabbed their ropes, and headed for the Epstein's car. David got his camera and fresh supplies of film.

The road wound through low rolling hills. Soft, waving prairie grasses flowed over them, and bison dotted the distant slopes. Shadows were lengthening, and a soft, cool breeze moved through the car.

"This sure is pretty," Fritz said. "It's kinda nice to see some prairie that ain't all plowed up."

"Yes, is good to keep this land as is," Josif said.

"And the buffalo," Michael-Joseph added.

The group spotted pronghorn antelope, more deer, bison, and a huge prairie dog town. David took pictures with his Speed Graphic, and the others used their Brownies.

About halfway around the loop, David pulled over at a level area with a small stand of ponderosas. There were a few stumps and broken branches on the ground. "How does this look for roping practice?" he asked.

PRAIRIE DOG TOWN   JMD

"Just right," Fritz said, getting out of the car with his rope.

Several stout broken branches were found to use as horns. After warming up on stumps, the roping began in earnest. The boys were first enlisted as steers, then the men. The boys' roping skills had improved to adequate. Josif and Fritz were good enough, and David was accomplished.

David showed everyone the trick roping he had learned from Will Rogers. He could do a flat spin, which he stepped in and out of. He brought the loop over his head and moved it up and down his body. Then he did a vertical flat spin to each side and the front. He ended his performance with several flat spins over his head, and the roping of a snag.

"Papa," Daniel said in amazement, "you really know what you're doing."

"I should, I've been practicing for about a year, depending on the weather."

"So, Deborah and I didn't have to convince you to come?"

"I was ready as soon as you and your sister got home and wanted to go back."

Josif laughed and clapped David on the back. "That's good. We will see more of you then."

"Do we all feel ready to take on Wyoming?" David asked.

"I guess we're about as ready as we'll ever be," Fritz said.

All nodded in agreement.

*   *   *

At the Game Lodge, the women had bathed and were trying on Rebecca and Deborah's clothing. Rebecca had convinced Izabella to wear something of hers to dinner. None of the Dacias knew they might be eating at a nice restaurant on the trip. Rebecca and Deborah had extra new clothes; why not share?

Izabella was in a blue skirt and blouse, liberally trimmed with silver fringe. She had on blue cowgirl boots, a red scarf, and a silver cowgirl hat.

Rose and Caroline were in similar outfits; Rose in blue and silver, and Caroline in yellow and gold.

Rebecca and Deborah were in pink and silver.

The men and boys almost didn't recognize them. When they did, they were slack-jawed. Rebecca explained her reasoning, and Josif had to agree. "Is very nice of you," he said. "We did not bring nice clothes because wedding is at rodeo. Izabella and girls look beautiful."

"David and Daniel have clothes for you and Michael-

Joseph," Rebecca continued. "I'm sorry we don't have anything to fit you, Fritz."

"I got a Western shirt and new pants for my weddin', Fritz said. "I'll wear that and my Stetson that August brought me back from New York."

* * *

At dinner, Joseph was wearing a dark blue shirt with light blue fringe. Michael-Joseph was in red, Daniel in silver. Spirits weren't high among the men, except Fritz who looked perfectly dressed and ruggedly handsome.

Daniel brought up the rear of the group as they entered the dining room. An older man with a heavy mustache and bowed legs approached him. "You folks entertainers or somethin'?" he asked.

Daniel looked at him glumly. "No," he said. "New Yorkers."

The man chuckled and patted Daniel on the back. "Good luck, son," he said. "You're gonna need it."

* * *

Three tables were again pulled together and the group was seated. The dinner menu had local game items, mostly buffalo. Platters of buffalo steaks, rainbow trout, roast pheasant, walleye pike, and a small plate of rabbit and rattlesnake sausage were brought to the table. David took a photo of the food. After explaining that he was doing a story for the *NY Times*, he was given a menu to take with him.

Everyone enjoyed the food. Deborah, Daniel, and David were imagining reactions of their friends back home to them eating buffalo and rattlesnake. Rebecca tried some of the buffalo, but mainly stuck to the trout and mashed potatoes. Michael-Joseph was trying to find a piece of rattlesnake in the sausage.

* * *

In their room that night, Michael-Joseph and Daniel compared notes about the trip. "So far, things couldn't be much better," Daniel said. "I think Mama is holding up pretty well; having fun, even."

"Yes," Michael-Joseph replied. "She and my mother seem to like each other. And your mother rode Sky. That was really good. I bet your father puts her picture in the paper."

"I bet he does too. And the picture of our parents together in their cowboy outfits that he had Fritz take."

Daniel told Michael-Joseph about the comment the old cowboy had made. "Have you been practicing your mental jabs?" he asked.

"All the time. Even when we're eatin', I'm picturing how to knock the waiter out."

"Me too. I feel kinda bad about it, but it helps to have a target. We haven't done any push-ups yet," Daniel reminded Michael-Joseph. "I don't want my parents to know that we're planning for a fight."

"Me either. We haven't exactly had much privacy, though. Wanna do some now?"

"Do you think it'll make a difference at this point?"

"Not really, but we have to be able to tell August we did some," Michael-Joseph replied.

The boys got on the floor and began their exercise. After about a minute they decided it would be more productive to practice their jabs. They took turns holding the pillows and gradually perfected their technique, although the mule kick aspect was weak.

"I think we have to depend on speed and surprise," Daniel said, "if cunning and reason don't work."

"Yeah, we may have to fight 'em off, back to back, sendin' 'em flyin'," Michael-Joseph said.

"Maybe we could rope them," Daniel suggested.

"Naw, that'll just make 'em ambush us later," Michael-Joseph said. "We have to take care of it the first time. No question about who won."

"Well, let's try to talk our way out of things first, Tarzan, if things get rough," Daniel said.

"Sure thing, Captain Nemo," Michael-Joseph replied.

CHAPTER SEVEN
The Setup

While the boys were punching pillows, August was sitting down to a friendly little game of poker. Three fellow performers were gathered in a room at the Prairie Gold Hotel, smokin', drinkin', and playin' some poker. August was persuaded by promise of a low-stakes game with amateurs to wind down after the performance.

August noticed the other players weren't the big names; they were backup performers. He was pleased that Floyd and Trixie weren't among them. Conversation was about making a living. "What I make singin' and playin' sure helps when a fella's tryin' to farm nowadays," one of them said.

"You got that right," the other one added. "You pretty much gotta be workin' two jobs to make it."

"Whaddaya do besides writin' songs and singin'?" the third asked August.

"I do some farmin'," he replied. "I just got married and we're settlin' in at a farm near Centerford."

"Over easta here. I hear that's some pretty good farm country over there."

"When we get rain it is," August replied.

"I heard you got a coupla racehorses over in Montana last year," the first one said. "That must come in handy for a little extra dough."

"We don't race 'em." August said. "Bill and Sky are mine and Marie's personal ridin' horses."

"What kinda horses are they?"

"Appaloosas. Indian horses. They've got black and white spots."

"I've seen horses look like that. Pretty fast, are they?"

"Oh yeah, they can tear up a track if they want to."

"You and Marie must have fun racin' 'em by yourselves."

"We sure do."

"I bet you got the fastest one."

August laughed. "Turns out Marie's got the fastest. Sky always beats Bill by about a neck."

* * *

After about thirty minutes of play, August was ahead by ten dollars.

A knock on the door stopped the game. One of the players opened it to Floyd and Trixie. Floyd pulled up a chair and sat down. Trixie sat on his lap, crossed her legs and smiled at August. Her red, curly hair hung to her shoulders. A red sequined bow was still in her hair from the show. Her black fringed skirt was above her knees, and she was swinging her foot in a lazy motion. She was wearing red cowboy boots.

"Deal me in," Floyd said, filling glasses for Trixie and himself with whiskey. "Get off," he said to Trixie. She made a pouting face and stood up behind Floyd, whiskey glass in hand.

Floyd won the first hand with a pair of eights. August won the second with a straight. Other players won a few hands, and after another thirty minutes, August was back to his initial stake of fifteen dollars.

During the playing, Trixie had made a show of bending to peer over Floyd's shoulder to look at his hand. She was wearing a low-cut blouse, and August was the intended recipient of the view. Floyd didn't seem to mind.

It was getting late and the group decided to play

one last hand. The betting was soon between August and Floyd. August bet all his money on four threes. The pot was up to sixty-five dollars. When it came time to show, Floyd had a full house, and August was the winner.

"I wanna chance to get my money back, Wagner," Floyd said. "Tomorrow night after we get paid. Okay. with you fellas?" he asked the other players.

"Sure, Floyd, who wouldn't want a chance to double their pay?" one of them said.

August vowed to himself to only bet the fifty dollars extra he just won. He wasn't going to risk his pay playing poker with Floyd Delaney.

CHAPTER EIGHT
Wyoming

The group stopped in the State Game Lodge gift shop on the way out. The men and boys got rattlesnake rattle key chains for themselves and those at home. The women and girls got handfuls of lucky rabbits' feet. David bought a history of the park and the Game Lodge and one about Peter Norbeck.

This time they ordered a case of pop, steaks, short ribs, and rolls for when they camped that night. These were stowed near the ice bowl, which was refilled.

* * *

The wedding party headed out the long scenic drive to Deadwood, a mining town. Although the town was only fifty-eight years old, it had an historic look and feel. It got its name from early prospectors who found a *gulch of dead trees with a creek full of gold.*

SITTING BULL   GEORGE A. CUSTER   Probable CRAZY HORSE Image

The Black Hills had been part of the Sioux and other tribes' sacred territory, given to them in the Sioux Treaty of 1868, also known as the Treaty of Fort Laramie. But the discovery of gold there drew prospectors. General George A. Custer and the Seventh Cavalry were given the assignment to make it safe for them. Thus, the devastating Sioux War, including The Battle of the Little Big Horn, from 1876 to 1877.

Deadwood had a long street through the center of town. Many buildings had been preserved and saloons and dance halls were prominent. There were also gift shops and a museum. "I've been savin' a real important purchase for here," Fritz said. "I'm gonna get Flora's wedding ring here. I wanna get her a ring of Black Hills Gold with the pink, green, and yellow gold. It'll always remind us of our weddin' in the Black Hills."

Fritz found a jewelry store specializing in Black Hills Gold. He picked a ring with the traditional tricolor grapes and grape leaf design. Izabella seemed to have hands the size of Flora, and Fritz selected a ring which fit her. Then he went to the engraving counter and had it engraved. The ring came in an ornate box, and he pushed it deep in his pocket.

David bought books about the history of Deadwood and those buried at the Mount Moriah Cemetery. Wild Bill Hickok and Calamity Jane were two of them. Josif got a book about the people and history of the Black Hills. Fritz got a booklet about the Homestake Gold Mine and one about Wild Bill Hickok. David and Josif also got small beaded purses for their wives. The others got postcards.

After lunch at a Western-themed restaurant, David followed the map to the cemetery. There, everyone spread out and searched through the headstones. Wild Bill Hickok and Calamity Jane's graves were fenced off and easy to find. Everyone took pictures.

* * *

The next stop was Devils Tower. Although it looked small on the horizon, one could see that it was gigantic. It stood high above all other features around it like a looming sentinel. Thought to be the lava plug of an ancient volcano, it rose eight hundred sixty-seven feet to a flat top. Igneous rock had formed massive hexagonal columns from top to bottom. From a distance the tower appeared to be evenly grooved along the sides.

Teddy Roosevelt had valued the tower so much that he made it America's first national monument. Six Indian tribes considered it sacred and often associated it with grizzly bears, due to the columns, which resembled deep grooves made by bear claws.

Everyone was awestruck and frustrated they could only take a few photos due to their limited film supplies.

It was early, around two o'clock, and the area at the base of the tower was shaded. There was less than a mile and a half trail around the base of the tower, and the group decided to follow it.

The children climbed over remnants of broken columns at the side of the trail. The Dacia children were in their normal playclothes. As they would be camping that night, Daniel and Deborah were in their borrowed clothing. Rebecca was wearing a skirt and blouse borrowed from Izabella. She had been persuaded to save a good outfit for their arrival at the ranch the next day.

David had also gladly borrowed normal clothing from Josif. The plan was for the group to camp near the Belle Fourche River that night. In the morning they would get cleaned up and go to the Doyle ranch. It would be Sunday, and they hoped to get there by mid-morning. The ranch was to the north, towards Hulett.

With frequent photo and rest stops, the group returned to their vehicles around four o'clock. They got situated and headed north along the Belle Fourche River.

* * *

At the Doyle ranch there was also a plan: clean and fix up better than a spring cleaning. The fixing-up part had been going on for months. Boards on the front porch had been hammered down; the railing had been painted. The walls in the spare bedroom where the female guests would be staying were repapered with a floral design.

The bathroom was painted, and all the fixtures scrubbed. The bathtub and sink had permanent hard water stains that no amount of scrubbing could remove. Flora put a bar of pink soap on a small, pretty plate by the tub. It helped some.

Rugs were hung over a fence and thrashed until dust stopped billowing from them. Curtains, sheets, towels, and blankets were washed. All the best clothing was washed and ironed. Floors were swept, firewood cut and stacked.

The business part of the ranch was being readied as well. The Doyles were putting on a rodeo on the Fourth of July, as well as Flora's wedding. Everything was to be perfect.

All fencing was inspected and tightened. Existing bleachers were painted white and several more tiers were constructed and painted.

Bunting was nailed to the announcer's stand and over the boxes where animal and rider would emerge.

The bunkhouse was scrubbed, mattresses beaten, the stove cleaned, sheets and blankets washed, and firewood hauled and stacked. The barn loft was cleared in the center and swept. The stable and barn were cleaned more deeply than usual, and tack cleaned and oiled. Horses were curried and hooves cleaned. Arrangements were being made for neighbors to bring bulls, calves, sheep, and horses that needed breaking. Excitement and exhaustion prevailed.

Flora lived with her father, Finley, and two brothers, Frank and Fred. They joked that Flora was marrying Fritz because she'd finally found a man whose name began with an "F."

All the Doyles had thick brown hair but Flora had long blond hair like her mother. The men had mustaches; Finley's was bushy and greying. They were all slim and muscular-looking.

Flora hadn't considered Fritz's name as a marriage qualification. She first met his brother, August, at Pioneer Days in Billings, Montana. She was later introduced to Fritz in South Dakota. Fritz wasn't as handsome as August, but he was impressive. He had large, rugged features and was six foot four. He was one of the heroes mentioned in August's famous song, *The Dakota Six*, so had some fame. She was attracted to him and loved hugging the huge bulk of him.

Flora had seen the Wagner farm that Fritz would inherit. It was large by farm standards, three hundred and twenty acres, although not compared to their ranch of twelve hundred acres. The farm was well-maintained and the farmhouse large and comfortable. There would be plenty of room to raise some horses and children.

Foremost in her attraction to Fritz though was his attention to her. Fritz treated her with gentleness and seemed almost in awe of her. She had seen him with the Dacia and Epstein children the year before and knew he liked them.

There were things she would miss about the ranch and her friends and family. But she was twenty-two and was ready to be married. Perhaps she would join her family in the fall to help with the horse racing they did at the fairs. Perhaps she and Fritz would race some horses of their own.

* * *

Flora was musing about her future when she wandered into the stable. Their foreman, Slim Stanton, intruded on her thoughts. "You 'bout done tryin' to impress them New Yorkers?" he asked her while currying one of the horses. "You really think they'll even see everything we've cleaned up as nice? They'll prob'ly be in some fancy duds too nice to get any dirt on. They'll be weak and won't have one callous, 'cept on their money countin' fingers."

"Slim," Flora said, "you better be decent, or I'll tell Papa to fire you! I met the Epstein kids already, and they're fine. There was nothin' high or mighty about 'em. The boy was one of the kidnap victims and the girl faced down a gangster. They learned to ride bareback. I like 'em. They've got grit."

"You think their parents are gonna be the same way? They're New Yorkers, Flora. City slickers who won't know a steer's tail from a pump handle. Not that they'd ever stoop to pumpin' water," Slim muttered.

"You might be surprised," Flora said. "Maybe you

should wait to pass judgement 'till you meet 'em. Seems like you got your mind made up already."

"Oh, I guess I'll be meetin' 'em all right. Ruin a good rodeo's what they'll do. Get in the way and complain that we're hurtin' the steers. It's gonna be grand."

Slim was in his forties, six foot two, lean, hard, and weathered. He had worked all over Wyoming from Yellowstone and the Big Horn Mountains to Jackson Hole and the high plains west of the Black Hills. There was nothing he didn't know about cattle and ranching, and he was the boss. He lived in the bunkhouse with the two ranch hands and was leery of strangers.

"Look, Slim, I'm gettin' married. I want beautiful memories. I won't be puttin' up with you startin' fights and makin' trouble with my guests."

"Yeah, sure. I'll behave, but I'll bet you my bronc-bustin' championship belt buckle those New Yorkers are gonna be a pain."

"I was hopin' you'd kinda help me look out for everybody. I don't want anybody to feel embarrassed or get hurt," Flora said. "That would be a very unhappy wedding memory."

"I s'pose you're also referring to that big farmer you're marryin'?"

"Well, sure, I 'specially wanna keep him in one piece."

"And that family of Bohunks too, I s'pose?"

"Of course, Slim."

"I don't know if your papa pays me enough."

"Think of it as bein' your weddin' present to me."

"I already got ya somethin'."

"Slim, please, I need your help."

"You're askin' an awful lot. But as I taught ya most everythin' ya know 'bout ridin' an ranchin', I feel responsible. I'll try."

* * *

The country north of Devils Tower was gentle and beautiful. Grasslands merged with foothills dotted with stands of ponderosa pines. Higher tree-covered hills and mountains rose in the distance. The Belle Fourche River flowed gently through grass-covered banks and meadows. The soil was rust red in most places. In spots, the river appeared wide and shallow with banks up to four feet high.

David stopped the car on such a bank. The river flowed gently below, around boulders and a snag. There was a twenty by fifty-foot-wide area of raised white ground between the river and the bank. It looked like an oasis floating on the river, serene and so close to the gentle water that one could lie on the warm ground and trail their fingers in it. Birds sang from nearby cottonwoods. The sun would soon sink behind the tallest peaks and shadows were lengthening.

"What does everyone think of this spot?" David asked.

Fritz replied from his truck by stopping the engine and untying the tarp.

The Dacias got out of their car and looked over the bank. "This is beautiful, David," Izabella said. "We will hear the soft sounds of the river as we sleep."

"We can gather soft grass to put under our sleeping bags," Rebecca said.

* * *

Fritz climbed onto the bed of the truck and handed down their camping supplies. The men handed the items down the bank where the boys took them and set them out. Blankets were spread and the cookstove set up on a flat rock. The boys set up the tents, being sure to kick away any stones. Two ropes were tied to the fenders of the cars and draped over the bank to help with climbing up and down the bank.

Fritz gathered dry branches from the roadside and started a fire. The girls gathered wood for the evening, then grass for their beds.

Rebecca and Izabella decided that the buffalo short ribs should be boiled before grilling. The steaks would have to be fried and the stove rack put over the coals for the short ribs. Rebecca got water from the river and put it on the stove to boil.

In the meantime, the women headed to patches of soft waving grasses hanging over the riverbank to gather for their beds. The girls had already covered the tent floor with a thin layer of grass and were collecting more. Izabella and Rebeca each made two more trips. The grass looked about four inches deep on the tent floor.

Rebecca returned to the stove to put the ribs in to boil. Izabella and the girls spread out the sleeping bags as blankets. The large bed looked soft and inviting.

"I'm going to put my good outfit for tomorrow on top in my suitcase with my cowgirl boots and hat," Deborah said. "I don't want to leave them out and let bugs or snakes get in them tonight."

Izabella and the girls looked around the tent. "Let's block the back entrance with our suitcases now and move some to the front when we go to bed," Rose suggested.

"Good idea," Izabella agreed.

"I'm closing mine and Mama's real tight," Deborah said, zipping the suitcases and buckling their straps. "Mama wouldn't like it at all if she found a snake in her clothes."

"Ugh," they all said, and closed their suitcases. They stacked them at the back of the tent, trying to block all openings.

The girls ran to a new area of soft grass to gather for the other tents. Izabella joined Rebecca at the cookstove.

* * *

The campsite with its three tents, campfire, cookstove, lazy river, and pink sky looked idyllic. David took a picture. He then scrambled up the four-foot bank to his car and got a shot from there.

"It would be good to put cameras and books in the cars tonight," he called to the group. "It can get damp by a river at night."

Josif and Fritz climbed the embankment and deposited Brownies, postcards, books, and souvenirs in their vehicles.

Josif and Fritz got out their bottles. The three men gathered at the edge of the river and passed Fritz's whiskey bottle around. "This sure is a pretty river," Fritz said. "If it weren't for the mosquitoes, it'd be damn near perfect. I know what. I'll light a cigarette and blow some smoke around. That might scare 'em off."

Fritz pulled his bag of tobacco and packet of rolling paper from his shirt pocket. He rolled a smoke and snapped a match alight with his thumbnail and lit his cigarette; he took a deep breath and blew smoke at a small swarm of insects. "I see we got some gnats too," he said, chasing them with a stream of smoke.

As the sky changed from pink twilight to deep blue, the biting and stinging increased. Everyone gathered around the fire where the heat and smoke kept the pests away.

"Don't scratch," Rebecca said to her children. "It will get bigger if you scratch."

"Well, that ain't gonna happen," Fritz said. "Not scratchin's pure misery." He scratched hard at his arm. "I hear clay and bear fat are good at keepin' bugs away," he said. "At least, that's what I heard the Indians used."

"No, thank you," Rebecca said. "I prefer to cover up more." Rebecca went to the tent and got a folded-up sweater she had prepared as a pillow. She put it on and buttoned it to the neck. She tied her neck scarf to cover her head and stuck her hands in her pockets. "There, that will be better," she said.

* * *

Dinner was a drawn-out affair. They ate in the glow of the fire, nibbling on ribs, steak, rolls, and cookies. The children had pop, and the adults sat around the fire and passed a bottle. The women joined in until tension left their bodies and thoughts of their soft, cozy beds beckoned.

Josif got a stick and pushed the remnants of the burning fire together. The unburnt sticks flared up, then joined the bed of coals. Fritz gathered up the buffalo ribs and steak bones and flung them into the darkness of the river. "You know the Indians didn't call Devils Tower *Bear Lodge* for nothin'," he said. "I bet there's nothin' a bear wouldn't like better'n gnawin' on some buffalo bones."

The girls squealed and headed for the tent. The boys looked over their shoulders into the darkness and headed for the mens' tent. "If you have to go durin' the night, go in pairs and make a lotta noise," Fritz instructed. "That'll scare 'em away."

Rebecca grabbed a pot and spoon. She gave the

other pot and a spoon to Daniel. "For noise-making," she said. We'll keep them by the front of the tents."

Izabella and Rebecca joined the girls in their tent. The beds weren't soft, but they were certainly more comfortable than those in the Badlands campground. Except for whining mosquitoes in the tent and annoying itching under the covers, it was pleasant. The sound of the Belle Fourche River flowing nearby was soothing. A breeze through the pines made a soft lullaby, helping the full and relaxed travelers stop slapping and scratching and slip into sleep. The moon and stars shone brightly overhead.

CHAPTER NINE
Closing the Trap

August had little choice but to join the poker game on Saturday night. Two of the backup singers he'd played poker with the night before jovially escorted him to the room. Inside were the third player and Floyd and Trixie Delaney.

The performers had all been paid after their last performance in cash. Only a few performers were scheduled for the Sunday matinee; August was one of them. He had one hundred dollars pay plus his fifty-dollar winnings from the night before. He had put his pay in his boot and the fifty in his pocket, determined to bet only that.

Floyd pulled a quart of whiskey from his coat pocket and poured everyone a glassful. Trixie stood behind Floyd, smiling at August. One of the backup singers pulled out a deck of cards and they cut for deal. August won with an ace; everyone anted up a quarter and he dealt.

After an hour the whiskey bottle was empty, and August's winnings had gone from fifty to one hundred. It was decided to take a break. The players got up and stretched, then left to visit the bathrooms down the hall.

Except Trixie.

August had about two fingers of whiskey left in his glass. Into this Trixie pored chloral hydrate, better known as knockout drops, which she kept in her drawstring purse. Then she slipped out the door, headed for the ladies' room.

Another bottle of whiskey was produced by one of the returning players. The glasses were refilled and the playing resumed.

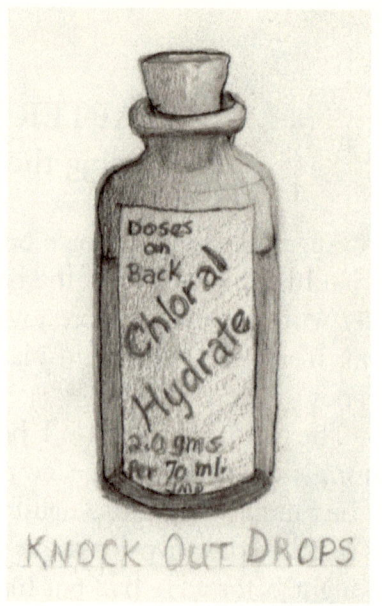

* * *

The last thing August remembered was trying to play a losing hand. He didn't even have a pair. He felt woozy and confused. "Looks like you used up all your luck, kid," were the last words he heard.

* * *

August awoke in the morning to the sound of someone pounding on his door. He was in his room on his bed; his boots were on the floor. He sat up on the edge of his bed, rubbing his face and aching head. He couldn't remember coming to his room or taking off his boots. "Who is it?" he called.

"Floyd," was the response.

"Go away," August said. "I don't wanna see you or your wife ever again."

"Afraid that's not gonna happen, bucko. You owe me a lotta money."

"What're you talkin' about?"

"Why don't you open the door, so we don't have ta yell. Unless you want everyone to know you're tryin' to welch on a bet."

August got up and opened the door. He felt queasy. "What the hell are you talkin' about?" he asked Floyd. "I was ahead last night." Floyd came in the room and shut the door.

"For a while you were, then you weren't. You started losin' and didn't stop. You kept bettin' on pairs and tryin' to bluff. You're not very good at that, you know."

August tried to find memories of the game but couldn't. He didn't know what had happened. He grabbed his right boot and shook it. It was empty. "You and your crooked buddies robbed me," he said. "I wouldn't never bet my pay."

"Afraid you did, kid," Floyd said. "You were kinda desperate. You wanted to win your horse back."

"Win my horse back?" August felt feelings of anger and anxiety. He didn't remember the night before, but he knew he would never bet Bill or Sky.

"Yeah, you got a little loose and said you bet Sky could beat most any horse around. I took you up on that bet."

"If I said that, I wasn't serious," August said. "I wouldn't never bet Sky."

"You did though, I got four witnesses."

August lunged at Floyd, grabbing him by the collar. He brought his fist back, ready to deliver a knockout blow.

Floyd drew back and smiled. "I wouldn't do that unless you wanna explain to the sheriff and get written up in the papers. Performers who have reputations as drinkers, fighters, and gamblers don't go far in the business. 'Specially when they lose their wife's pet horse in the process."

August let go of Floyd. He realized he was dealing with a professional. It seemed like his whole life was at stake. He had to be careful. He used his boxer's training to get himself under control.

Floyd continued. "You might not remember the sweet deal I made you. I gave you a chance to get Sky back, and another horse as well." He smiled, but his eyes were calculating as he assessed August's reaction.

"What're you talkin' about?"

"A claim race. I've got an old Quarter Horse might have some speed left in 'im. He's eight though and a little swaybacked. Buddy's his name. We agreed that I'd race him against Sky. If you win, you get Buddy. If I win, I get Sky.

"Why would I do a dumb thing like that?

"Because you kept thinkin' you were on a winnin' streak. You didn't seem to think you could lose, until you did, that is. Then you lost a lot. Almost everything you might say. You pulled off your boot and bet every last dime of what you made on this gig. But you still didn't win. Guess you're a loser, Wagner not such a big *Dakota Six* hero anymore."

August felt sick. He couldn't believe what he was hearing.

"But hey, I like to give a guy a chance," Floyd said. "You can place some side bets on the race maybe make your pay back and keep your horse."

August couldn't think clearly.

"So, like we agreed last night, Trixie and I'll come by your place in Centerford with Buddy. We'll have us a little race and see who owns what horse in the end."

"Get outta my room," August said.

"Sure, kid. Just remember, you gotta pay up. If you can't cover your bets, you're nothin'. Your reputation will stink. Your friends and family will disown ya. And if you ever have any kids, they'll hear their daddy bein' called a bum." Floyd laughed and closed the door behind him.

* * *

August sat on the edge of the bed with his head in his hands. If what Floyd said was true, he could lose Sky. Losing Sky would break Marie's heart, and that would break his heart. He didn't know how to tell her about the Delaneys and the poker game.

He had a matinee performance and would be done by 3:00. August got cleaned up and went out for breakfast. He hoped coffee and food would help clear his head.

The pain he could be causing Marie was all he could think about. He had made a huge mistake. After her frustrations with Chicago and the *World's Fair*, she might leave him and go back to her family. He had done nothing but fail her. All he wanted was to hold her and tell her it would be okay. He had never felt so bad.

* * *

Marie stayed by the kitchen radio all day. The *Country Jamboree* August was performing in was being broadcast over the radio. She was pleased to hear August introduced, although surprised he had written a new song.

Even though he didn't say it, she knew it was for her. The name of the song was *Don't Let Me Go*. She listened with pleased expectation, which soon turned to puzzled concern.

"*I'm a fool.*
I'm a fool.
I'm too dumb to count to two.
I'm the world's biggest fool.
But I love you so much, dear.
Don't let me go.

I make mistakes.
I get bad breaks.
I let you down.
I make you frown.
But you're the best I'll ever know.
Don't let me go.

Don't let me go.
Don't let me go.
I love you more than you'll ever know.
Don't let me go, my dearest one.
Don't let me go.

No fella's as dumb as me.
I'm the worst could ever be.
I don't deserve one good as you.
But my love for you is true.
Tell me what I long to hear.
Don't let me go.

I'll make everything up to you.
I'll make it just like new.
My heart breaks to hurt you so.
A fool I'll be no more.
Please know I love you so.
Don't let me go.

Don't let me go.
Don't let me go.
I love you more than you'll ever know.
Don't let me go, my darling one.
Don't let me go.

Don't let me go.
Don't let me go.
I love you more than you'll ever know.
Don't let me go, my darling one.
Don't let me go."

Marie stood at the sink and looked out the window. Bill and Sky were grazing in the pasture. Everything looked fine, but it might not be for long. What could August's song be about? He sounded desperate as though he had ruined things so much that she would leave him. Could he be trying to tell her he'd been duped, like in Chicago? What was wrong? She felt ill. Her heart ached. She wished he was home.

CHAPTER TEN
We're Here

Fritz was awakened by the sound of rain on his tent and distant thunder. He lay still for a moment, then he jumped up and looked out through the tent flap. The ground was wet and the distance between the river and the top of the ground they were camped on had lessened.

"Flood!" he yelled. "Flood! Flood! Run! Run now! Hurry!" Without putting on boots or jacket, he crawled out of the tent. "Flood," he yelled again. "Everybody get up and get to the cars right now! Don't get dressed. Run for your lives! Flood! Hurry!" His booming voice was more effective than beating on a pot.

Fritz tried to stand but couldn't. The white ground they camped on was clay. It was slick and the increasing rain was making it slicker. Every time he tried to stand, he fell on his face. His hands and clothes were coated, and he couldn't get a good purchase with his feet.

Sounds of alarm were coming from the other two tents. The adults pushed the children out of the tents and told them to run for the cars. But no one could run. All fell in the wet clay and struggling to stand only made it worse. "Get sleeping bags," Izabella called. "We make bridge."

Sleeping bags were pulled from the tents and thrown on the ground to walk over. The bags helped, but also began to slip, and the river water crested the dry ground, making the sleeping bags float and slide over the clay.

The adults, on the verge of panicking, yelled to the children to run and climb up the bank to the cars. Little progress was made. Some of them made it to the ropes hanging from the bumpers, but their slick hands couldn't grasp them. The four-foot bank was impossible to climb. Small rivulets of water were flowing down it.

Fritz struggled to one of the ropes and was able to tie it around his waist. He braced one foot against the bank and leaned back against the rope. He kept a tenuous balance with his other foot. There he stood, grabbing everyone who came close by the neck of their shirt and pants' waist. Then he swung them up onto the bank where they landed on their fronts. Everyone slid and scrambled over to Fritz. Those who were rescued tried to reach over the bank to help the others. Finally, Fritz heaved Josif onto the bank; the last one but himself, safe.

Josif lay on the bank and reached for Fritz. He could reach his arm and grab his hand but couldn't get a grip. Izabella reached for his other arm. A distant roar was no longer distant. A massive force of muddy water, broken trees, and rocks was within sight. Fritz tried to dig his toes into the bank to climb out, but the clay crumbled. Josif and Izabella reached out as far as they could, trying to grasp Fritz's belt, but it wasn't far enough.

The sound of the Epstein's car starting was drowned out by the crash of the flood. Fritz was pulled out of the water and onto the bank by the rope around his waist. He had received only a glancing blow on his leg from passing debris. All had gotten out alive.

* * *

The flood and its debris had risen about three feet up the bank. The entire camp and all their suitcases had been washed away. The travelers were covered in white clay from head to toe. They had no shoes and were wearing the clothes they had worn to bed, now imbedded with wet clay.

It was just after dawn, but the sky was leaden grey,

especially over the mountains. The beautiful Belle Fourche River was running amok. The group was stunned, trying to understand what had just happened, and what they would do now. The noise of the water was deafening and frightening.

"Go to cars and drive to higher ground," Josif yelled over the roar. The roadside had some gravel on it, and dirt rather than clay. All ten got into the vehicles. Fritz in his truck led the way. The group soon reached a safe elevation and Fritz stopped the caravan. He got out of his truck and everyone joined him.

"Man, that was really somethin'," he said. "That was a little too close for comfort."

"Way too close," Daniel said.

Rebecca and Izabella were hugging their children. Rebecca was crying. "We all could have died," she sobbed, squeezing them tighter.

"We're okay, Mama," Deborah said.

"For once it wasn't my fault," Michael-Joseph said, trying to lighten the mood.

Josif patted him on the shoulder. "No, you not at fault. I should see the danger."

"Me, too, Joe," Fritz said. "It was just so doggone pretty, and it's been so doggone dry, who'd a thunk it'd flood?"

"We all should've thought about it and realized the danger," David said. "I know that I thought that such a beautiful spot would always be beautiful. Thinking back on it, I suppose that snag in the water might have been a clue."

"And a four-foot riverbank," Fritz added.

"Thank God all are alive," Izabella said. "We lost everything else but are all okay. That is what matters. Thank you, Fritz. You save all our lives."

"I'm glad it worked out. I'm especially glad David remembered the rope was tied to the car. We sure weren't gettin' any grip with that clay all over everythin'."

"No," Josif said. "Was almost too late."

"Yeah, I noticed," Fritz said.

All were silent for a moment. Rebecca was emotionally drained. Daniel had been kidnapped when he visited the Dacia farm the previous year. Now this year the whole family had almost died. They had lost all their possessions. She had no control over anything and would be meeting strangers looking like this. She wished she was back in New York in her clean, comfortable apartment. She hoped she would never come out west again and hugged Deborah more tightly.

"I figure we're about twenty miles from the Doyle ranch," Fritz said. "I've got the directions memorized. I hadn't planned on greetin' my fiancée lookin' like this, but I don't guess I have much choice."

"I'm so embarrassed," Rebecca said. "Coming to someone's home looking like this. What a horrible first impression we'll make."

"I'm sure they'll understand," David said. "Let's untie our ropes from the bumpers and keep on."

* * *

The Doyle household had been up since five. Flora had everyone dress in their Sunday best and her father and brothers looked awkward.

"I don't see why we have to dress like we're goin' to church when we're not," Flora's younger brother, Fred, complained. "We can't compete with New Yorkers; why try? We'll just look like we're tryin' to put on airs."

"And not very good airs compared to them," youngest

brother Frank added. "We've met Fritz and the other Wagners. And the Dacias too. They're regular folks, they won't care if we're dressed up or not."

Flora's father, Finley, ran his finger around the inside of his collar, loosening it a bit. "Now look, boys," he said, "we've been over this before. Some a these folks are from back east; they like to dress nice. Heck, they like to sit around dressed nice all day. It's natural for 'em. They prob'ly wouldn't know what to do if they ever got any dirt on 'em. We don't wanna shock 'em; might faint."

"Papa, you're just as bad as Fred and Frank," Flora said, sounding defeated. "Can't everybody just settle down and act civilized for a few days? Is that too much to ask? This is gonna be my weddin,' ya know. I'd like it to be memorable for nice reasons."

"Well, that's the problem, Flora. It's your weddin', and a rodeo, and the Fourth of July. It's bound to get rowdy. Ain't no way 'round it."

"Please, Papa, make 'em behave. Make Slim and the hands too. Don't let 'em make my last memories of here be angry."

Finley put his arm around his daughter. "Don't worry, honey. We'll all be on our best behavior and try to make you proud. Just remember we can only change so much. You can't expect us to turn into different people; we only know how to be us."

"Thanks for tryin'. I know we can only spruce this place up so much, and gettin' married in the middle of a rodeo ring ain't exactly elegant. It makes sense to me and Fritz, but it might not to them. I wanna be able to hold my head up as much as possible at my weddin'. I don't want anybody to think we're backward or don't know how to do things proper." She looked at the floor. "I'm gonna need all the help I can get."

"Flora, honey, we're gonna do our best. That's all we got to offer. If anybody makes fun a your weddin', we'll take 'em out back and show 'em what's what. We'll all be lookin' out fer ya. Right, boys?" Finley asked.

"Sure, Flora," the boys answered.

"We won't put up with folks who look down on us for the way we dress or cuz we got dirt under our fingernails," Finley assured her.

"Papa, that's not what I mean. I don't want anyone to get beat up, even if they're rude. I want everybody to get along and be polite to each other."

"Like I said, honey, we'll try," Finley repeated. "But you gotta remember this is a weddin', rodeo, and the Fourth of July. I only have so much control over the inevitable."

* * *

The sound of multiple vehicles coming up the long driveway stopped the conversation. Flora peered out the window with Fred looking over her shoulder. "Looks like that's them," Fred said.

"Kinda early," Finley remarked. "Not even 6:00. That's surprisin'."

The vehicles pulled up in front of the house, but no one opened their door or got out. People inside the cars looked strange, as though they were wearing masks.

Finally, the door to the truck opened and a tall, mud-covered man got out. "I think that's Fritz," Flora said. The man paused by the truck and looked at the cars. Slowly the doors opened, and nine various-sized, mud-covered people emerged. They stood by their vehicles, heads hanging.

Flora opened the door and went out onto the porch. "Is that you, Fritz?" she called.

"'Fraid so," he replied. "We had a little run-in with a flash flood and some wet clay. All our stuff got washed away. We're sorry to show up like this. We had hoped to make a better first impression."

"Is everyone all right?" she asked.

"Yeah, we made it through by the skin of our teeth, but we're all here," Fritz said.

Flora went over to Fritz and looked up into his eyes. "I'm sure glad to see you again," she said. "Although I remember you bein' a little cleaner."

Fritz smiled; some dried clay cracked and fell off his face. "I'm mighty pleased to see you again too," he said.

Flora suddenly remembered her duties as hostess. She studied the group. "Frank, go get some a yours and Fred's clothes for our men guests to wear. Fred, go out to the bunkhouse and see if Slim can round up some clothes to fit Fritz and the boys. Bring back soap and a stack a towels too. Papa, would you show the men where to wash in the river? Fred and Frank, bring their clothes over there. Oh, and tell Pete and Hank to start heatin' water and come pour it in the shower barrel. Ladies, come with me."

The men headed off, following Flora's instructions. Izabella, Rebecca, and the girls followed Flora into the house.

* * *

The Lucky D was set in rolling grasslands, studded with clumps of ponderosa pines, aspen, and bur oak. The red soil framed the dark pines, and there were numerous red sandstone outcroppings working their way out of the hillsides.

A small tributary of the Belle Fourche River wound its way across the ranch effectively dividing the hills from the flatter land where the ranch buildings were located. The exception was at the ford where the river dipped away from the hills at a shallow angle and flattened out.

Here, the water was only around eighteen inches

deep in a twenty-foot-wide natural ford of the river, which was twelve feet across from bank to bank. Other parts of the small river were three feet deep, only four feet across with one-foot banks.

A long, dusty and pot-holed driveway led from the road to the ranch house, which wasn't far from the ford. From the ranch house, all the other buildings were easily approached. A wide road connected the house to the barn, going past the corrals and animal pens. The barn was actually the most handsome building on the ranch. It had been built during a more prosperous time when the Doyle family had first homesteaded there. A symbol of prosperity, it had been built to exhibit quality and substance. The other buildings looked like poor cousins next to it.

Behind the barn were the windmill and the plain-looking rectangular bunkhouse. Made of rough-hewn lumber like many of the other buildings, it was utilitarian without any attempt at charm. A thin stand of trees rose behind the bunkhouse.

* * *

The Doyle Barn with Lucky D Brand

The Doyle ranch house was a rambling affair. It was constructed of the same rough-hewn local lumber as the other buildings with a deep porch on two sides. It had begun as a small claim shack, which was now the kitchen. Five bedrooms, a sitting room, and recently a bathroom with a claw foot tub and commode had been added. There were mudrooms at each door and a laundry room next to the kitchen. The furnishings were basic, but comfortable and neat.

Izabella introduced Rebecca to Flora. "I'm pleased to meet you," Rebecca said. "We're so sorry about our appearance and any mess we make."

"Oh, don't worry about that. It's real easy to get covered in somethin' when you're dealin' with nature," Flora said. "I'm just glad everyone's okay."

She studied the girls. "Let's see, goin' by size, I'd say you're Rose, you're Caroline, and you're Deborah."

"You got it perfect," Rose said. "It's nice to see you again."

"Yes," said Caroline. "Now we can see what your ranch and horses look like."

"And maybe you'll show us more about riding," Deborah said.

Flora laughed, "We'll get started on that right after we get everyone cleaned up and fed. It sure is nice to see all of you again, and to meet you, Rebecca."

* * *

Flora ushered the women into the laundry room and brought in chairs. "I'm gonna ask you ladies to stay in here until we can get things set up for ya. I'm gonna make a call, then get you some coffee and breakfast."

The women were glad to be out of sight, and eager for

the promised breakfast and coffee. They sat silently and tried not to shed more clay.

Rebecca had spent much of the night scratching and knew she wasn't the only one. Izabella and the girls had also been scratching their heads, arms, and legs. The lovely soft grasses had been inhabited. She feared she would be covered with red bite marks which would itch. They would be everywhere, including her hair. Worse yet, they might be hard to get rid of. She felt infested and considered running outside and jumping in the river. She again longed for Manhattan.

* * *

Flora went to the phone on the kitchen wall and ground the crank. She listened to the earpiece for a moment. "Hi Velma," she said... "Yes, they're here already...

No, it wasn't good. They got caught in a flash flood on the Belle Fourche. Lost all their belongings, clothes and everything. Didn't even have time to put on their boots... Yeah, if you'd call around it'd help a lot.

"We're just gettin' the water heated to clean up the women, so as soon as possible I guess... There's three men, two kinda average, and a real big one. That's Fritz, he's about six four; he's mine. Then there's two women, slim and average-sized. There're three girls the size of your three, and two boys about the size of Tim and Tom Olson.

Nope, no hats, boots, socks, drawers, shirts, pants, skirts, blouses, jackets, or gloves. No nothin'... No, they're not naked. They're wearing what they were sleepin' in; it's just not in very good shape anymore.... Thanks, Velma. Bye." Soon various *rings* were heard as Velma put out the word.

Flora filled a large pan with warm water from the stove and grabbed a couple towels. She took them to the laundry room and set them on a table by the women. Why don't you all get your hands and faces clean," she said. "I'll get you some drinks and fry up some potatoes and eggs. Flora grabbed two mugs and filled them with coffee. "You ladies want cream in yours?" she called to them.

"Yes, please," was the subdued response.

"And fresh milk for the gals?"

"Yes, please."

The women and girls were relieved to clean their faces and hands. The coffee, milk and food soon revived them. Flora looked out the kitchen window. "The hands are bringin' some hot water for the shower barrel. A couple more trips and some cold water from the river and we can get your showers started. You might wanna draw straws to see who's first."

Rebecca looked in the direction Flora had indicated the shower was in. It didn't seem to be in the house. "Is the shower outside?" she asked. She tried to keep her tone neutral.

"Yeah, but don't worry, it's real private. We have a bathtub in the house, but we can't have all that clay go down the drain. We have to be mostly clean to use the tub.

"What does *real private* mean?" Rebecca asked.

"The opening faces a wall of the house. You only go there for a shower. You can't see in from where you pour hot water in the barrel. It's real private."

"Is there a blanket or something we could hang over the entry?" Rebecca asked.

"Well, sure. We can do that." Flora said.

"We should wait for clothes first, shouldn't we?" Izabella asked.

"Either that or I can lend you some a my things," Flora said.

"You're trying to pack your things to take to your new home. We don't want to wear the things you've been packing," Izabella said. "We can wait for clothes to arrive."

"Yes, we can wait," Rebecca said, trying not to sound too resigned.

* * *

In about thirty minutes, two cars showed up with stacks of clothes. Louise drove one car and Lorene the other. Both were neighbors and friends of Flora's.

The women carried the stacks of clothes into the Doyle ranchhouse. Flora organized them in the sitting room by sex and size.

There were piles of everything, including very broken-in cowboy boots and sweat-stained cowboy hats. Leather gloves that would naturally curve around a rope or reins; chaps and even some spurs were included.

"Are they here?" Lorene asked.

"Of course they are."

"Can we meet 'em?"

"Let's let 'em get cleaned up first," Flora answered.

"Aw, why? We wanna see what they look like all covered in clay."

"Well, Lorene, the men and boys are out washing in the river. You could go out there."

"Flora, you got nerve. We just wanna see 'em."

"Well, when everyone's ready we'll all meet each other," Louise said, leading Lorene toward the door. Let's let 'em get settled."

"Thanks for bringin' things over," Flora said. "You're a big help."

Flora picked through the clothes and gathered outfits, which she showed to the women and girls. Everything had been well-used. Rebecca knew that any reluctance on her part would be seen as insulting. She accepted an outfit with a calf-length brown gabardine skirt, blue blouse, and neck scarf. A broken-in leather cowboy hat, belt, and boots completed the ensemble. She noted some old stains that could never be removed on the skirt.

"Two more things you'll need," Flora said, rooting around in the pile, "are a jacket and gloves." She held several choices up with her back to the laundry room. "Ah, here's a nice one for you, Rebecca," she said, and turned around. Flora was holding a beautifully tanned, soft, brown leather jacket. It had leather fringe on the sleeves in a V shape down the front and across the back.

Rebecca was stunned. It was beautiful and powerful. It had a style and energy of its own. "It's truly beautiful," she said. "Someone was very kind to lend it to us."

"Well, that'd be Louise LaVoi. She and her kids make 'em. They're kinda for dress-up, but these next few days'll be special. Plus, she's gotta heart a gold," Flora said. "And since you've got an outfit, let's get you cleaned up first." Flora grabbed a towel and two blankets from a shelf. She opened a drawer and picked out a hammer and two nails. "Just follow me," she directed.

It was a short walk from the door out the laundry room to the shower enclosure. Flora led Rebecca past a ramp up to a fifty-gallon barrel. A pipe from the bottom of the barrel went to the top of the shower stall. They walked to the stall and stopped. There were about two feet between the enclosure and a windowless wall of the house. A bench was against the wall, and there were several nails in the wall used as hooks. Flora put a blanket and towel on the bench, then nailed the second blanket across the shower opening.

There was a slatted wooden floor to the stall and a soap shelf. The bar of soap needed washing. It was cracked and grimy and may have once been white. A knotted rope hung from a lever overhead.

Flora held out her hand and gave the rope a little tug. A small stream of water trickled from the sprinkler head onto her hand. "That feels pretty good," she said. "Just pull the rope when you want water. I'm gonna tell Pete and Hank to keep the barrel full of nice warm water. They can't see you from the tank. They wouldn't even try, so don't worry about bein' seen. Just wrap yourself in the blanket when you're done and come on back through the laundry room. I'll have your clothes waiting for you in your room."

"Do you have any shampoo?" Rebecca asked.

"Not really," Flora answered. "We've got some stuff we use on horses, but that's about all. I'm sorry we don't have all the conveniences you're used to."

"I'm sorry, Flora. I don't mean to find fault. There aren't many places that have such a variety as New York City. This will be fine, and I'm going to be so happy to get this clay off me. What should I do with my clothes?"

"Just put 'em in a pile to the side and we'll wash everybody's stuff at once." She laughed. "We can start at the river and add some clay to the bottom." Flora turned to leave.

"You know," she said, turning back, "you might like how that clay treats your skin. It'll leave it nice and soft and clean. It's called bentonite and even ol' Chief Gall himself used it. Was real proud of his smooth skin, they say. It should help with those bug bites you were talkin' about too."

* * *

Flora left Rebecca to her shower. She went back to picking outfits. For Izabella she found a dark green skirt, green checked blouse, yellow scarf, and brown vest. Her boots had some tooling on the side; there was a small silver cabochon on the hat band. There was another fringed jacket in tan leather and Flora added it to Izabella's pile.

The girls were beside themselves with excitement about their new clothes. They crowded each other at the laundry room door to see the selections. Flora patiently picked out combinations and set aside their outfits.

Soon Rebecca returned covered in her blanket. Flora directed her to the bedroom and retrieved the blanket for Izabella who was next.

* * *

Rebecca found her clothes on a bed next to what she assumed were Izabella's. Three sets of girls' clothing were on the other bed in the room. She wasn't used to this closeness but had already camped as a group. She would endure and not embarrass her family or the Dacias.

Flora had added undergarments to the piles and Rebecca gritted her teeth and got dressed. The clothes smelled of fresh air and were worn and soft. They fit her comfortably.

There was a dresser with a brush, comb, and hand mirror, as well as a full mirror on a stand. Rebecca brushed her wavy black hair and looked closely at her skin. She expected to find numerous red and itchy bites. She didn't;

her skin looked clean and felt smooth and soft. In fact, her skin had seldom looked so good, even after a beauty treatment at Wanamaker's.

Rebecca stepped back and looked at herself in her outfit with boots and hat. It was a new look, but she liked it. She looked and felt tough and strong. She briefly imagined a picture David could take of her on a horse.

Then she slipped on the fringed leather jacket and fell in love. The fringes swung freely and looked beautiful. The leather was soft and supple. All her movements seemed graceful.

As she finished dressing, Izabella came in covered in the blanket. Rebecca took it from her as she handed it out the door and went into the sitting room. The girls and Flora gasped in amazement. "Mama, you look beautiful! Like a real cowgirl. Right, Flora?" Deborah asked.

"It'd be hard to look more real unless you were covered in somethin'," Flora said, laughing. "You look real nice."

Izabella's arrival also brought exclamations of joy and admiration. The girls could hardly wait for their turns. They were thrilled when they, too, came out of the bedroom in their long cowgirl skirts, boots, country blouses, and hats. Everything Flora had picked had a little extra flair.

Izabella and Rebecca searched through the piles and found outfits for the men and boys. "Where are the men and boys?" Rebecca asked. "They must be clean by now."

"Oh, I'm sure they are," Flora said. "Pete's prob'ly feedin' 'em, and gettin' 'em settled in."

"Settled in?" Rebecca asked.

"Yeah, I guess we haven't had a chance to show you around and fill you in on everything yet. We've only got the one guest room in the house. The men and boys'll be stayin' in the bunkhouse. They'll eat there. There's gonna be a lotta guys stayin' over cuza their horses and stock. The bunkhouse'll fill up and there'll be camps set up all over, especially down by the river. They're gonna get a real feel for the wild west."

"They all be pleased," Izabella said.

* * *

Daniel and Michael-Joseph knew they were in a different world. Bathing in the river with their fathers and neighbor was a new experience. They soon discovered that the trick was not to look at anyone. The bars of soap were passed around and the creek turned cloudy with the clay. It was with relief that the boys dried off and got into their borrowed clothes.

Josif and David had clothes that fit. Daniel and Michael-Joseph's were large and rolled up at the sleeves and legs. Fritz's clothes were short and tight.

Their breakfast had been steaks and eggs with biscuits, coffee, and milk. Pete was one of two hands and was the cook. He was in his forties and had years of experience cooking for cowboys, both on cattle drives and in bunkhouses.

Pete was short and like the others, bowlegged. He was mostly bald and not counting his mustache, mostly a day or two behind being clean-shaven. Pete was good-natured and a self-starter. He needed little direction to fulfill his duties and was always ready to help. He played a guitar.

The visitors ate at the large, solid pine table that ran through the center of the bunkhouse. Bunkbeds lined the sides of the thirty-foot walls. There was a potbellied stove near the door and a pile of wood between it and the cook stove.

Pairs of small chests of drawers stood at the wall between the beds, and pegs on the wall held jackets, hats, gun belts, ropes, or anything else that would hang from a peg.

There was a distinctive aroma to the bunkhouse and although comprised of many layers, all blended together and could be identified by anyone who'd ever spent time in a bunkhouse on a ranch. The first impression was smoke, both wood and cigarette; then was the smell of beans, onions and potatoes forever steamed into the walls with the coffee. Horses, cattle, sweat, manure, and hair treatment odors appeared around the room in varying intensities, as well as whiskey, smelly feet, and saddle soap. It was a man's world.

Daniel and Michael-Joseph would be sharing a bed, heads at the ends and feet in the middle. They sat on their bed after breakfast, all eyes and ears, not wanting to miss a thing.

Finley knew the Dacias and Fritz. He introduced them to Slim, Pete, and Hank. Hank was the other hand and was lanky and younger than Pete. He was an orphaned local boy who'd found a job with the Doyles and was a thankful and willing worker.

Then Josif introduced David to everyone.

Slim sized him up. "So, what kinda work do ya do?" he asked David.

"I'm a reporter and editor for *The New York Times*," he said. "I'm writing articles about the Black Hills in both South Dakota and Wyoming."

"You gonna take pictures and write about us?" he asked.

"If you don't mind," David said. "I'd like to show the folks back East what a real rodeo is all about, what life is like in Wyoming."

"Is that so? You think you're gonna get it all figured out in a coupla days?"

"No, of course not. But I would like to give an introduction. Get some quotes from you, so that it's said the way you want."

"What if we say sumthin' you don't like? What if you say sumthin' we don't like?" Slim asked.

"Then we'll talk about it. We'll come to an agreement."

"We got your word on that?"

David stuck out his hand. "You do," he said.

Slim shook his hand, giving David a look that said *We'll just see if you do.* He said, "You got yourself a deal."

* * *

"Glad to see you boys gettin' along," Finley said. "That'll make Flora happy."

"Speakin' of makin' Flora happy," Fritz said, "now that I'm cleaned up, I'd sure like ta see her."

"She's lookin' forward ta seein' you too," Finley said. "Maybe we should head over ta the house."

* * *

The change in the travelers' appearance was remarkable. They fit in. Except for the size problems with the boys and Fritz, they were dressed like locals. Izabella and Rebecca gave their husbands and sons a stack of clothes that would fit.

Flora gave Fritz a pile as well. "These clothes belong to Moose Johnson. You'll be meeting him soon," she said.

Fritz took the clothes. He wanted to pick Flora up and hug her, but not in front of everyone. "Come on out to the truck," he said to her. "I wanna show you somethin'."

Frank snickered and Finley cuffed him. "Straighten

up," he said.

"You can all come," Fritz said. "Lucky for all of us, some things weren't down by the river." He climbed onto the truck, untied the ropes, and pulled off the tarp. "You can thank *The New York Times* for all a this grub. They didn't wanna put a strain on ya with all your extra company and celebratin'."

Flora gasped with surprise, and Finley's eyes widened. He was struggling with whether he should feel grateful or offended. He decided on grateful. If a big outfit like *The New York Times* didn't carry their weight, then he'd be offended.

"That sure is neighborly of 'em," he said. "Looks like they thought of everythin'."

"They did their best," David said.

Flora went to the porch and rang the triangle, signaling for Slim and the hands to come. Slim was also surprised by the food, and a little offended. He didn't like charity.

David sensed the discomfort. "Times are hard across the country," he said. "The paper wants to share the stories of many Americans. I was lucky enough to get this assignment. I could've poked around this area on my own and not learned much. Being included in this wedding party, a rodeo, and the Fourth of July is a dream come true. The paper wants to show its gratitude. It sent this stuff along as a contribution to the festivities. We don't want our presence to make life any tougher."

"Thoughtful of 'em," Slim said. He and the hands helped the Doyles unload the truck. Many of the supplies were taken to the bunkhouse. Josif's box of carefully packed jars were given special attention. The specialty items stayed at the ranch house. Fritz and Josif took their saddles to the barn.

Everyone was putting their new belongings away and gradually relaxing after their earlier brush with death. Rebecca still felt shaky. She was longing to just sit and enjoy another cup of coffee. It was still overcast outside and not ideal for touring the ranch. She decided to rest on the bed first for just a few minutes.

CHAPTER ELEVEN
Fire!

Rebecca awakened to the sounds of serious discussion. Concern was in the voices. She got up and went to the kitchen doorway. Flora was cranking the phone. Slim and the Doyle men were in the room.

"Velma, we got smoke in the hills above our place," Flora said. "Call over to the Richardsons and have one of their boys ride up to the CCC camp. Tell 'em to truck a buncha them fellas up the Hardy's road to that big ridge behind us. We're gonna start movin' our cattle down outta there. Get 'em across the river and away from the trees... Thanks, bye."

"We better get everybody that can ride saddled up and on the way," Slim said. "Flora, you organize the ones who stay here. Set up a line to keep the cattle headin' toward the river crossing and not at the buildings."

Rebecca became aware of distant thunder. The sky was dark. She heard one of the men ringing the triangle. "But won't the rain put out the fire?" she asked from the doorway.

"Not if it don't rain," Flora said. "It don't always rain. Sometimes we just get the thunder and lightning. It's bone dry out there now."

"Are we in danger?" she asked. Her stomach twisted with a strong feeling of anxiety. "Is the fire coming our way?"

"Not us so much as our cattle. We're across the river from the fire, and there ain't any trees along the banks to jump it. We gotta direct the cows toward the ford and away from the buildings."

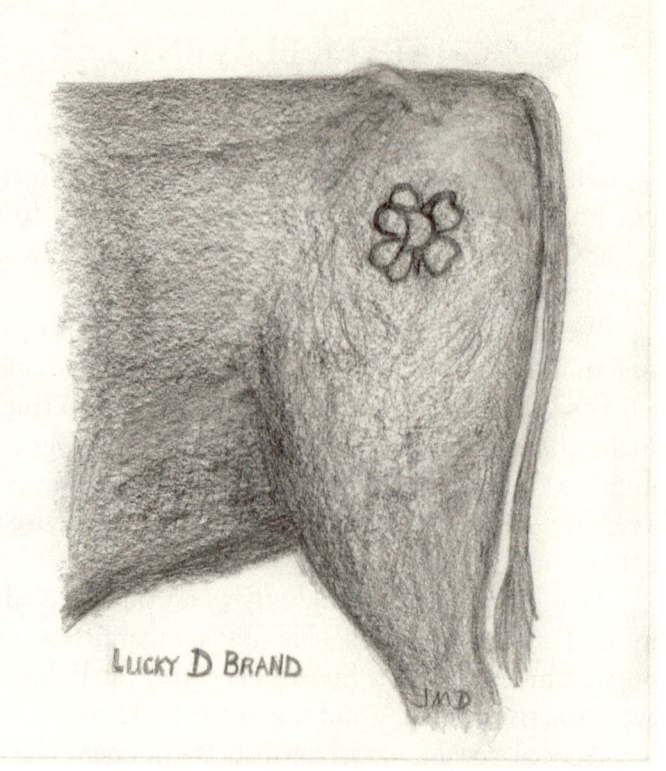

LUCKY D BRAND

"We? Is there something I have to do to help?" Rebecca flashed on her Manhattan home. She wanted so much to be there.

"Come on out to the corral. We'll get organized there."

Rebecca grabbed her jacket from the bedroom and followed Flora. She didn't want any part of this but had to make sure her children were safe.

* * *

Slim, the hands, and the Doyles were saddling their horses. They had strapped on chaps. Each saddle had a coiled rope hanging from it. They were wearing leather gloves and had rifles in their saddle scabbards and pistols on their hips. As soon as they were saddled up, they kicked their mounts into a gallop and charged up the slopes behind the ranch.

* * *

Deborah happened to look up as Slim rode by on his black stud, Diablo. The sky behind him was gray and charged with danger. Even though she only saw him for a moment, Slim's image was forever imprinted on her mind.

He was the most natural example of a leader of men she had ever seen. He was handsome, mature, confident, strong, and in control of man and horse. He rode his black horse as if one with him, powerful, unstoppable, almost a force of nature. His jaw was strong, and his outfit was well-worn, showing his muscles. His hat was lightly rolled on the sides, his boots black.

Deborah watched as he led the men up the hills behind the ranch. Diablo led the way, clearly the top horse of the herd. Slim moved with his horse and seemed to be leading him even though he was riding.

She was smitten. Slim would forever be her private standard of manliness to which all men she would ever meet must be compared. She felt a little disoriented.

* * *

The Dacias, Epsteins, and Fritz gathered around Flora. "Fritz, you and Mr. Dacia go in the barn and bring back eleven bridles with bits. They're hangin' on pegs on the south wall.

"Mr. Epstein, you and the boys go back to the

bunkhouse and grab five holsters with loaded pistols. Izabella, would you get my gun? It's hanging on the wall by the back door."

The girls and Rebecca stayed with Flora. Thunder growled in the distance and lightning flashed in the black clouds. It seemed to be coming closer. Rebecca's skin crawled; it seemed she could feel every hair on her head and neck. She felt about to explode and very much out of her element. She focused on her children and what Flora had said.

Soon everyone returned with their burdens. "Here's what we're gonna do," Flora said. "You men are gonna get saddled up and follow the others after the cattle. Don't be heroes. Just convince the cows to head downhill away from the fire. Send 'em toward the river crossing where you got cleaned up. "Your pistols are to scare a cow to change direction, or for a rattlesnake. They come out during a fire. Stay out of the fire. If you do fire your guns, see where you're shootin' first. There's gonna be a lotta smoke and dust. And you may come across the CCC boys. They'll be the ones fightin' the fire.

"The rest of us are gonna be on horses making a line to keep cattle goin' in the right direction. Nothin' hard. Just sittin' on a horse yellin' at the cows as they wander out of the hills.

"Ladies, you're gonna have pistols too, in case you need to scare a vagrant. So, let's start by gettin' everyone's guns on."

Rebecca also felt disoriented. This was so strange, but she did as told.

"Now, instead of us haulin' a bunch a saddles outta the barn, let's bridle 'em up here. Then we'll take the horses to the saddles." Flora studied the herd of restless horses in the corral. "Fritz, I'm gonna give you Aces High to ride.

I'll help you corner 'im. Mr. Dacia, see if you can get ahold of any of them Appaloosas and get bits and bridles on 'em. Take any that you catch into the barn and start saddlin' 'em up."

Flora sweet-talked Aces High, and Fritz approached him at eye level, calmly and confidently. Flora put the bit and bridle on Aces High and handed Fritz the reins. "Help the others saddle up when they get there, hon," she said, giving Fritz a quick smile.

Josif had bridled two horses and was headed for the barn. Daniel and Michael-Joseph captured and bridled a horse, then got another one and led their horses to the barn. Flora gave one each to Izabella and Rebecca.

The girls were petting a horse, which was soon bridled and given to Rose, then one each for Deborah and Caroline. Flora whistled to one of the few remaining horses. It was a Quarter Horse, a pinto, solid and strong and eager to run. This was Flora's personal horse, Sundance.

* * *

The group saddled up in the barn. Fritz, Josif, and David put on chaps, mounted up, and headed out on their horses. They didn't carry rifles, but they had ropes and handguns. David clung to the saddle horn and reins and tried to do what Josif and Fritz did. Gradually he felt more comfortable, letting go of the saddle horn, sitting back and going with the motion of his horse.

The three stayed within easy sight as their horses climbed the first slope. The sky was leaden gray. A wind came up at the top of the rise. There the ground flowed down into an irregularly-shaped bowl of land. Lines of pine followed dry creek beds. Over the top of the next rise, smoke rose thick and dark from several clumps of trees. Others were burning brightly with orange flames and white smoke. A few cattle were trotting away from the flames.

The men let these cattle continue. They moved around the burning clumps, deeper into the hills.

Six cattle were trotting across the face of the fire. Fritz rode between them and the flames. Aces High crowded them into moving in the right direction. Josif and David followed them yipping and yelling until they were firmly headed away from the fire.

David was jubilant. He and Josif turned their horses back in the direction of the fire. The smoke was becoming thicker, but glimpses of cattle through the smoke and dust drove them on. Fritz spotted a bunch going in the wrong direction and raced after them. Josif headed through the smoke after another bunch.

David was going to assist Josif when he spotted a horse and rider going after a panicked bull heading down a steep ravine, which curved and led into an unseen burning stand of trees. The smoke and dust were thick. The rider had pulled his neckerchief up over his mouth and nose. David did the same.

The bull had stopped between burning trees, confused and uncertain. The path behind him was narrow, but the walls of the ravine had opened up. The way forward was barely open, but passable.

The rider spurred his horse ahead and fired his pistol in the air. The bull began to move toward safety.

The path it had to go lay under a burning snag, which was leaning on another burning tree. The rider pressured the bull, forcing it forward. With the bull's first few steps, the snag shifted and slid down the supporting tree. It rested on another burning branch. The space under the snag now wouldn't be high enough for the bull to pass. There would be no way to make it try. The horse and rider would have no chance. To make matters worse, a burning tree fell across the rider's path of retreat.

David saw what had to be done. He urged his horse around the burning trees to where the bull and rider's exit was blocked. David grabbed the rope hanging from his saddle. He played out the line and opened the loop. There was a strong branch near the top of the snag. If he could rope it, he could pull the snag down, away from bull, horse, and rider.

He swung the loop over his head, waited for the right moment, and let it fly. The rope caught the branch. Without knowing how it happened, his horse stopped and set his feet. David coiled the slack and wrapped the rope around the saddle horn. The horse backed up, quickly and decisively. The snag fell to the ground and the horse pulled it out of the way. David said, "Whoa."

The bull plunged through the opening, his eyes wide with fright. The rider followed. He looked at David as he went by and seemed to do a double take. David thought he looked like Slim. The rider pursued the bull, and David could see through the smoke that he had it under control.

David shook the rope and was able to coax it off the end of the branch. He coiled it up and examined the loop. It was singed and damaged. He hooked the coil over the saddle horn, then rode on, deeper into the hills.

As he topped another rise, he saw a line of men with shovels, axes, and hoes working the edge of the fire. More men were along another side. There were no apparent cattle here. David headed back the way he'd come. More CCC men were spread out around burning areas, bringing them under control. He could see a few riders herding stragglers toward the river. David wove his way through more trees and shrubs, looking for cattle. Any that he found were easily directed to safety.

* * *

As the men galloped off, Flora was helping saddle horses for the women and children. Michael-Joseph and Daniel had saddled one horse and were working on another. Rose had hefted a saddle up on a horse, and Caroline and Deborah were straightening the saddle blanket on another. Izabella was busy with a horse and saddle, and Rebecca looked overwhelmed. Flora inspected all the saddles and tightened cinches and straps.

She instructed Izabella to get on a solid wooden box and brought a horse over to her. Izabella easily stepped into the stirrup and threw her right leg over the saddle. She took the reins and moved her horse out of the way.

After the children were mounted, Flora gestured at the box and smiled at Rebecca. "I've saved the most gentle horse for you," she said. "This little mare is called Honey." Flora had a beautiful golden tan horse with black mane, tail, and legs. She had delicate features and was slightly smaller than the other horses. "She's a buckskin Quarter Horse," Flora said. "She's sure-footed, fast, and gentle. You won't have any problems with her."

Rebecca mounted Honey and was surprised at how easy it was. Honey's smaller size made her much less imposing, and being a mare, in her mind, less threatening. And Rebecca had to admit, Honey was beautiful. Her black mane and tail highlighted her golden honey color. Her muscles were well-defined, and she looked eager and intelligent.

Flora led the mounted group out of the barn. There were eight riders. She took them to the edge of the ranch and set them out at fifteen-foot intervals. "Your jobs are to just make noise and keep the cows heading down hill towards the river. We don't want 'em runnin' around the buildings. The fire's pretty far away, so I don't expect they'll be comin' fast. Ladies, in case one doesn't get the idea, just fire your pistol in the air. That oughta turn 'im."

Rebecca remembered that she had belted on a holster with a pistol in it. The gun was on her left although she was right-handed. She reached across her body and felt the handle. It was cold and hard. A tool in this wild country, a common item.

She looked around at the children and Izabella. Everyone seemed calm. The horses were still. She was located between Deborah and Daniel. Izabella was between Michael-Joseph and Caroline. Rose was next to Flora who was on the downhill end.

A few cattle began to show up at the top of the first hill behind the ranch. They weren't grazing, but they weren't running either. The children began yelling, and the women joined in. The cattle moved downhill away from them. Some cattle were far enough away to not pose a problem and headed toward the river without urging.

After about an hour, the cattle seemed to be coming more closely grouped together. They were coming faster, but not running. Flora would frequently leave the line to redirect them and escort them down the hill.

The men from the ranch began to appear behind the cattle. They were yipping and yelling and keeping the cattle moving.

* * *

Rebecca watched every steer, ready to intervene if one approached her children. She watched Flora's movements as she left the line again to move more cattle.

From her right she heard Daniel yelling; there was urgency in his voice. Rebecca turned to the right and saw a steer, wild-eyed and panicked, heading for Daniel.

It had gotten separated from the others. The steer wasn't responding to the yelling and didn't seem to be aware of its surroundings.

Rebecca saw it had a broken branch hooked around a hind leg. With every step it seemed to respond to the pain by going faster. It was bawling and coming closer.

Rebecca kicked Honey's sides and urged her forward between the steer and Daniel. Honey responded instantly. Rebecca reached for her pistol. She didn't think about what she was doing. She pointed the pistol at the steer's head and pulled the trigger. The animal stopped in its tracks and fell to the ground, a bullet between its eyes. It was less than fifteen feet from Daniel.

* * *

The men coming down the hill behind the cattle had seen the incident. One could almost hear them gasp. They hurried the cattle down the hill and headed toward Rebecca. David had already left the group and headed for her.

He arrived at her side before the others to find his wife in as much disbelief as himself. Daniel and Deborah were speechless. "I don't know how it happened," she said. "That cow was heading right for Daniel; I had to stop it."

Finley rode up and looked Rebecca in the eye. "I'm sorry I killed your cow," she said. "It was coming right for my son."

"We'll be happy to pay for it," David said.

"You don't owe me nothin' for that steer," Finley said. "We needed one for the barbecue anyway."

"I've never killed anything before," Rebecca said.

"Well, gal," Finley said, "you sure have now."

"There was no other choice, I had to."

"That's how it is out here," Finley said. "You do what

you gotta do to survive. It ain't always easy." It seemed to Rebecca that Finley understood her. He knew that she had never even imagined such a thing. He seemed to see her now as a person. She had never felt so full of life.

David also seemed excited. He was looking at Rebecca with new eyes, and she knew the look. She hadn't seen it that intense in years.

Finley looked at David and Rebecca and stifled a grin. "You know," he said. "You two've had a busy day. When that happens 'round here we like to take a little trail ride an' relax. If you follow that trail that heads off to the southeast behind the bunkhouse, you'll get a real pretty view of the tower."

"Would you watch the children?" Rebecca asked Izabella.

"Of course," Izabella said.

The two headed their horses toward the bunkhouse. David turned in his saddle and called back to Flora. "What's my horse's name?" he asked.

"Stud Poker," she called back. "We call 'im Stud."

* * *

Smoke had all but disappeared from the distant hills and the sun was pushing through the clouds. David and Rebecca rode along the trail until they reached a flat area with a view of Devils Tower. White, fluffy clouds highlighted the distant monolith.

They found a shady area under the pines and got off their horses and tied their reins to a branch. They untied and spread out the blankets tied to the backs of their saddles, settling down together. Rebecca didn't notice that they were dirty.

"Rebecca, you're incredible," David said. "You showed such courage. You were beautiful!"

"Thank you, David," she said. "I didn't know I could or would do such a thing. I hate that I killed that steer, but I feel so alive now. I'm not so eager to go home."

"I'm so glad to hear that. I saved Slim and a bull from the fire by roping a burning tree. I think we've both proven our mettle."

"I hope so," Rebecca said, "I was feeling so out of place, like such an outsider."

"You know, I think it's a good thing we lost our clothes. It helps to be in disguise and look like everyone else."

"I agree. I actually like them. Someone lent me this beautiful fringed leather jacket. It's magical."

"You're magical," David said, reclining on the blankets.

"You looked so strong and handsome galloping your horse over to me," Rebecca said lovingly.

"Come here, Becca," David said and gently pulled her to him.

CHAPTER TWELVE
Unwelcome Company

After hearing August's song earlier, Marie had been able to do nothing but fret. She wandered around the house seeing things that needed doing but couldn't find the will to do them. *What had August been so upset about? What had happened?*

Aunt Magda who was staying with her while August was away, was at the Dacias fixing lunch for Uncle Jon. When he returned to the fields after lunch, Magda would call Gina to bring her back to Marie's. She didn't really want Aunt Magda to be there when August got home, but she longed for company.

At the sound of a vehicle coming up the driveway, she ran to the kitchen window. It was a car, not August's motorcycle or even Gina's car, pulling to a stop in front of her house. Marie stared at the car; she didn't recognize it. A man and woman were inside. They got out of the car and looked around, then ambled over to the pasture fence.

The man called to Bill and Sky who ignored them. He picked up some clumps of dirt near the fence and threw them at the horses' feet. The horses squealed and hopped out of the way. Marie had never seen the horses angry before. Bill and Sky had turned around ready to kick. They were staring at the man over their shoulders, their ears flattened.

Marie hurried to the door and rushed onto the porch as the couple were coming up the steps. The man was of medium height, in his forties, with a receding hairline and restless eyes. He was wearing a cheap cowboy-themed suit and seemed to be appraising everything he saw.

The woman looked to be in her early twenties. She had red hair, long and loose, a short-fringed cowgirl skirt, and boots. Her red top was low-cut. She was chewing gum.

"Don't mess with the horses," Marie said angrily. "What do you want?"

Marie had opened the screen door on her way out and was standing with her hand on the door handle.

"We've come about a horse race," the man said.

"We're not interested," Marie replied.

"You sure?" he said. "Have you talked with your man lately?"

"What are you talking about?" Marie asked, feeling her stomach clench.

"Ol' August went and gambled his pay away after he lost Sky over there on a bet." He gestured with his head toward the pasture.

"You're lying!" Marie said. "He wouldn't ever bet Sky."

"I've got witnesses."

"I still don't believe you," Marie said defiantly.

"Why don't you let us in, and we'll talk about it over something cool," the man said.

"Go to town for something cool. I don't want you here," Marie replied. She tried to pull the door shut, but the man grabbed it and kept it open.

"If we go to town, we'll be talking to the locals. Tellin' 'em about what a four-flusher your man is. A whole lotta nothin', a cheat and a fake. That should travel around pretty good." He leered at Marie and pulled the door open, out of her hand.

"I'm Floyd Delaney. This is my wife, Trixie," he said as he pushed by Marie. "We've come for a little visit."

Floyd pulled out a kitchen chair and sat at the table with his knees apart. Trixie perched on one of his knees, her legs crossed and foot swinging.

"How 'bout somethin' cool to drink?" Floyd asked Marie, while running his eyes over her.

Marie went to the phone and cranked the handle. "The Dacia farm," she said into the mouthpiece.

Floyd watched her with narrowed eyes. Trixie looked around the kitchen and fixed on Marie's refrigerator.

Marie spoke into the phone in Romanian. The word *Magda* was clear, as well as their names. Floyd looked at Trixie. "Look out, Trix," he said in a mocking voice. "She's tellin' *Magda* on us — prob'ly some old bohunk aunt. We better be careful." He laughed harshly.

Marie hung up the phone and crossed her arms. The phone rang once, then after a pause, again. They were different rings, and Marie knew who they were for.

Marie stayed standing. She was by the sink near the drawer she kept the knives in. She planned to stay there.

"Floyd," Trixie said. "She's got a refrigerator. I want one too."

"Keep your shirt on, Trix, you never know what might develop," Floyd said, looking around the kitchen.

Marie was feeling desperate. These people were threatening everything she cherished. They were rotten and greedy. She wanted them gone but didn't know how to make them go. She was afraid if August returned while they were there, someone could get hurt. She was afraid it

1920s
Monitor Top

might be August. He could do something stupid out of concern for her. Marie maintained her position and kept watch on the Delaneys.

Trixie was loudly chewing her gum and looking around Marie's house. This kitchen's too small," she said. "I wanna house like this, Floyd, but with a bigger kitchen." She looked at the refrigerator and leaned out trying to see into the other room. "It's okay, but I'd want the kitchen wallpapered with flowers, not painted like this." She continued chewing and swinging her foot. Whenever she looked at Marie, it was with a smug grin.

In what seemed like an hour, but was only ten minutes, a car pulled into the driveway. Marie recognized the sound as Gina's car. She heard three car doors open and close, then footsteps coming up the porch steps. Marie walked to the door and opened it just as Magda arrived. She stepped back and ushered her in. Evalina was behind her, with Gina behind her.

Magda took one look at the Delaneys, contempt clear on her face. She walked past them into the sitting room.

Evalina sat across from the empty chair next to Floyd. Gina sat across from Floyd. Evalina looked at Trixie's legs with her skirt above her knees. *"Che vergogna!"* she said under her breath, making a face like she'd stepped in something foul.

Magda returned from the sitting room with a blanket. She flung it onto Trixie's lap. "Have you no shame?" she asked and stood by Marie at the sink. Magda's arms were crossed, her right hand on the knife in her belt.

Trixie blushed and spread the blanket over her lap. "Get off," Floyd said. "Stupid broad, you don't hafta do whatever they tell you."

Trixie moved to the chair across from Evalina. She was at a loss for words. She was outnumbered by women who reminded her of her Irish grandmother. A woman who would have said much worse to her. She swallowed her gum and sat quietly with her head bowed, the blanket across her lap.

Gina was sitting back in her chair, her pregnancy obvious. She had her purse on her lap. It was unhooked and her hand was near it. She carried a .32 pistol in her purse, a holdover from her days with the mob. Her other arm was draped over the back of the chair. She regarded Floyd coolly.

"So, Floyd," Gina said, "what's *your* story?"

"No story. Trixie and I are backup artists for the big names," he said.

"Really? So why are you here?" Gina asked. "The show was at the Corn Palace, not here."

"Wagner lost a bet. He lost his pay and bet Sky against my horse, Buddy. We're here to arrange a claim race."

"Just as I thought, you're not backup artists. Your real game is con artists. It's written all over you. You're prob'ly planning the old bait-and-switch. Bring in a ringer, that'd be your speed." Gina stared at Floyd. He tried to hold her stare but couldn't. He blinked and looked away.

Another car pulled in the driveway. Two doors opened and closed. There were more sounds of approaching women. Marie went to the door and welcomed Grandma Wagner and Mrs. Epstein. Both women entered and stood by the table.

"Don't you have manners to give women a seat?" Magda spit at Floyd. "You have no quality. You think only of yourself."

Now Floyd was without response. He had heard this form of criticism from his own mother. Magda's comments hit a nerve. "Get up, Trixie," he said to her harshly. "We're leavin'. I'm not hangin' around some hen party." He spoke to Marie, "Tell August we'll be back. A bet's a bet, and I've got witnesses."

Floyd got up and left the room. Trixie got up, put the blanket on the chair, and followed him. They soon heard the sound of the Delany's car pulling out of the driveway.

* * *

Marie brought more chairs to the kitchen and made a pot of coffee. She told the women what Floyd had said. She also mentioned the song *Don't Let Me Go*, which August had sung earlier that day. They had all heard it and were equally as puzzled and concerned.

Gina told them what she suspected about Floyd. "We don't know all the details yet," Gina said. "We have to hear what August has to say."

"Yes, I hope he'll be home soon," Marie said.

"You know," Gina mused, "if this has anything to do with horses, you've got an expert in the family now. Your new sister-in-law, Flora, may well have heard of Floyd. When you travel the horse-racing circuit, you get to know the cons. Give her a call when August gets home."

"Yes," Mrs. Epstein said. "I didn't spend time with the Delaneys, but my first impression wasn't positive. They have an underhanded feel about them. Be very careful."

"Poor August," Grandma Wagner said. "Since he's become famous, he seems to attract a lot of riffraff."

"I think that comes with the territory," Gina said. "Flies always hang around money."

The women stayed with Marie until the sound of August's Indian was heard coming up the driveway. He parked in front of the house. The women rose and left, giving Marie and August privacy. He looked distraught as he came in the kitchen.

Marie ran to August and hugged him. She felt some of his tension leave as he hugged her back. "What happened, August?" she asked, trying to read the answer in his face.

"I've been robbed and conned," he said. "A fella named Floyd Delaney and his floozy of a wife, Trixie, did it. Them and three other backup singers named Chance Conroy, Trey Willette, and Lefty Willis. They musta slipped me some knockout drops. Then they stole my money and made up a story about me bettin' Sky."

"They told me," Marie said. "They were here."

"What?" August said. "Those lowlifes came here, to the house?"

"Yes, but first Floyd threw clumps of dirt at Bill's and Sky's feet."

"That son of a bitch!" August said. "Are they okay?"

"Yes, but they didn't like it. I've never seen them angry before. They were ready to kick."

"Good for them," August said, sitting down at the table. "What did you do?"

"I saw them from the kitchen window and was going out to yell at them. Just as I was opening the door, Floyd got to the porch. He grabbed the door and wouldn't let me close it. Floyd pushed his way into the house and brought that tramp, Trixie, with him."

"What?" August looked around the kitchen and at Marie. He reached for her hand, and she sat down next to him. "Are you okay?" he asked.

"Yes, I'm just good and mad."

"You're not the only one. First, I believed them—the part about me gettin' drunk and makin' bad bets, losin' everything. I was foggy from the knockout drops. I coulda done that, maybe, if I was drunk enough. But I couldn't believe that I'd ever bet Sky.

"I played cards on two nights. I won fifty dollars the

first night. I went to the game the second night planning to only bet my winnings from the night before. I put my pay in my right boot. That was off limits. Floyd said I got drunk and said I bet Sky could beat any horse around. He said he took me up on that bet and I lost. He said I bet my pay tryin' to win Sky back."

"That's what you'd do all right," Marie said, "if you ever bet Sky in a poker game. But I believe in *you*, August, more than their lies. You'd never bet Sky, and they can't make me believe it."

"Thank God you feel that way," August said. "After Floyd got done with me Sunday morning, I thought I'd done a terrible thing. If what they said was true, I was afraid you'd leave me. That's why I wrote that desperate song. I didn't want to try to explain on the phone, 'specially with a party line. I just wanted you to know what was in my heart. I hope it didn't upset you."

"It did, August," Marie replied. "I knew you were in trouble and were trying to talk to me. There was nothing I could do to help because I didn't know what the problem was. It was awful. And then when that Floyd showed up saying those awful lies, I didn't know what to do."

"It looks like you called out the ladies' militia," August said with a weak grin.

"I did," Marie said, laughing. "Those two were no match for them. Aunt Magda threw a blanket on that tramp's lap when she was sitting on Floyd's leg. She had her already short skirt up over her knee. Evalina said something that made Trixie blush, even though I don't think she understands Italian. The look she gave Trixie though was what did it. It was brutal. Trixie swallowed her gum." Marie laughed.

"Then Gina took care of Floyd."

"Did she shoot 'im?" August asked.

"No, but she figured him out in about two seconds. Called him a con artist right to his face. Said if he was arranging a horse race, it was prob'ly a bait-and-switch. She out-stared him and made him blink first."

August laughed. "Good for Gina," he said. "I bet she had her hand near her purse in easy reach of her gun."

"She did," Marie said. "She also had a good idea. She said we should call Flora. That she might have heard about the Delaneys on the horse-racing circuit. She might be able to help us."

"She's right," August said. "How about somethin' to eat, then we'll call the Doyles. It'll be gettin' dark by the time we call, and they should be done with their ranch work for the day."

CHAPTER THIRTEEN
An Evening at the Ranch

After supper the men adjourned to the bunkhouse and the ladies to the sitting room. There were several leather upholstered couches, stuffed with horsehair, and handmade chairs with cushions. Braided rugs were in front of the chairs and couches, with a large one in the center of the room.

The women and girls were catching-up and discussing Flora's upcoming wedding when the phone in the kitchen rang. Flora heard her ring and went to the kitchen. "Long distance call for me?" she asked. "Put her on, Velma."

"It's Marie," she called to Izabella. Everyone rushed to the phone.

Izabella looked concerned. "Is something wrong?" she asked.

Flora listened for a few moments. "Oh yeah, I've heard a them. Floyd and Trixie Delaney are a coupla cheats. They like to set people up for the old bait-and-switch." ... "That figures." ... "They say they got a horse named Buddy. An aging, swayback Quarter Horse, maybe got a race or two left in 'im?" ... "Yeah well, I'm not so sure ol' Buddy exists. Every time *Buddy* is supposed to race, he seems to pull up lame. Then his younger brother, Buster, shows up."

Izabella and the girls knew Floyd and Trixie from the Corn Palace. They had seen Trixie flirting with August and Floyd encouraging it. Now it seemed they were still causing trouble. Izabella was furious.

"I can help you out, Marie," Flora said. "I've seen Buster's tricks. He's a big brute, and he pushes against his opponent, trying to run 'im into a ditch or fence. He's fast, but you can slow 'im down. Here's how.

"When Buster is leanin' against Sky, let 'im lean. Have Sky take as much as he can. Then you just check Sky a little bit. Don't make him stop or change pace, just slow a bit. When you do that, Buster'll run off the road. You might want to race on a road with some deep, wide ditches along the side. As soon as Buster charges by you into the ditch, ask Sky to give you everything he's got. He won't let you down."

Flora reassured Marie some more, then handed the phone to Izabella. Izabella spoke to Marie in Romanian, concern evident in her voice. After a few moments' conversation, Izabella laughed outright. The names *Magda*, *Evalina*, and *Gina* were mentioned. Izabella laughed some more and spoke with Marie a few more minutes. She called Rose and Caroline over to say hello. When they were done, she hung up the phone and returned to the sitting room.

Flora explained the call to Rebecca and the girls. "We knew they were awful," Rose said. "I know Marie and Sky can beat those terrible people and their mean horse. Will we be home in time for the race?" she asked her mother.

"Marie said she and August would try to arrange the race for Saturday. We will leave on Thursday, the day after the wedding," Izabella said. "With no more sightseeing we should make it on time."

* * *

"Where'd ya learn to rope?" Slim asked David over supper in the bunkhouse. The question had an air of distrust behind it, suggesting a con from a New Yorker. All the men were there, including the Doyles and the hands, Pete and Hank.

"In New York," David replied. He could feel what he hoped to avoid: disbelief, ridicule, being written off as insignificant, a joke. He continued eating, waiting for Slim's reaction.

"Is that so? Who taught ya?" Slim studied David's face like he would the weather, looking for answers.

David dreaded this part; he knew his answer wouldn't be believed. "Will Rogers," he said.

"Will Rogers? Is that so?" Slim looked hard at David, then around at the other Wyoming men. Faces were unsmiling, unconvinced and distant. Will Rogers was a national hero and a cowboy. Anybody who dropped his name had better be on the level. "How'd ya happen to meet 'im?" he asked.

"Will does work for the *Times*. He comes to New York pretty often. I met him at the *Times* where I work," David replied.

"And one happy day he just decided to teach you to rope?" Slim looked skeptical. The other men stared at him, still trying to size David up.

"When he found out I was coming to Wyoming, he gave me two pieces of advice," David said.

"That bein'?" Slim asked, beginning to look irritated.

"He said if I hoped to get out of Wyoming alive, I better learn to ride and rope."

The ranchers guffawed and visibly relaxed. David had done the equivalent of giving a secret password.

Josif got out a jar of *tuica and* passed it around. Some drank from the jar, some poured it in their empty coffee cups. Finley tipped his hat back and grinned at David. "Well, you've sure got a feather in your hat that most folks would give their eye teeth for. Some might say you've been blessed. Ol' Will can say a few words and tell a whole story. I sure would be proud ta meet 'im."

"It's been an honor for me to know him," David said. "He's one of the kindest, wisest men I know."

Attitudes toward David softened. "Where'd he teach you?" Frank asked.

"Up on the roof at the *Times* ; then I'd practice on my roof."

"How long you bin practicin'?" Slim asked.

"Almost a year."

"Well, I guess you got the ropin' part pretty good." Slim looked at the others around the table. "You may not know it, but David here saved my life.today." Slim told the story of the burning snag and the escape of himself and the bull. "I wanna thank you fer that," he said.

The ranchers were quiet, trying to reconcile David's actions with their image of a New Yorker. They seemed to be having some difficulty. They quietly sipped their drinks, looking pensive.

Daniel and Michael-Joseph were watching the proceedings with both fascination and wariness. David seemed to be holding his own, winning over the ranchers. Daniel thought they just needed another little push. "Will Rogers taught my father some trick-roping too. He's real good!" he said.

All eyes fixed on Daniel. He realized he'd just thrown down the gauntlet for his father. He had to preform now in front of real cowboys. Daniel looked apologetically at his father.

"Let's see some," Finley said. "I sure enjoy some good trick-ropin'."

Pete fetched a coiled rope from a peg and handed it to David. David took it and stood up. He moved to the end of the room away from the table and chairs. David played out his loop and did a flat spin to the side, then to the front and to the other side. He did another flat spin parallel to the floor and stepped in the loop, bringing the loop up from toe to head, and back again.

The ranchers looked astounded. "This sure is hard to get my head around," Slim said. "Why'd you decide to learn ropin'? I ain't heard a too many loose steers in New York."

"Truthfully, I wanted to fit in. I wanted to be able to ride and rope like Will said. I didn't want to be the city slicker who couldn't do anything. I guess I wanted your respect, man-to-man."

There was an uncomfortable silence. Slim took a slug, draining his glass. "You're doin' pretty good," he said.

"Maybe not as good as your wife," Finley said, chuckling. "But you've got promise." The men all laughed appreciatively. "You two have sure been a bundle of surprises," Finley said. "I never in a million years would've expected yer first day on the ranch to be like this. You've shot holes in all a my pictures a New Yorkers, as well as one a my steers."

Hearty laughter and another round of *tuica* changed the conversation to Fritz. Finley turned to his sons. "So, boys," he said, "are you both ready for a brother-in-law?" He looked at Fritz. "Are you ready to call me Papa?" Finley slapped his thigh and doubled over laughing.

"Actually, I was considerin' callin' you *Daddy*," Fritz said, with a huge grin.

"And what're you gonna do about it if he does call you *Daddy*?" Slim asked.

"I guess I'll hafta call 'im *Sonny* and claim 'im as my own," Finley said, laughing. "I sure ain't gonna fight 'im over it!"

"We heard you flung everbody up a four-foot bank to get 'em outta that flash flood," Hank said. "Picked 'em up by belt and collar and let 'em fly."

"He save us all," Josif said. "We all die if not for Fritz."

"Sounds like a pretty handy fella," Finley said.

"And I'd a bin swept away in the flood if David hadn't remembered the rope around me was tied to the car. He got me out just in time."

"A heroic day all 'round," Slim said. "Hey, Pete, get us out a bottle a hooch. Let the celebratin' begin!"

"Is good idea," Josif said. "We get instruments."

"What kinda instruments ya got?" Pete asked.

"I have violin, boys have clarinets," Josif said.

"Papa sings," Daniel said. "He's a tenor."

"Is there anything yer papa can't do?" Slim asked.

"Shoot," Daniel said.

"Only cuz he never had lessons," Michael-Joseph added.

"Well, hell, we'll take care a that tomorrow mornin' right after breakfast," Slim said. "That's sumthin' else ol' Will could a mentioned; it's good to know how to shoot in Wyomin'."

"Let's hear some music!" Finley said.

Pete took his guitar from a hook by his bunk. Hank pulled a harmonica from his shirt pocket. Josif rosined his bow and the boys prepared their reeds.

"What'll we begin with?" Pete asked.

"*Yella Rose a Texas*, Finley said. "You folks know that one?"

"Yes, we know," Josif said. He began the song and the other players joined in. Everyone not playing clarinet or harmonica sang. The effect was pleasing, and the clarinets gave the song new depth.

"Sing us a song from your neck a the woods," Finley said to David when the song ended.

"Okay. I've got a new one by Cole Porter and Bob Fletcher," David said. "Cole Porter writes songs for Broadway musicals."

The ranchers looked ill and ready to bolt for the door. "You may've hit your limit," Slim said. "We don't know, or want to know, nothin' 'bout no Broadway musicals."

"I didn't think so," David said. "Cole Porter wrote the music; Bob Fletcher is from Montana and he wrote the words. The song's called *Don't Fence Me In*. It was just written this year. Daniel can play the tune and the rest of you jump in when ready."

The rich tones from Daniel's clarinet began the song and David's strong tenor provided the lyrics:

"O give me land, lots of land, under starry skies above.
Don't fence me in.
Let me ride through the wide open country that I
love.
Don't fence me in.

Let me be by myself in the evening breeze,
Listen to the murmur of the cottonwood trees.
Send me off forever, but I ask you, please.
Don't fence me in.

Just turn me loose, let me straddle my old saddle
Underneath the western skies.
On my cayuse, let me wander over yonder
Till I see the mountains rise.

I want to ride to the ridge where the West commences.
Gaze at the moon until I lose my senses.
Can't look at hobbles and I can't stand fences.
Don't fence me in."

The musicians played the song again and the cowboys soon learned the lyrics. They played and sang it over and over, the whiskey giving it the reverence of a hymn.

"Damnit," Finley said, "I may get to like this song as much as *The Red River Valley*. It sure is a dandy." He consulted his pocket watch. "Everyone's up at sunrise to feed the stock. Breakfast's after that around 6:00. I 'spect we better turn in."

The Doyles headed back to the ranch house, and the others visited the outhouse or a tree, then headed to their bunks.

Daniel and Michael-Joseph wanted to talk about their day but had no privacy. It would have to wait until tomorrow. Their heads were swimming with new experiences and information, but exhaustion took over and they were soon asleep.

CHAPTER FOURTEEN
Fittin' In

Most of the ranch was up at dawn. The men were feeding the livestock and tending to their needs. Roosters were crowing and doves cooing. The softly clucking hens were let out of the henhouse to forage in the weeds. The animals woke up and announced their presence. The noise level and activity gradually increased.

Izabella and Rebecca were up before dawn, Izabella making loaves of bread and Rebecca pastries stuffed with canned apricots and cream cheese, topped with almonds. They were ready by 6:00. Rebecca rang the triangle, and Daniel and Michael-Joseph were sent over to see what the ringing was for.

The boys were glad to see their mothers and regarded Rebecca with awe. "I guess I got my shooting ability from you, Mama," Daniel said. "You seem to be a *natural* too."

"I hope so when it comes to saving my children," she said. "I thank God I was there."

"Me too," Daniel said.

"What are the plans for today?" she asked the boys.

"Slim's gonna teach Papa to shoot right after breakfast," Daniel said. "Maybe he can shoot a hole in a can like mine."

"Then we might go for a ride in the hills," Michael-Joseph said. "We saw Flora out by the corral. She said we should go before everyone starts showing up for the rodeo."

"Flora said you could ride Honey again if you want to come with us, Mama," Daniel said.

"And you could come, too, Mama," Michael-Joseph said.

"Us too," the girls chimed in.

"First, let's have breakfast," Rebecca said. "Tell Flora to come in if she's hungry."

The women gave loaves of bread and pastries to the boys to take to the bunkhouse, then started on breakfast for themselves.

* * *

After their bunkhouse breakfast, Slim gave David a holster with a loaded pistol. He instructed him how far it should hang from his waist and the importance of the string tied around his leg. He unloaded the gun and gave it to David to reload. Then he took him out to the edge of the woods behind the bunkhouse and placed a rusty can on a stump. He showed David the sight and instructed him in aiming. "Now," he said to David, "aim and shoot. Be ready for a kickback."

David did as told. He held the pistol out, aimed, and fired. He hit the can low and on the outside.

Josif and the boys had come up to watch. The boys were sent after the can. They put it back on the stump and David tried again. This time he did better and almost centered the hole. The boys brought back the can and gave it to David.

"Not bad," Slim said. "You're gettin' it." He pointed to a chipmunk perched on a log a few feet into the trees. "There's a good target fer ya," he said. "Git 'im before he moves."

"I'd rather not, Slim," David said. "I don't want to kill something unless I'm going to eat it."

"Well, I guess we could fry it up for ya, but it won't

make much of a meal," Slim said. He aimed at the chipmunk and fired. It flew off the log. "Ain't good for much but target practice. Well, I got work ta do; see ya around," he said, and headed for the barn.

David was distraught. Another animal had died on his behalf. His heart was heavy. His bullet-holed can lost its luster. He had also lost ground with Slim. City slicker might as well be written on his back.

"It's okay, Papa," Daniel said. "You didn't kill it, it's not your fault. You just killed the can."

Fred and Frank had seen the incident as well as Pete and Hank. "We prob'ly see things a little different out here than in New York," Hank said. "We deal with death all the time. It's how we make our livin'. Ya get used to it."

"I suppose so," David said.

"Say, fellas," Frank said. "Fred an I've gotta go across the river and get some steers and a bull for the rodeo. Wanna grab Fritz and come along? We could use the help."

David's spirits soared again; he would be doing something useful. He would be cowboying.

* * *

Despite their protests, the boys were sent to the corral to go on the trail ride with Flora and the girls. "That ride sounded pretty good before you heard about the roundup," David said. "Do you really want your mother to join us with the cattle? She would, you know. I think it's best for you to go on the trail ride and look out for your mother while she's looking out for you."

The boys agreed and walked down to the large corral with the horses in it. Flora again gave directions. "You all seemed to do pretty good on the horses you had yesterday. Why don't you all go to the barn and get a bridle. When you get back, find your horse and bridle 'im up."

Izabella and Rebecca walked to the barn together. "You have changed, Rebecca," Izabella said. "You are even more a woman. You have found parts of yourself you didn't know you had."

Rebecca pondered Izabella's words. "You're right," she said. "I am slowly giving up fear. I'm following my children's example and experiencing life. I think I'll always appreciate luxury, but this wild life has its appeal. It makes you feel more alive."

Izabella laughed. "I think we will be seeing more of you and your family after this. You'll probably end up like Deborah, wild for horses."

"I certainly do like Honey," Rebecca said. "She's so beautiful and sure-footed; I feel safe on her."

* * *

Everyone led their horse to the barn. Flora addressed the group. "If there're no objections, I'd like to ask you all a favor. That is to take care of your horses while you're here. They'll be your horses to ride all day if you want to. But with all the action goin' on, Pete and Hank won't have time for it."

The children looked at their horses with new eyes. They felt immediate ownership and affection. Rebecca was surprised to find she had similar feelings towards Honey, as did Izabella for her horse, Queenie.

Flora handed out curry brushes and demonstrated on Sundance how to clean a horse's back and stomach to prevent saddle sores. Then detailed instructions on how to saddle a horse and wiping them down after riding. She showed them how to lean into a horse to make them exhale while saddling them, as some tended to hold their breaths. Not doing so could result in saddle slippage while mounting if the horse were prone to such tricks.

Rebecca curried Honey, breaking up the hair clumped with dry sweat, and feeling pride at bringing her coat to a golden shine. The strong smell of horse didn't bother her, and she also identified the scents of hay and straw as pleasant. Rebecca admitted she had changed. She was feeling the joy and confidence she had seen in her children. Becoming immersed in the messy business of basic survival now a worthy challenge.

* * *

The eight riders mounted up and headed out. Flora led the way and the women brought up the rear. Izabella and Rebecca were again armed.

The group headed up a trail to the southwest of the ranch. It crossed a rocky outcropping with sweeping views of the valley below. There were occasional views of the Tower framed by galleon clouds in an ocean blue sky. Meadowlarks sang from shrubs, the crisp air was invigorating, and the scent of disturbed earth made one want to run with joy.

Flora led the group past the outcropping to an open meadow. Orange and yellow Indian paintbrush and yellow arrowroot dotted the landscape. The ground was level with no dog holes. "How about we go a little faster?" she called to the group. "Just give your horses a little encouragement, they'll be wantin' to keep up with Sundance." She urged her horse into a lope.

The children urged their horses to follow. Honey and Queenie followed along, and Rebecca realized that she was on a running horse. The ground flew by. Rebecca felt Honey's power, and instead of resisting it and tightening up in fear, she relaxed into the movement. She felt strong and capable and in partnership with Honey. She felt an elation she had never before experienced.

Daniel and Michael-Joseph were also loving the fast ride. They had ridden this fast on Bill and Sky, but they were easy rides. These horses were cowboy horses, used to riding hard under an experienced hand.

Deborah, Rose, and Caroline were doing fine on their horses. They had spread out and were riding next to each other, their horses keeping pace. Rose kicked her horse into a gallop and the others followed, tearing across the broad meadow.

Not to be outdone, the boys followed, and soon all were at a gallop. Rebecca grabbed the saddle horn as a precaution but knew she really didn't need it. Flora galloped Sundance into the lead and slowed the group down. "Well, I'd say you all got the hang of ridin'," she said. "You all did real well.

"If we go up the trail a little farther, we'll get a view of the Belle Fourche."

"What's the name of the river that goes through your place?" Rose asked.

That's called Turtle Crick; it's an offshoot of the Belle Fourche. It cuts off at about ninety degrees from the Belle Fourche. It doesn't get the force of water that you got, but it sure is handy for the ranch.

In a few minutes the river came into view. It meandered peacefully through soft grasses in a wandering valley. The view was spectacular, and Flora had everyone dismount to give their horses a rest. Those who brought their Brownies took pictures.

Michael-Joseph and Daniel sat next to each other on a log overlooking the valley. "What do you think so far?" Michael-Joseph asked Daniel.

"I think things are goin' pretty good," he said. "Mama seems to have changed like Deborah and I did. Papa is doing okay, but the *not killing* the chipmunk was hard."

"I don't blame him," Michael-Joseph said. "Papa always tells us the same thing. Don't kill anything you're not gonna eat unless it's tryin' to eat you. I didn't like what Slim did."

"I didn't either, but I think most folks around here are gonna see things Slim's way. Papa may have more trouble fitting in, even after he's done so many good things."

"Everyone loved *Don't Fence me In*; we'll just hafta keep 'em singin'," Michael-Joseph suggested. "Maybe we should carry our clarinets with us." "Good idea. We could at least startle someone pretty good," Daniel agreed. "But I could also see some kid using them to dig holes with. Maybe we should leave 'em at the bunkhouse."

"That seems smart," Michael-Joseph agreed. "Pete said folks would start showing up today, so we should keep our hands free, ready for action."

"Right," Daniel said.

"This is prob'ly the day we get in a fight," Michael-Joseph noted.

"Prob'ly. Makes me wish I'd done more push-ups," Daniel said.

"Yeah. Guess we'll hafta take 'em by surprise. Get the drop on 'em."

"Yeah and remember everything August taught us."

* * *

The girls were sitting together on a group of rocks looking at the horses and the view beyond.

"A bunch of kids should be showing up today," Rose said. "Maybe some of the girls can show us something we could do in the rodeo."

"Us, in the rodeo?" Deborah asked. "What can girls do in a rodeo? I don't want to ride a bucking bronco."

"Girls don't do that," Caroline said. "They do the barrel race or the egg in a spoon race like we did in Centerford last Fourth of July. Only they do it on horses. We could try those races."

"Wow!" Deborah said. "We could be in a rodeo; we have to find out more."

"Yeah," Rose said. "I hope these kids are friendly."

* * *

"A honeymoon in Yellowstone Park will be beautiful," Izabella said to Flora. "We wish you and Fritz many long years of happiness and all the children you want."

"Thank you, Izabella," Flora said. "It's hard to believe, but soon you and I will be neighbors! My life will change quite a bit."

"Yes, it will. It is like to move to another country, but you will speak the language and come already having friends and family there."

"I will. And Fritz and I plan to visit here often, maybe do somethin' with horses together with my family."

"That would be good," Izabella said. "This is good country to visit often."

"Do you have everything you need for your wedding?" Rebecca asked. "Will you want help with your hair or anything? We'd be glad to help."

"Well, maybe with my hair. I'm wearing my mother's wedding dress, veil, and shoes, so I'm all set there."

"Is someone making you a wedding cake?" Rebecca asked.

"Well, no one's really offered. I suppose Thelma

wouldn't mind workin' somethin' up," Flora said.

"Would you mind if I make it for you?" Rebecca asked. "I took a class in New York about decorating wedding cakes, and just love making them whenever I have the opportunity."

"That would be wonderful!" Flora said. "Thank you so much."

"I would like to contribute something to your wedding too," Izabella said. "Do you have a handkerchief I could embroider your new initials on?"

"I have a hankie of my mother's, and some of her embroidery thread too," Flora said. "Thank you, Izabella, I will always cherish it."

"When did your mother pass?" Rebecca asked.

"She died in 1918 from the Spanish flu. Fritz's parents died then too. We have that in common," Flora said.

"It's a hard thing to have to share," Rebecca said.

* * *

Fred and Frank led Josif, David, and Fritz to the river crossing and down the gentle slope where they had sent the cattle. Fred rode next to Fritz. He pulled a flat bottle of whiskey from his inner vest pocket, took a slug, and passed it to Fritz. "You know, big brother," he said, "as your new kin and as a favor to Flora, we're supposed ta look out fer you."

"Uh-oh," Fritz said. "Sounds like somethin's comin'."

"Actually, two somethin's," Frank said, riding up. Josif and David also came closer to hear. Fritz took a long swallow and sent the bottle on its rounds.

"The first one is the fella whose clothes you're wearin'," Frank said. "That'd be Moose Johnson, and you can tell how big he is by how loose his clothes are on you."

"Yeah, I figure he's got about thirty pounds on me, judging by the crease in his belt," Fritz said. "Kinda fat and sluggish, is he?"

"Not really," Fred said. "He's pretty fit and he loves ta fight. He think's he's the top dog in these parts cuza his size."

"He ain't top dog?"

"Hell no. Slim's top dog. Make no mistake about it. He's the stud in this neighborhood."

"What about your father? He must carry a lotta clout."

"Oh, he's Mr. Doyle, the owner of the Lucky D. He's just too old to be the stud anymore," Fred replied. "Ol' Slim's the boss. You don't wanna get on his bad side."

"So does this Moose need an excuse to fight?" Fritz asked. "Or can we just get at it. I enjoy a good fight, and since my brother, August, got married, he can't be counted on."

"Oh, Moose'd be happy to just get on with it," Frank said.

"I'm likin' Moose more and more," Fritz said. "Lookin' forward to meetin' him. So, what's the second somethin?"

"That's a sneaky little weasel called Wade Wilcox," Frank replied. "He got Flora to go on a date with 'im once, couple years ago. Now he claims you're stealin' her from 'im. She can't stand 'im. Says he tries to take without askin'. I know she came home from that date madder'n a hot hornet, and ol' Wade had a black eye and scratched face. He carries scars on his face from that encounter. He's feelin' vengeful 'bout that too."

"Now him I don't like already," Fritz said. "I'd like ta meet him too."

"Just be careful a that bastard," Fred cautioned. "He don't play fair. Watch yer back when yer around 'im."

The bottle made the rounds again. Josif addressed the Doyle brothers. "After wedding, we will be what is called shirttail relatives with you. Our daughter, Marie, is married to Fritz's brother, August."

"Say, ain't you one a the *Dakota Six* too?" Fred asked.

"Yes, I am in song."

"That'll be a good story for the bunkhouse tonight," Fred said. "That and the kidnappin' and about the mob. That'll be great to hear, and now we'll be related kinda. That's really somethin'."

"And more of your song, David," Frank added. "That's a humdinger of a good song."

"What will you men do without Flora to run the house?" Josif asked.

"We'll eat at the bunkhouse. Pete can sure cook bettern' either of us," Frank said.

"Pardon to ask, but is not one of you brothers ready to marry?"

Frank and Fred looked at each other with sheepish grins. "Fred's been seein' Phoebe Greco for about two years," Frank said. "She'd be happy to take Flora's place."

"What would you do?" Josif asked Frank.

"I bin thinkin' a buildin' a place next door and raisin' and racin' horses," Frank said. "Fred could handle the cattle part and I'd take care a the horses. That way we'd have two ways to make money case one a them went belly up."

"Slim knows ranchin' and horse raisin' and trainin'. It could work out real good."

"Do you have wife in mind?" Josif asked. "You will need woman to help you."

"You sure do hit on the right questions," Frank said. "Turns out I bin gettin' along real well with Phoebe's sister, Penelope. They get along swell together and seems like the family ties are already there."

"That is good idea," Josif said. "Make strong family business. Have many children to run ranch. Everybody share in work and profits."

"That's what we were thinkin'," Fred said. "We may have two announcements a week or so after Flora's weddin'. But we haven't asked Phoebe or Penelope yet, so keep it under yer hats."

The bottle was passed again, then stowed back in Fred's vest. "Well, I guess we better go round up some cows," he said, and led the group into the trees on their task.

CHAPTER FIFTEEN
Fights and Friends

Shortly after noon, the locals began showing up in trucks and on horseback. Some of them carried camping supplies. The bunkhouse filled up and overflowed to camps set up along the river near the ford.

* * *

Michael-Joseph and Daniel didn't know where to turn next. The good news was that they were both on horseback. They were both riding Quarter Horses and becoming very comfortable living in the saddle. Michael-Joseph was on a pinto named Champ, and Daniel on a black horse named Midnight.

They pulled up to the corral fence and watched various animals being put into smaller pens with chutes opening into the corral. There were pens for steers, calves, unshorn sheep, bulls, cows, and horses.

Some of the bulls were in smaller pens by themselves. These weren't the fat, solid blocks of meat like the white-faced Herefords. These were a Texas Longhorn mix — solid, rangy, and with a bad attitude.

The bullpens had openings into a chute, which led to the box. This was the place where a mounted cowboy and wild animal plunged into the corral when the word was given. There was a chute for the horse pens as well, and the Doyles had built seats with good views next to and over the boxes.

* * *

The boys noted all the kids that had arrived. A few were on foot, but most were mounted and feisty, racing each other along the driveway yipping and whooping. Two of the boys rode up to Michael-Joseph and Daniel. They were of their same size and rode so easily it looked as if they exerted no control over their horses but moved as one.

"You must be the kids from South Dakota and back East," one of them said. "You're wearin' our clothes."

"You guys must be Tim and Tom Olson," Michael-Joseph said. "Thanks for the loan. I'm Michael-Joseph from South Dakota and this is Daniel from New York City."

The boys didn't smile. "That's what we heard. What're ya doin' way out here?" one of them asked.

"We're friends of the groom," Michael-Joseph said, "and the bride. We met Flora last summer, as well as her father and brothers."

"Don't he ever talk?" the other boy asked, referring to Daniel.

"Sure, I talk," Daniel said. "I say all kinds a fuckin' things."

Tim, Tom, and Michael-Joseph all stared at Daniel. Daniel felt like he was staring at himself. What had he said and why? It sounded like a challenge. He had used the worst word possible and presented himself as tough. He sensed a fight in his immediate future. *Get it over with,* he thought.

"You sure got a filthy mouth," one of the boys said. "Follow us down to that grove in the meadow and let's talk about cleanin' it out."

The four boys kicked their horses into a gallop, racing down the grassy slope toward a group of trees. Michael-Joseph and Daniel soon realized they were in a real race, and hunkering down and grabbing their saddle horns, kicked and urged their horses to go faster.

All four arrived in a group without a clear winner. Tim and Tom jumped from their horses, and Daniel and Michael-Joseph did the same. The horses moved away from the boys and began grazing.

Without preliminaries, the fighting began. Tom punched Daniel in the eye and Michael-Joseph hit Tim in the gut. Daniel visualized the perfect jab and delivered it to Tom's stomach. Tom let out a blast of air and took several steps backward. Tim was also holding his stomach. The two ranch boys glared at the strangers.

"You asked for it now," Tim said. He aimed for Michael-Joseph's jaw and gave him a bleeding lip. Michael-Joseph blackened his eye.

Daniel, wanting to leave his mark on Tom, hit him in the eye, then began a series of jabs in the gut, hard and fast, and often.

Tim got Michael-Joseph in the eye right before Michael-Joseph began his series of hard, fast jabs in Tim's gut.

The fight soon ended, as August had predicted, with Tim and Tom sitting on the ground holding their stomachs.

"I hope you learned your lesson," Tom said to Daniel. "It'd hurt too much to teach you anythin' else." The boys all laughed. Tim and Tom held out their hands and Michael-Joseph and Daniel grabbed them and pulled the boys to their feet.

"I'm Tom," said the boy who had fought with Daniel.

"And I'm Tim," said the other.

"Are you two brothers?" Daniel asked.

"Naw, we're cousins. His pa and my pa are brothers," Tim said. "And you two aren't related?" he asked.

"Naw, we're friends. We've been through a lot

151

together," Michael-Joseph replied.

"Like what?" Tom asked.

"Like getting kidnapped by gangsters. Then this trip, nearly getting washed away in a flash flood, and getting in a fight with a couple a ranch kids," Daniel replied.

They all laughed.

"Do you swear like that back in New York?" Tim asked.

"No, I learned that from the gangsters," Daniel said. "They talked like that a lot, and sometimes those words are the first ones that come to mind. I'd appreciate it if you didn't spread that around; my parents would feel obliged to make a public apology."

"We heard your mother shot a steer right between the eyes," Tom said.

"We never thought New Yorkers'd be like that," Tim added. "Pretty tough livin' there, is it?"

"Not really," Daniel said. "Our family's full of quick learners. We might have a violent streak, too, everyone but Papa, that is. He's a pacifist."

"What's that?" Tom asked.

"Someone who doesn't believe in violence. He believes in reason over fighting."

"That's not gonna go over too good around here," Tom said.

"It doesn't go over too good anywhere," Daniel replied. "But that's how he feels, and he won't change. He said if my mother or my sister or me were being attacked, he'd fight to prevent it. He'd die to prevent it, but he wouldn't kill in vengeance or try to do harm."

"I never hearda anybody like that," Tim said. "I wish him luck."

"So, who's wearin' whose clothes?" Michael-Joseph asked.

"You're both wearin' some a each a ours," Tom replied. "Daniel's got my boots; Michael-Joseph's got Tim's."

"They fit perfectly; thanks again. Are you guys camping here for the rodeo?" Michael-Joseph asked.

"Yeah, we're camped down by the river with our fathers," Tom said.

"Well, if you come to the bunkhouse tonight, Daniel and I are supposed to tell 'bout our bein' kidnapped by the gangsters," Michael-Joseph said. "Plus, Daniel's father taught everyone a new song that they really liked, called *Don't Fence Me In*. We'll prob'ly sing it again tonight."

"Are you two gonna do anything in the rodeo?" Tim asked.

"We'd like to, but don't really know what we could do," Michael-Joseph responded. "What're you guys gonna do?"

"We'll be doin' calf ropin'," Tim said.

"Wow, that'll be fun to watch," Daniel said. "Is there anything Michael-Joseph and I could do?"

"Well, you might be able to handle barrel racin' but that's mostly for girls. You'd need to find about four more boys to race with you so'd you wouldn't lose to girls. Try to avoid that," Tim advised.

"Where could we find guys to race with us?" Michael-Joseph asked, looking at his new friends.

"I knew you two would be trouble," Tom said. "I guess we could round up a few more fellas."

The four mounted up and loped back up the slope to the ranch. They met smiles of appreciation and even laughter as the four black eyes were noted. "Glad to see you fellas gettin' along," Finley said when he saw them.

"Say, Mr. Doyle," Tim said, "can we set up for barrel racin' in the corral for a bit? We got a coupla greenhorns here need ta practice."

"Sure thing, boys, we can set up two courses; the girls'll wanna practice too. I'll get Slim to get it set up." Finley rode off toward the barn to make arrangements.

* * *

The four girls were riding their horses in a group, watching all the activity. A group of mounted local girls rode up to them. "Are you the visitors from back East and South Dakota?" one of them asked.

"Yes, I'm Rose, and this is my sister, Caroline. We're from Centerford, South Dakota. This is Deborah, our friend from New York," Rose said.

"Pleased to meet you," the girl replied. She introduced herself as Daisy, then introduced the rest of the girls. "We heard you got caught in a flash flood. That musta been awful."

"It was," Caroline said. "Everything got washed away. We would've died if Fritz hadn't saved us by throwing us all up on the bank."

"I bet we're wearing some of your clothes," Deborah said. "Thanks for sharing."

"That's okay," Daisy said. "We're glad to help."

"Are you girls gonna be in the rodeo?" Rose asked.

"Yeah, we always enter the barrel racin'," Daisy said. "Can you do anything?"

"We heard about the egg in a spoon race; we've done that before on foot," Caroline said. "We could probably try it on horses."

"Is barrel racing hard?" Rose asked.

"Depends on how good you ride and how fast your horse is," one of the girls answered.

"Looks like they're settin' up barrels," Daisy said. "We'll show ya how to do it."

BARREL RACING

* * *

The local girls lined up and took turns running the cloverleaf course, their horses leaning dramatically as they rounded the barrels. Then a breakneck run for home. A Quarter Horse at full gallop, a rider leaning into the horse's neck urging it to go faster, reins slapping its rump, then a dusty slide to a stop.

"Now you try it," Daisy said to Rose, "but don't go full out. Just get a feel for how to go 'round a barrel, both for you and the horse. Be sure you follow the clover leaf pattern and go 'round all the barrels. Keep your balance and grab the horn goin' round the outside. You can try gallopin' some on the way back."

Rose rode her horse around the course at a lope. She could imagine how much harder it would be at a gallop, and did gallop the last stretch down the center of the course. Then Caroline and Deborah took a turn.

While the girls were practicing, Michael-Joseph, Daniel, Tim, Tom, and four other boys entered the ring and gathered around the starting barrel of the second course. Michael-Joseph and Daniel acknowledged their sisters with nods, then faced the other boys. Tom explained how to run the course and Tim demonstrated, followed by the others.

The girls watched. The boys were in their best Western clothing with bright checks, plaids, and stripes freshly ironed. As did everyone, themselves included, they wore cowboy hats. Well-used and formed hats with the owner's particular roll or fold of the brim. Hats that made a statement and carried an attitude. Cowboy boots were clean and polished, the heels well-worn. The smell of a sweet hair treatment floated above the smell of horse.

Rose, Caroline, and Deborah felt like they were window shopping in a strange new store. When dressed up, the boys back in South Dakota had an equal flaunt of masculinity, but it was different here. Here, a horse completed everyone's outfit. Cowboy hats, not Fedoras and caps, were worn on a daily basis. Boots and spurs meant for riding, not work boots for plowing, were all that was considered. The cowboy look was definitely more romantic than the farmer look, and the girls couldn't stop staring. The boys were staring too.

Eventually the boys and girls' practice runs coincided and they ended up racing each other. The locals were fastest, but the visitors improved with practice and made a decent showing. The local girls were as fast as the boys.

When the practice ended, the two groups mingled, and everyone was introduced. Rose was pleased to meet Billy Cooper, a lean young man her age. She had admired his riding ability and they had exchanged distant smiles during the races.

Caroline and Deborah were also exchanging shy smiles with the boys, as were the local girls with Daniel and Michael-Joseph.

* * *

When Rebecca had shot the steer, it was dragged off to the barn for butchering. The hide was saved for Louise and her family to tan and work; the entrails were fed to the hogs. The meat was cut for pit roasting, barbecued ribs, and hindquarters to be slow roasted on a spit.

Pete and Hank had built a fire in a pit the ranch used for this form of roasting. The pit was next to the barn and was already lined with flat rocks. They had shoveled out the old ash and started a new fire on top of the stones; green alder branches were put to soak. The brisket and shoulders were seasoned with Pete's secret spices, wrapped in brown paper, then in wet burlap and fastened with chicken wire.

When ready, the coals were evenly spread, and wet alder branches laid on top. The meat went on top of that, then a metal sheet, the sod and dirt from the pit and an old saddle blanket over all.

The meat had been slow cooking all night and half the day. Pete figured it must be ready. He and Hank had set up a picnic area between the barn and the corral in the shade of an ancient cottonwood. Women had been bringing dishes to a large central table all morning.

Pete had been cooking beans in a huge pot in the bunkhouse, and Rebecca and Izabella had provided many loaves of warm bread and six apple streusels. The women were now ready to relax. They had left Honey and Queenie tied up in the shade by a water tank in front of the ranch house.

Now they put on their hats and boots and headed for the horses, having decided to look for their husbands to have lunch together. As they approached the corral, they saw the Doyle brothers, Fritz, and their husbands. They had just herded a group of steers into an enclosure for the bull doggin' contest. David and Josif joined them, and Fritz went in search of Flora.

The four rode over to the picnic area and tied their horses to the barn fence. The roasting pit had just been opened and the meat unwrapped. The aroma was pervasive and mouth-watering. Pete sliced off fork-tender pieces of meat as the celebrants came by with their plates,

Rebecca noticed that many seemed to be talking about her in reference to the meat. She was both embarrassed and proud. She still couldn't believe what she had done, and she couldn't imagine explaining it to her New York friends. She wouldn't know where to begin, especially after the tale of the flash flood. They would look at her with unbelieving eyes, marveling at the experiences, which had influenced her so much and which were so foreign to them. Now seeing her as different and changed.

Rebecca looked at her clothes and the clothes everyone else was wearing. A stranger would think she was a local. She liked that feeling. *Which would she prefer, she wondered? A trail ride with David with a gallop across a golden meadow followed by a picnic under a shady tree. Or a concert at Carnegie Hall in elegant clothing, followed by dinner and drinks at a fine restaurant?*

Just asking the question told her a lot. She saw her children eating with other children and appearing perfectly happy. What a sequence of events her mother-in-law, Ida Epstein, had begun when she suggested Deborah and Daniel spend a summer with the Dacia children. It had changed all their lives, and for the better. Her whole family had become more confident and open minded, even though they had all faced terrible danger to get there. She liked the feeling of strength and self-reliance; it was new and intoxicating.

* * *

Fritz and Flora sat by themselves to eat. They held hands across the table and had eyes only for each other. Fritz ate half his usual amount. They discussed their honeymoon plans, and Flora told Fritz about a little cabin her mother had that sat by the river under the trees. It was in a private spot and she had fixed it up for their wedding night. They could leave from there early Thursday morning, get breakfast on the road, and head for Yellowstone.

After a four-day honeymoon, they would return to the ranch for one of its heavy-duty, dual rear-tired trucks. They'd fill it with Flora's three horses, and Fritz's with her belongings, then head for the Wagner farm. Mr. and Mrs. Fritz Wagner of Centerford, South Dakota, going home.

The arrival of three more duallys with horses brought Fritz and Flora back to the present. Flora wanted to give Sundance a good grooming, and Fritz decided to check with Fred or Frank to see if anything else needed doing. They parted at the barn.

* * *

Fritz rode over to the livestock pens to evaluate the bulls and broncs. He was leaning on his saddle horn, appreciating the neck on a longhorn mix, when "Hey you!" caught his attention. "You," the deep and challenging voice said, "Shorty! Too bad you can't fill out a man's clothes." The voice came from behind him, loud and insulting.

Fritz smiled to himself. Moose Johnson must be here. He turned to face the speaker. "True, your clothes were pretty big at the gut, but kinda tight in the men's department," he yelled back, getting off his horse. Moose was his height, and very solid. The extra pounds weren't fat. He looked like a Viking with a cowboy hat for a helmet, large-boned and fierce.

Both men tied their horses to the rail and squared off. They had looks of serious combatants, but with a subtle underlying feeling of pure joy. They circled each other, growling. Once within reach, they put their heads down and pushed each other's shoulders. Neck and arm muscles bulged, boots dug into the dirt, but neither moved.

Fritz dropped his arms, shifted to the side, and punched Moose in the jaw as his weight carried him forward. With an indignant look, Moose regained his balance and delivered a solid blow to Fritz's gut. The fight was on. Soon the two were wrestling on the ground, then breaking apart and standing to punch some more.

Cowboys gathered 'round, and word of the fight between the two giants spread like wildfire. This had been a much-anticipated fight. One of the cowboys began collecting bets.

The fight was moving away from the corral toward the campsites and the river. It was at the stage of powerful punches sending the other flying. No clear winner was emerging. There were shouts and cheers with each punch.

The two squared off again. Fritz charged Moose, hitting him in the stomach with his shoulder. As Moose folded, Fritz slung him over his shoulder and pushed him off into the river. Then he jumped in after him. Hoots and cheers erupted.

* * *

One of the other new arrivals had been Wade Wilcox.

He lived twenty-five miles away and had hauled his horse in his truck. He unloaded his saddled mount. Looking around he was happy to see the crowd watching the fight, not him. He grabbed a knotted burlap bag from the floor of his truck and got on his horse. He carried the bag away from his body and rode around to the back of the barn.

Wade felt he had luck on his side. As he'd pulled into the Doyle ranch, he'd scanned the crowd. He'd spotted Fritz saying good bye to Flora at the barn door; she'd gone into the barn.

Wade knew his chances for revenge on Flora were disappearing. He also knew that he wouldn't let her leave, having done what she did to him, without payback. Wade carried four parallel scars down his left cheek. They had never paled to white, but always had an angry redness, which was darker than his thin, blond hair and coarser than looked natural against his sharp features.

The scars had clearly been caused from deep scratches; a tactic seldom used by men. Wade wore his approach to women on his face. He hated Flora for it, and deadly revenge was all he could think about. He wanted the witness and cause of his shame gone, dead and buried.

If this opportunity hadn't presented itself, Wade was going to put the snake under the seat of Fritz's truck, or in Sundance's stall. Hurting something she loved would be better than nothing.

Wade tied his horse at the back of the barn and staying in the shadows, snuck up to where Flora was grooming Sundance in his stall. He opened the door to the stall and stood blocking the exit. Sundance whinnied in warning and stamped his feet. Wade held the bag out toward Flora.

"What're you doing here, Wade?" Flora asked, immediately realizing her peril.

"I came to see *you*, Flora," he said. "I got a dandy little

weddin' present for you an' that big clodhopper a yours."
Wade untied the bag and tipped it over. A two-and-a-half-
foot prairie rattler slid out. It was startled by the sudden
light and immediately coiled into a striking pose. Wade
held still, but Sundance didn't; he whinnied, and reared.
Flora tried to calm him, but avoiding his hooves took her
closer to the snake.

Wade was watching with joyful anticipation. With
any luck, both Flora and her horse would die. As soon as
the snake struck Flora and her horse, he would leave. He
would probably have to knock Flora out to keep her from
talking before she died. People would think her horse had
kicked her accidentally, in a panic.

* * *

Slim sat on Diablo watching the fight between
Fritz and Moose. It was turning out to be a good one. He
scanned the crowd to see if Flora was watching and was
surprised she wasn't there. He noticed Wade's truck was
parked, but he and his horse weren't present. Without a
second thought, Slim galloped his horse toward the barn.

As he got closer, Slim heard Sundance, clearly upset,
hitting the side of his stall with his hooves, neighing
urgently. Slim rode Diablo into the barn. He saw Wade in
the stall door and Sundance rearing in fear of something
on the floor in front of him. Flora was trying to calm her
horse but was also clearly afraid of something near her
feet.

Slim immediately understood what was happening.
Then he heard the rattle, loud and deadly. A strike was
imminent.

Slim aimed Diablo at Wade and charged. At the last
minute, he turned him, and Diablo's hindquarter hit Wade
in the back, throwing him to the ground inside the stall.

PRAIRIE RATTLESNAKE

Slim hadn't seen where the snake was but knew a sudden movement would cause a strike.

Slim turned Diablo around and rode back to look in the stall. Wade had fallen on the snake, part of it, that is. The body and rattle were under his body, but the snake's open mouth was fixed to Wade's neck. It had its fangs sunk into Wade's jugular vein. Wade turned onto his back, screaming and pulling at the snake. It only sunk its fangs in deeper, coiling its body around Wade's hand, rattling furiously.

Slim pulled his pistol and shot the snake at the base of its skull, between Wade's neck and hand. The mouth released and Wade shook his arm hard, flinging the carcass against the stall wall. He tried to get up, but collapsed, his breathing desperate, coming in high-pitched wheezes.

"You and Sundance all right?" Slim asked Flora.

"We're fine, but that sure was close. Thank God you came along," Flora said, soothing Sundance and looking at Wade with revulsion.

Wade was writhing on the floor; his neck was swelling. He was gasping for air and trying to scream.

* * *

When the gunshot was heard, the fight ended. There was a stampede to the barn and a crowd gathered around Sundance's stall. Wade's neck and face were red and swollen. He was fighting for air, making high-pitched, raspy sounds and clawing the straw in pain. There were bite marks in his neck and a dead snake a foot from his outstretched left arm. The open burlap sack near Wade told the story.

The crowd parted for Doc Worley and Finley. The doctor made a point of attending all local rodeos and had his medical bag with him. He opened it and got out a vial of Morphine and a syringe, drawing up a small amount and injecting it into a vein in Wade's arm. In moments Wade's hands relaxed and his breathing eased. He took one last, long, thin high-pitched breath, and died.

"Well, that's the end a that," Finley said. "You guys drag 'im outta the stall so Flora kin git out and throw a blanket over 'im."

A dripping Fritz worked his way through the crowd. Flora came out of the stall behind Wade's body and Fritz hugged her, asking if she was okay and what had happened. Still holding her with one arm, he looked around at the scene, and at the wound in Wade's neck.

"Wade Wilcox up to his mean and evil ways," Frank replied.

"Looks like he got caught in his own trap," Fritz said. "Good riddance." There were murmurs of agreement.

Someone went out to the back of the barn and got Wade's horse. Wade's cousin, Earl, got Wade's truck and left with his body for the funeral parlor in Sundance. The crowd dispersed, now subdued.

Flora regarded Sundance's stall. The horse was still upset and restless, his eyes moving nervously. Slim had removed the snake, but its blood was in the straw. The place where Wade had fallen held his presence.

Fritz saw that Flora still felt uneasy and upset. He gathered the grooming brushes and handed Flora Sundance's reins. "Looks like Sundance could use some more curryin' and fresh air," he said. "Looks like you could too. Let's get you set up in the shade out there and I'll give this stall a good cleanin'."

Flora put her arms around Fritz and kissed him. "I love you, Fritz," she said.

CHAPTER SIXTEEN
Sad Songs on the Range

Although not well-liked because of his mean and selfish ways, Wade had been a decent cowboy. He had worked on his cousin Earl's ranch and was hard-working and knowledgeable about ranching. However, he wasn't a team player and always looked out for himself first. Although reliable on the job, he was a washout as a friend. He seemed to be in competition with everyone, bringing uneasiness to all his relationships.

The scars had made him worse: defiant, angry, and aggressive. If Flora had an alternative, she might have used it. The normal ranch dirt under everyone's nails would surely result in an infection and scarring.

But Wade was forcing himself on her. Her arms were pinned, and he was getting down to business. Flora had managed to free her right arm. Using her one available weapon, she clawed his face with the terrible strength her fury gave her. Wade had stopped immediately. He dropped her left hand and felt his face hot with pain and streaming with blood.

He immediately backhanded Flora. She reacted by hitting his eye socket with a powerful head butt, a technique Slim had taught her. It had knocked Wade out. Flora fled his truck and made her way home.

The community knew this story and girls who did not only ever went on one date with Wade. None of them spoke about it, though their hanging heads and loss of joy told their stories.

If Wade hadn't been killed essentially by his own hand, he would soon have been found among the castrated calves where he belonged. He would have been culled from the herd.

The snakebite had been immediate retribution from God. It was proof of a just God and had prevented a cowboy from doing another harm. The rodeo-goers recognized the holiness of the death and settled on quiet activities for the rest of the afternoon.

Some sat around their campfires and sang hymns. *Shall We Gather at the River, The Old Rugged Cross,* and *Amazing Grace* were all sung as a group as they performed their tasks. A quiet gentleness descended on the ranch.

Bottles were passed and thoughts of eternity entertained.

Izabella and Rebecca rode back to the ranch house. Izabella sat in a rocker on the porch and began work on the embroidered hankie she promised Flora.

Sitting quietly in the shade on the porch and listening to the gentle music coming from around the ranch was a welcome comfort. So much had happened in such a short time. And these were big things: flood, fire, and death. Rebecca shooting the steer. And more was coming. A two-day rodeo, the Fourth of July, and the wedding. She focused on her embroidery and the soft breeze stirring her hair.

* * *

Rebecca searched through the kitchen for items she would need for the wedding cake. She was delighted to find three square cake pans with two-inch differences in diameter. These would allow stacking with room for decorations around the edges.

A search of Flora's pantry turned up small bottles of food coloring and some tiny silver-colored candy balls. Rebecca grouped everything she would need together. She planned to make the three tiers on Tuesday and decorate the cake shortly before the wedding on Wednesday afternoon.

It would be white with pink rosebuds and green leaves on the edges, and a fully open pink rose on top. The silver candy balls would be lightly sprinkled on the flowers and leaves to look like dew drops.

The cake would be white French vanilla with a pineapple cream cheese filling and white buttercream frosting. Luckily, the class included tips on cutting the corners off envelopes to make various shapes. Rebecca found a large crystal platter for the cake and all was ready.

* * *

Activity remained light for the rest of the day, although a few riders took off into the hills, and several more trucks arrived. Izabella watched two riders with what looked like suitcases tied to their saddles. They had come out of the hills and were heading for the ranch house. She called Rebecca.

"We found these suitcases rammed into a big snag about a hunderd yards down from where you musta camped," one of them said. "They were kinda muddy, but not too wet. Figured they must be yours." The cowboys untied the suitcases and brought them to the porch.

Rebecca thanked the men and asked them to send Flora over if she was free. She laid her suitcase on its side and opened it. Mud was caked in the zipper, but she managed to force it open. Miraculously, the contents were undamaged. It appeared that the suitcase had been carried by mud versus water, and the leather and flap under the zipper had kept the thick mud out.

Rebecca looked at the clothes with new eyes. She

saw how much out of place they were. They would be useless in daily ranch wear. She felt relief that she and her family had been spared from wearing them when they first arrived. If the clothes hadn't been lost, they would have been wearing them every day. They would have stood out, never coming close to fitting in.

"What can I do with these?" she asked Izabella. "They're an embarrassment really."

"They wouldn't work for everyday around here, but they are pretty. They could be special for big events, not church, but...

"Rodeos!" Flora said, coming up the porch steps and seeing the satiny colors in the suitcase. "We always begin a rodeo with a grand entrance around the ring. Everyone dresses in their best duds for that."

"Oh, you mean some of the ladies would like these?" Rebecca asked.

"Sure, they would, for any parade or rodeo they're in. We don't see clothes like that too much around here. Folks wouldn't spend what little money they've got on 'em anyway. Clothes like that are a real luxury, even if you make 'em yourself."

"Let's see if Deborah's clothes are okay," Rebecca said, unzipping the second suitcase. There was a trace of dried mud on the inner flap, but the clothes were unharmed. "I would love to give these clothes to the girls around here," Rebecca said. "But how do I choose?"

"Tomorrow is youth day," Flora said. "The winners of the events could get a nice outfit. Then they'd have somethin' special to wear for The Fourth of July."

"I would love that," Rebecca said. "Will there be women my size competing?"

"Oh yes, women compete in the barrel racing but not as many as girls. Don't worry, there'll be winners for everything," Flora said.

"I want to give these things away, but then everyone will know what clothes we wore here," Rebecca lamented. "They'll see us as Easterners again."

"You mean you brought these to *wear*? I sure thought these were more gifts from *The New York Times*," Flora said. "As far as I'm concerned, you're still missing a couple suitcases, the ones with your real clothes."

Rebecca and Izabella laughed. "Thank you, Flora," Rebecca said. "You are very kind."

"I don't know what you're talkin' about," Flora said, laughing "Let's take these in the house and sort them into prizes. Then we can make sure all the winners get somethin', even if it's only a pretty pink neck scarf."

* * *

Leftover food from the noon meal was finished at the evening one. As darkness fell, the cowboys either stayed at their fires singing and visiting or went to the bunkhouse. The bunkhouse was always good for a game of poker, telling stories, drinking, and singing. It soon filled up.

After a bottle made the rounds, Finley said he'd been waiting to hear the story of the boys' kidnapping. "All I heard is talk about you boys bein' kidnapped," he said, "but none a the details. Let's hear the story."

Michael-Joseph and Daniel both told the story, adding details and descriptions of the gangsters. The part about Michael-Joseph smoking and puking on the gangster nearly brought the house down. With the addition of the effects of the beans on Daniel, some nearly fell out of their chairs.

Then the boys demonstrated their clarinet-playing disaster, which had alerted the horses to their presence from several miles away and allowed the girls to rescue them. There were immediate hoots and demands to knock it off, followed by more laughter.

Deborah's bravery at beating on the hideout door to make the gangster come out was noted. Remarks about the grit of the Epstein women made David proud. He loved their strength.

Both David and Josif were listening to the story and hearing new details. Each time they heard the story, they learned more. They were grateful their sons escaped and sometimes wondered who was more miserable, their sons, or the gangsters.

"Say, what was that song you were tryin' to play?" Pete asked. "I ain't never even heard any part of it."

"That was our aim," Daniel said. "We wanted to make them so miserable they'd be falling down drunk. Then we thought we could untie ourselves and make a break for it. The music is an adaptation of a song called *Bolero*, written for clarinets. It's very beautiful, but we made it awful."

"Let's hear it the right way," Finley said.

The boys positioned their clarinets, settled themselves, and with a slight nod from Daniel began the sensual melody of Bolero. The cowboys looked at each other and raised their eyebrows. This was not really campfire music; it was like nothing they had ever heard. But it did go good with liquor. The rich tones of the well-played clarinet duet, the repetitive melody with embellishments and increasing intensity had the cowboys on their feet cheering. "Play those licorice sticks, boys, ride "em hard!" Finley yelled as the song ended with a crescendo of harsh harmonies.

"Now play *Don't Fence Me In*," Slim said. Those who had learned the song sang along, and the others soon learned it. It was sung five times.

"*Red River Valley* was next, and everyone thought of Flora who would soon be leaving them. A few wiped away a tear and Fritz understood what a treasure he was removing from their lives.

Then came thoughts of Wade, in cold storage in the Sundance Funeral Parlor. "Play *Streets of Laredo*," Wade's cousin, Earl said. Pete began with his guitar and the others joined in:

> As I walked out on the streets of Laredo,
> As I walked out on Laredo one day,
> I spied a young cowboy all wrapped in white linen,
> All wrapped in white linen as cold as the clay.
>
> I can see by your outfit that you are a cowboy.
> These words he did say as I boldly walked by.
> Come an' sit down beside me an' hear my sad story.
> I'm shot in the breast, and I' know I must die.
>
> It was once in the saddle, I used to dashing.
> Once in the saddle I used to go gay.
> First in the card-house and then down to Rose's.
> But I'm shot in the breast and I'm dying today.
>
> Get six jolly cowboys to carry my coffin.
> Get six dance-hall maidens to bear up my pall.
> Throw bunches a roses all over my coffin.
> Roses to deaden the clods as they fall.
>
> Then beat the drum slowly and play the fife lowly.
> Play the dead march as you carry me along.
> Take me to the green valley and lay the sod o'er me.
> I'm a young cowboy and I know I've done wrong.

Another bottle made the rounds, and someone began, *Oh Bury Me Not on the Lone Prairie*. This left the group pensive and feeling the possibility of a cowboy's fate, dying and being buried in the prairie. Alone, unmourned, becoming part of the vast expanse of grasslands. Part of the land they loved, but lost in it and gone, turned to prairie dust.

* * *

"Let's sing *Abide with Me*," Finley said. "Then I'm turnin' in. The rodeo starts tomorrow and I'm announcin'. Need my beauty sleep."

CHAPTER SEVENTEEN
A First Rodeo

By sunrise everyone on the ranch was up and busy. Izabella and Rebecca were baking. Izabella had made eight loaves of bread. Rebecca mixed the cake batter and poured it into the three graduated cake pans. She put the pans in the oven to bake while the bread was rising.

The girls were also up, dressed and ready to immerse themselves in the rodeo. They had seen the contents of the suitcases the previous night and Deborah was pleased to give the clothes away as prizes.

The three ate a quick breakfast and headed to the corral to get their horses saddled. They had spent the previous afternoon combing their horses' manes and braiding them with Daisy and her friends. They had told the girls about the grand opening and charge around the ring. That day's participants would be mounted and in their best outfits. They would gallop around the ring, stopping in front of the grandstand for the *Pledge of Allegiance*, national anthem, and announcements.

All three of the girls were going to compete in the barrel racing and egg race. The boys were also going to try barrel racing but hadn't braided their horses' manes.

There was a brief damp coolness in the morning air. The rising sun soon turned it to heat. The boys arrived at the ranch house to pick up bread for the bunkhouse. They were happy and excited, and their mothers paused to drink in these happy images.

Rebecca explained about the found suitcases and the white lie that the other suitcases with their normal clothes had been lost. These fancy things would be awarded as prizes to the girls and women, and if David or Daniel's things were found, they could go to the boys and men. The boys were happy to keep this secret and said they'd tell their fathers and Fritz.

With everyone's chores done and breakfast eaten, folks wandered to the corral. Seating was in the bleachers or on the fence around the enclosure. Izabella and Rebecca climbed to the top row of the bleachers to get the best view.

All young people in attendance would be in at least one event. The youths and other contestants mounted up and formed a line outside the corral. Those leading the charge would be carrying the US flag and the Wyoming state flag.

Finley mounted the steps to the announcer's box located in the middle of a long side of the ring. Being two rows above the boxes where the cowboys would mount the bulls and horses, it offered a great view of the action.

He flicked a toggle switch on a box and picked up the microphone, tapping it and adjusting the volume. Speakers at the far ends of the ring responded. He studied the line of riders, and seeing that all was ready, said, "Let 'em in."

Riders with flag supports on their saddles galloped into the arena, the flags unfurled and waving. A complete lap of the ring brought the flag bearers and riders to the announcer's stand where they stopped in a cloud of dust, facing Finley.

"We're about to get started with the rodeo now," Finley said. "But first we'll say the *Pledge of Allegiance* and sing our national anthem. Then we'll sing my new favorite song, *Don't Fence Me In.* Pleased murmurings.

"I'm gonna ask David to lead us off. Josif will be playin' violin and a course you know Pete and his guitar." Finley handed the microphone down to David. Hats were removed for the *Pledge* and national anthem. With the help of the instruments and David's singing, all notes were hit squarely.

Next was *Don't Fence Me In*. Josif played a few opening notes, Pete played some chords and David began singing. Most of the crowd had already learned the song and jumped in. Beginning the rodeo as it did, it felt like a cowboy anthem.

"Welcome everbody to the Lucky D's annual Fourth of July Rodeo," Finley said into the microphone. "It's gonna be a goodun this year. We've got some guests from our neighbor state, South Dakota. That includes my future son-in-law, Fritz Wagner, and the Dacia family. Fritz is the other big fella besides Moose. We'll be seein' what he's made of and if he's good enough for our Flora."

Hoots and cheers from the audience.

"Mrs. Dacia's responsible for all that fresh bread we've bin gettin' ever mornin'." Enthusiastic applause. "Josif Dacia's bin workin' like a hand. Their kids bin ridin' all over the place, gettin' in a few fights, braidin' manes, stuff like that. Surprisingly normal for South Dakotans." More hoots, laughter, and applause.

"Then we got the Epsteins from New York City. Put yer guns away, pards, they're real nice folks." Laughter and applause. "They wanted to see Wyoming so much, they jumped right in with a flash flood and a fire. Came to the house all caked in mud. Got cleaned up and helped with the forest fire." Applause. "David roped a burning snag and saved Slim and one a our bulls. Not to be outdone, his wife, Rebecca, shot a steer between the eyes for our barbecue. I'm startin' to think a her as *Becky the Kid*."

Gunshots, standing applause, and cheering. Rebecca blushed and tried to sink out of sight. But with the standing ovation, she finally stood and waved at the crowd.

"She's also bin the one makin' them strudels and other tasty things." More applause.

We're gonna start the rodeo today with the kids' events. Then we'll get to the rough stock tomorrow.

"Let's give these contestants a big hand and get on with the show."

The audience cheered and the young riders turned toward the exit and galloped out of the ring.

* * *

To give contestants time to prepare themselves for barrel racing, wooly ridin' or mutton bustin', was the first event. Unshorn sheep were brought into the ring one at a time and the youngest cowboys and girls set down on them. The children would hug the sheep and hold tight to the wool. Then the sheep would be released, and the child staying on the longest would be the winner. Most ended the race while riding from the side of a sheep.

MUTTON BUSTERS

One toddler was able to hang on like a burr on a sock. His sheep took off for the far end of the ring, and he had to be plucked off when the sheep tired. A clear winner.

Cowboys rode into the ring after each contestant to herd the sheep out. Hank, Fred, and Frank set up the barrels for the next event. It would be girls' barrel racing, divided into three age groups: nine to thirteen, thirteen to sixteen, and sixteen to adult.

Rose, Caroline, and Deborah would be in the first category. The race began with the youngest group, and although none of the visitors had winning times, they made a good showing and received hearty applause. Teenage girls raced, and some young women.

Daniel and Michael-Joseph gave it everything they had in the boys' barrel racing but didn't win either. The cowboys recognized their courage and willingness to try though and rewarded them with cheers and yells of encouragement. Rebecca realized that she was much calmer now seeing her children doing brave things. She was amazed at her growth.

It was now around 2:00PM, and the ribs, which had been slow-roasting on a huge covered grill, smelled done. The rodeo was adjourned for lunch. Pole-bending, and the egg in a spoon races would begin after lunch. Boys' calf roping would be the last event.

David and Josif sat with their wives discussing the rodeo. All their children had done well in the barrel racing, and David had great photos. Rebecca had imagined riding with Deborah on her race. She felt the speed, the turns around the barrels, the horse leaning, then the fast gallop home. *Maybe another time*, she thought, and again surprised herself.

Finley tapping on the microphone alerted the crowd that the rodeo was about to continue. The women went back to the house to use the facilities, as Rebecca hadn't totally changed, preferring indoor plumbing. Josif and David lingered behind to use the outhouse and for David to get more film.

On David's way back from the privy, he passed by two cowboys sitting in the shade of a tree sharing a bottle. Not having children in the races, they had spent the morning drinking. They were pretty well hammered.

"Hey," one of them said to David. "You the one that won't fight?"

David knew what this would turn into. He had been here before; he was about to get beaten up. "I always make hurting someone the last option," David said. "I don't believe in violence to solve disagreements. I like to find solutions."

"I'll show you a solution," the first cowboy said, staggering to his feet. "You'd let somebody come 'n kill your granny and not lift a finger. We call those kinda folks cowards around here. This is a man's world out here. We got no use for cowards." The man lurched toward David and threw a punch. David sidestepped and the drunken cowboy stumbled when his fist didn't connect.

Another fist did connect with David's jaw, knocking him down. The second cowboy had gotten up and joined the fight. The first cowboy regained his balance and hauled David off the ground by his shirt. As soon as David was partially upright, he hit him in the gut, then the jaw. David fell to the ground again.

"Put 'em up, you damn coward," one of them said. "We're not done with you."

"Perhaps you not understand English," Josif said, returning from the privy. "This man does not like to fight. He is very brave." He smiled at the cowboys. "He does not like to fight, but I do." Josif threw the first punch and the fight was on. Drunk as they were, the cowboys could fight in almost any state out of habit. Josif had his hands full, keeping them under control.

The sounds of a fight, even as far away as behind the barn, were picked up by cowboys. They were drawn to it as lemmings to a cliff. It was almost instinct. As soon as they found the fight and saw two against one, they joined in. Fights were supposed to be fair, and they were all determined to make it so.

Fritz showed up, then Slim, then Moose. Fritz and Moose restarted their fight from the day before, and Slim headed for a knot of combatants. Soon, all men over the age of sixteen were involved.

Finley was aware of the fight and looked over his shoulder toward the barn more than at the ring. He finally couldn't take it anymore. "Flora, honey," he said into the microphone, "come up here and announce for a while. There's a fight goin' on an' I better go an' stop it."

* * *

Flora took the microphone and tapped it. "Well, kids and ladies," she said, "this seems to be the time in the rodeo for the big fight. Every year our daddies, brothers, husbands, sons, male cousins, and now my fiancé, try to beat each other up. It ain't a regulation event and there ain't no prizes, no belt buckles, but they all participate. Every year."

The ladies clapped, cheered, and booed. There were several gunshots.

"So, I figure we got time to hand out some ribbons and prizes."

Cheers from the crowd.

Flora had a Stetson hat box, which everyone recognized. It was full of ribbons and rosettes. The Lucky D always kept a good supply for their rodeo.

This year she also had two suitcases. They'd been sitting on the bench between her and Rebecca and been a topic of quiet conjecture. Now Flora opened them. Bright colors of satiny fabric shown from inside.

Oohs and *aahs* from the crowd.

"We got three events left, but the Epstein family has brought along some special prizes, and I wanna hand 'em out before the men get back. Lucky for all a us, the only suitcases showed up after the flood were ones with the prizes. So, I'll be handin' out a ribbon to the winners, as well as a shirt, boots, hat, or neck scarf.

"There are some real pretty things that'll perk up yer outfits next time yer in a parade or rodeo."

Murmurs of anticipation from the crowd.

"I'll be saving out prizes for the last two youth events, so don't worry if you haven't competed yet."

Flora called out winners and handed out prizes and ribbons. The girls loved their store-bought clothes, and tried on boots, hats, and blouses over their shirts. Imperfect fits could be hand-corrected. But none of them would have bought the fabric to make them entirely by hand.

"They brought prizes for the men and boys as well, but those suitcases weren't found," Flora said. "Start lookin', boys."

The fight hadn't petered out yet, so Flora got the last two races underway. The Dacia and Epstein children didn't win in either of them. The egg race was lost in about ten feet, if that. The visitors had no chance in the pole bending but were cheered on by audience and fellow competitors. The boys' calf roping would be postponed til the morning when cowboys would be around to wrangle the calves.

* * *

Michael-Joseph and Daniel were still riding with Tim and Tom Olson. Milling around on horseback with ranch kids, talking about the rodeo and racing, filled them with pride. Billy Cooper had joined them. He and Rose were noticing each other. Caroline thought both Tim and Tom

182

were cute, and Deborah still had a crush on Slim. Michael-Joseph and Daniel thought Daisy and all her friends were cute. The group was having a great time together.

* * *

Shortly after the youth events were finished, the cowboys wandered back to the corral. They were all a mess: shirts ripped and untucked; eyes blackened; lips bleeding; hats missing; and a few teeth. They headed for the river and their camps to get cleaned up. Bottles came out to ease the pain, and the women brought food to the picnic table under the cottonwood.

Pete brought beans from the bunkhouse, and any leftover meat. Everyone ate and got lazy. Instruments came out, the cook fire was fed, and the cowboys eased into the evening. People broke into small groups and visited, forgave each other for hard punches, and passed the bottle. Music and singing came from around the ranch.

Fritz found Moose in his camp by a nice fire and approached him smiling. "You come back for more, did ya?" Moose asked, rolling a cigarette.

"Naw," Fritz said, handing Moose a bottle of whiskey. "I come to ask ya a favor."

"Stop callin' ya Shorty?" Moose said, uncorking the bottle and taking a slug, then handing the bottle back to Fritz.

"Naw. I was wonderin' if you'd be my best man at the weddin'?" Fritz said, watching Moose over the top of the bottle as he took a healthy swallow. "Josif will be playing violin an' David'll be takin' pictures. I'd like someone I respect and trust at my side, an' from the way you fight, that's you." He handed the bottle back to Moose.

"I liked you right from the start," Moose said, guzzling the whiskey. "Maybe it's the way you dress." He handed the bottle back to Fritz. "Sure, I'll be your best man. I'd be proud to. Whadda I gotta do?"

"You gotta stand up next to me by the preacher. I give you the ring to hold on to. When the preacher asks for it, you give it back to me. Then I put it on Flora's finger."

"When do you give me the ring to hold on to?"

"Right before the weddin', I guess. I hate to let it outta my sight. I had it in my pocket during the flood," Fritz said.

"Is that all, just hold the ring?" Moose asked, handing the bottle back to Fritz.

"I guess you kinda look out for the groom too."

"You mean in case anybody says you can't marry Flora, I should talk to 'em?" Moose asked.

"I'll take care a any of them," Fritz replied. "I mean like if the groom steps in cow shit or somethin', you could help get it off."

"So, the best man is supposed to clean cow shit off the groom's boots?"

"Only if he steps in it before the weddin'; otherwise, the groom's strictly on his own," Fritz assured Moose. "You help make sure the weddin' goes off good and kinda keep an eye on the groom. Make sure his pants are buttoned-up and stuff like that." Fritz tossed down a large slug of the whiskey and handed the bottle back to Moose.

Moose laughed.

"Then there's a custom of the best man making a toast to the bride and groom. You could do that too."

"A toast? You mean somethin' like, 'Here's mud in your eye?' Somethin' like that?"

"Well, for a weddin', I was thinking of something a little more elegant. Somethin' more like, 'I wish the bride and groom many long years of wedded bliss and happiness, all the children they want, and the money to raise them.' Whaddaya think of that?"

"I guess I could say that. When do I gotta say it?"

"I think sometime right after the wedding cake is served," Fritz said. "Ol' Finley might say somethin' too. If he does, you can go right after him."

"So, does that mean I hafta be your best man until after the toast? Do I still hafta keep an eye on your boots and buttons until then?"

"I'd appreciate all the help I can get, Moose. I ain't never done anything like this before," Fritz said. "I don't wanna embarrass Flora or her family in any way. I want Flora to have a beautiful weddin' and for everything to be done just right."

"Well, I can't refuse that," Moose said. "Flora deserves a happy weddin' and nice send-off."

"There's one more favor I need from you," Fritz said. Moose looked skeptical. "I left my Stetson in my truck the night of the flood, but my good clothes were in my suitcase in the tent. They got swept away. Might you have any more clothes I could borrow that're a step above work clothes?"

"Not since my confirmation suit, and that's kinda small for me now." Moose thought a while. "I ain't got nothin' good enough for a weddin', and we buried my pa in his best suit. Now, Grandpa's closet might have sumthin'. He was big as me, so there's no problems there. Grandpa was a travelin' preacher. He's got a coupla nice ridin' coats and some black boots and hats. A white shirt or two. I could run back home in the mornin' and pick you up some stuff."

"Thanks, Moose, that'd be swell," Fritz said. He pulled out his bag of tobacco and rolling papers and prepared and lit a cigarette. "Now where'd that bottle get to?" he asked.

* * *

185

In the bunkhouse, the occupants had broken into small groups and were either playing poker, telling stories, or singing and playing instruments quietly. Michael-Joseph and Daniel were sitting at the dining table with Tim and Tom, looking at a folder showing brands. Tim and Tom were enjoying being the experts and explaining how to read the parts of a brand.

Josif was playing the violin and practicing the *Wedding March* with Pete.

Slim rose and grabbed a bottle from the shelf and a rope from a hook near his bed. "Come on out with me," he said to David., "I wanna show you somethin'."

David knew a summons when he heard one. He followed Slim outdoors to some log rounds sitting around a fire. He and Slim sat down. Slim uncorked the bottle and handed it to David. David had a feeling he was about to get drunk. He took a hearty swallow of the burning liquid and handed the bottle back to Slim. Slim took a sizable slug and gave it to David. David took another shot, almost coughed, and figured he was about ready for whatever Slim had in mind.

"David," Slim said," you singed my rope. It ain't no good anymore, burned almost all the way through. Probably break with any stress on it a' tall. It's gotta be fixed, an' I'm gonna show ya how."

"Thanks, Slim. I could get you a new one, but I'd be pleased to learn how to fix one. That'd be better."

Slim passed the bottle again. "Around here we don't think about gettin' a *new* anything. We fix things. He pulled his knife from a sheath at his belt and cut off the burnt end. Then he took a piece of antler tip out of his pocket. "This is what you need to fix a rope," he said. "We call it splicin'."

David realized he was being let into the inner

knowledge of being a true cowboy. He knew this was an honor. David was having trouble differentiating between the strands of rope Slim was loosening and weaving ends back through. But he saw the principle behind the technique. Slim finished off the end of the cut rope. It was now smooth, rounded, and impossible to unravel. He gave it to David to examine.

"That's one of the most perfect things I've ever seen," David said. "What a good thing to know."

"That was the first part," Slim said. "Now I'm gonna show you how to tie a *honda* knot."

"Great!" David said. "What's that?"

"Have another slug first," Slim replied, and handed David the bottle. "That's the knot that makes the loop you feed yer rope through. It's also called the *cowboy knot*. You can't be a proper cowboy if you can't tie it. You ever meet anyone says he's a cowboy, ask 'im to tie one. If he can't, he's a liar. No two ways about it."

Slim showed David how to tie the knot a couple times. David was sure he'd do better if he weren't drunk; Slim agreed. Finally, he was able to tie the knot twice in a row. David beamed, and Slim felt he'd made a contribution to humanity. He'd showed someone an important tool in the art of survival. He felt David understood its significance.

David was admiring the knot and stuck the folded long end of the rope through the loop in the honda knot. He opened the folded rope into a loop and did a small flat spin between himself and the campfire.

Slim gave him the rope and the cut-off burnt part. "Have some souvenirs from yer trip to Wyomin'," he said. He pulled out his fixin's and rolled a cigarette.

Slim lit the cigarette and took another slug. "David," he said, looking him in the eye, "I got some things to say to ya. Before ya got here I was sure what you were gonna be like, and it wasn't particularly nice. I'll spare ya the details, but it had to do with bein' a sissy and not carryin' yer weight."

David squirmed a little and took another drink.

"Well, I was wrong," Slim said. "There's nothin' sissy about ya, even though ya won't fight. Your boy said you'd fight to protect family or friends and die for 'em but not seek vengeance. You took the punishment so you wouldn't have to deal it out. That's standing up fer yer true self like a man."

"You wouldn't kill a little critter because you didn't need to. It's different from how I'd do things, but that don't make it bad or wrong. You worked hard to learn ropin' and ended up savin' my life. If that ain't bein' a cowboy, I don't know what is."

Slim looked hard at David. "You're not a Christian. You don't love Jesus. In fact, was your people that betrayed him. But here's what I figure." Slim took another drink and handed the bottle to David. "You got the heart of a Christian. I don't think there's nothin' unkind about ya. Yer not hurtin' others is probably somethin' Jesus'd like. Even though it was a Jew betrayed 'im, that's somethin' you'd never do, and I can't blame ya fer that. And I suppose a fella's gotta admit, Jesus started out Jewish."

David nodded. "That he did," he said.

"So, what I'm tryin' to say is you're A-okay with me. I'm sorry I misjudged ya, and I'm proud to know ya."

David wiped a tear from his eye.

"Now don't start that kinda thing," Slim said. "I won't have no men cryin'; I'll leave if ya keep it up."

"I'm done," David said. "But I got somethin' to say to you." He took a good-sized swallow and handed the bottle back to Slim.

"You weren't the only one who came with his mind

already made up. I thought everyone would see me and my family only as New Yorkers. I was afraid we'd be avoided and made fun of, or worse. Those two guys were drunk and looking for a fight, they were the exception. I didn't realize how fair and kind everyone would be.

"Yes, there were some hard moments, but we've been treated with great kindness and generosity. Coming here and meeting everyone has been one of the biggest thrills of my life. I especially appreciate your honesty and integrity, Slim. I hope you will honor me by letting me call you my friend."

Now Slim wiped a tear from his eye. "Cut that out!" he said. "One thing you gotta learn 'bout cowboys right now is they don't cry. No way. No how. Ever! You make one cry, they might hit ya." He stared at David. "I'd be pleased ta be yer friend," Slim said. "Now stop talkin' about it."

CHAPTER EIGHTEEN
Back to the Rodeo

Wednesday was the big day: men's events in the rodeo; the Fourth of July; and Flora's wedding.

Most cowboys were suffering from hangovers and aches and pains from the big fight the day before. Fresh bread, beans, eggs, and coffee, as well as a few hairs from the dogs that bit them, revived their spirits.

Finley was sporting a black eye and was slow and stiff climbing the stairs to his seat. After the *Pledge* and national anthem, he made the day's announcements.

"Welcome back for the second day of the Lucky D Rodeo. As you know, this is a special day. It's the Fourth of July and the day my little girl, Flora, gets married to that big fella over there, Fritz Wagner." Applause and cheers.

"Now, we got a little sidetracked on our schedule yesterday due to the big fight and all." Cheers and pistol firing. "So, we gotta stick to business today. We're gonna start with boys' calf ropin', so you cowboys out on the fence there can start gettin' them doggies in the chutes. After that event, we'll have the men's calf ropin', the wild cow milkin', then the bull ridin', followed by bull doggin' and bronc bustin'.

"We'll stop fer lunch when them haunches on the spits smell done. We'll finish up the events and hand out the prizes after that. The weddin's scheduled for six; there'll be more eatin' and the weddin' cake after that. Then the big dance in the loft for the rest a the evenin' or however long we last." Cheers, whoops, and more guns fired in the air were the response.

* * *

Tim and Tom as well as Billy Cooper were in the calf roping event. Michael-Joseph and Daniel wished they were also but were realistic about their rodeo skills. It was clear a lot of practice was involved. They cheered on their friends, and the Olson brothers placed well.

Rose had eyes only for Billy and took several pictures of him with her Brownie. He joined her on the fence after his performance.

Many cowboys were in the men's calf roping. The Epsteins were appreciating seeing the abilities of a Quarter Horse in action. They were well-trained and focused. David now understood why his horse needed so little guidance during the roping of the burning snag.

The next event was wild cow milking. Two teams of four would compete at the same time. Fred and Frank helped herd feral cows into chutes. Each team had one mounted member with a rope. That person would rope the cow, then dismount and help with the milking. The rope would be removed from its wrap around the saddle horn and could be grabbed by another team member. Two of the team would try to hold the animal in place; the other two would try to milk it. Three drops in a pop bottle could win the event. There was a two-minute time limit.

After watching the first group, Josif, David, and Fritz decided to give it a try. Fritz got Moose to join them. It was decided David would rope the cow, Fritz and Moose would hold it in place, Josif would milk it, and David would hold the collection bottle and run it home.

The ropers waited at the proper distance and those on foot were at their starting lines. Wild cow milking was a fun event, hysterical at times, but it could also be dangerous. Cowboys could be stepped on, kicked, or trampled. But it was a worthy event, and required skill, speed, and courage.

David studied the cow in the box for his team. She was clearly agitated. His heart went out to her, but the angry look on her face suggested that his team would be in trouble. When the signal was given, the gates were pulled open and the cows erupted from their boxes.

David rode with the cow and roped her. He wrapped two dallies, his horse stopped and backed up, the rope went taut, the cow spun in place and halted. Fritz and Moose grabbed the cow. David unwrapped the rope from his saddle horn and jumped off his horse. Fritz was at the head of the cow, holding her by the horns; Moose had her by the tail, and Josif was regarding the bucking cow's udder with distrust.

David joined Josif who handed him an empty pop bottle for milk collection. The cow was being held in place fairly well by the grunting efforts of Fritz and Moose, but that didn't mean she was still. She was bawling and kicking, sometimes with both hind feet, trying to buck and wrench her head from Fritz's grasp. Moose was at the end of the cow's tail, but still had to jump and dodge to avoid being kicked.

"Milk 'er," Moose yelled through clenched teeth, as he evaded another hoof aimed at the family jewels.

Josif crouched and warily reached for the udder. As soon as he touched it, the cow kicked forward with a hind leg. Josif hopped backward away from the cow just in time.

Josif slowly approached the udder again. "Get ready," he yelled to his team. David held the bottle out and also crouched near the udder to collect any possible drop that Josif might be able to milk. The cow continued to push Fritz with her head and kick at Moose.

Josif grabbed the teat closest to David. David quickly positioned the bottle. Josif milked the teat. The cow bucked and kicked forward in indignation; both David and Josif were thrown backward into the dirt. David managed to keep the bottle upright. He studied the bottle. It looked like a small stream of milk had flowed down the inside.

He and Josif scrambled to their feet and away from the cow. David took off for the finish line. Fritz and Moose happily released their holds on the cow, moving away from her. Mounted cowboys herded her into a pen.

The thin stream of visible milk triumphed over a small muddy blob in another team's bottle, and David's team was declared winner.

Cheers and gunshots erupted from the crowd. Relief flowed from Flora and the wives and children of the visitors.

Daniel was mentally composing a new paragraph for his report on his summer vacation. He would have a photo to accompany it, thanks to his Brownie camera.

* * *

Next up was bull riding. This was a very popular and dangerous event. Bulls weighing two thousand pounds or more would do their best to throw off their rider and cause him harm. In spite of their size, bulls' athletic moves included leaping into the air while throwing their rear legs to the side and exposing their underbelly. On a *sun-fishing* bull, the cowboy usually falls off, now in danger of the bull landing on him.

Riders could be thrown coming right out of the chute, even while in the chute. Cowboys often hit the ground hard or even upside down. The bulls sought domination and could cripple or kill a rider.

The eight-second ride was up to the cowboy, but saving his life was often up to the rodeo clowns. These cowboys would try to distract a bull from killing the rider while a pick-up man rode in to pull a contestant up onto his saddle and away from the powerful and erratic kicks of a bull or horse. They would drag a rider from the ring and put themselves in danger to get a bull away from a fallen contestant. If the cowboy somehow got hung up on a bull, it was up to the clowns to move in and save him.

There were metal barrels scattered around that a clown could jump into. Volunteers were always welcome and needed.

* * *

The wild cow milkers were still pumped with adrenalin from their event and entered the corral to join others as rodeo clowns. They stood around the chute and farther into the ring, ready to distract a bull or aid a fallen cowboy.

David watched the experienced clowns approach the bulls to keep them away from a fence or chute wall where a rider could be crushed and battered. When Finley announced that the eight seconds were done, someone would ring a bell and the cowboy would dismount. If the cowboy had problems establishing his balance or got off to a poor start, the official could allow the ride to go longer in hopes the rider could get a good eight-second ride.

There were at least two judges as both the cowboy and bull got scores of one to twenty-five. A bull got a high score if he gave a good ride and the cowboy if he rode that good ride for eight seconds. One hundred points was the highest score; eighty-five was considered good.

Doc Worley was the second judge. The local country

doctor, he had seen more rodeos than any of them and was a fine judge of both cowboy and animal. He and Finley sat next to each other in the judging box with pads and pencils. Finley continued to announce.

"Well, folks, we got the big event comin' up now — everbody's favorite, bull ridin'. This event separates the studs from the boys and the bulls from the steers. We've got some good an' rank rough stock here today. You all might remember Tornado, High Flyer, Flapjack, Full House, an' Big Boy. They've been loungin' around makin' calves, eatin', and lookin' for a good fight for some months now. We got some cowboys like that, too, so it's time to get 'em together."

Cheers and gunshots.

"First up we got Gene Wilson. He drew High Flyer from the Olson Ranch, the Double O, so look for a grand entrance." Finley looked down into the chute where Gene was wrapping his gloved hand into the bull rope. A flank man was securing the flank strap at the proper tightness with an easy release knot.

"Looks like he's 'bout ready to go."

Gene gave the nod, the chute door flew open, a red flag dropped, and the timer started. High Flyer leapt into the ring. His forelegs were two feet off the ground and his hind legs about seven. Gene had his feet forward and was almost lying flat on the bull's back. His right hand was secure and his left hand in the air.

"So far, so good, folks," Finley said.

High Flyer landed with a jolt and jumped and bucked again, this time higher. First, Gene found himself flying upward through the air, his right hand free, no bull beneath him. Then he hit the ground and rolled. A mounted cowboy moved between Gene and the bull, and two clowns ran to Gene and hurried him out of the ring.

"Nice try there, Gene," Finley said into the mike, "but you only got six seconds; you didn't cover that bull. Better luck next time."

Finley conferred with Doc Worley. "We're gonna give High Flyer forty points between us. He's turnin' into a pretty high scorer. Nice job over there at the Double O."

Big Boy was next. He weighed about three hundred pounds more than the other bulls. He was broad and heavily muscled. His neck was barrel thick, and he seemed to wear a constant scowl.

Big Boy bucked and kicked, his movements hard and powerful. The rider stayed on, but occasionally lost his balance on the bull. He completed the ride leaning heavily to the side. He was awarded thirty points for riding a hard bull but received none for style. Big Boy earned forty points, giving the rider a seventy-point ride.

Flap Jack was a huge brute whose specialty was sun-fishing or rolling to the side in mid-air. Flap Jack flipped to his side moments after he charged out of the box. The cowboy landed on his back. Flap Jack landed inches from the rider; his head lowered with murderous intent. The cowboys on the ground moved in. Two grabbed for the rider who'd had the wind knocked out of him. The others distracted the bull by waving their arms and hats in front of him. Two mounted cowboys roped the bull and directed it to a small side pen.

David followed the others' lead, distracting the bulls and protecting the fallen riders. He had never seen such powerful animals before, let alone get in a ring with one and try to attract its attention. He regarded the barrels that he could jump into if a bull charged him. It made him think of what a ride over Niagara Falls in a barrel might be like, minus the water, if a bull kicked or tossed it.

Full House got his name from his repertoire of bull tricks. He could do them all. He started with a drop, lowering his head and kicking high and hard behind. Then he spun, sun-fished, and bucked. The rider managed five seconds. Full House scored forty-five points.

"Let's give Dick Miller a big hand," Finley said. "He sure had a lotta try." Applause and gunshots.

The last bull was Tornado. He was known for spinning. Ned Smith drew him. With Ned's nod, the chute sprung open and Tornado entered the ring with a high jump and buck. Then he spun while bucking and kicking. Ned gripped the bull rope hard, but the constant spinning forced his hand to the side where it became wedged. The force of the spin was too powerful for him to overcome and he was stuck on the side of the bull. If he fell off with his hand hung up, he could dislocate his shoulder or rip tendons and ligaments. If he didn't get off soon in a controlled fashion, he'd be falling off while still hung up.

The cowboys on foot and mounted moved in to help, but Tornado's movements were too strong, fast, and erratic to approach. The bull was moving his circles toward David. David could see from the rider's face that he was weakening. The only thing in David's reach was a barrel. He grabbed it by the two ends and flung it at Tornado's legs. The bull stumbled and stopped bucking and spinning for a minute. Riders raced in and freed Ned's hand, scooping him off the bull and to safety.

Tornado now faced David head-on. David was too far into the ring to get out quickly. His barrel was about fifteen feet away. Not knowing what else to do, David tried his herding skills. He took off his hat and waved it in the air. He yelled at the bull, trying to sound dominant, spreading his arms and legs to look bigger.

Tornado stared at David. His flank strap was still on and he hadn't given up the fight. Just as the bull looked ready to charge, a rope landed over its head and a rider came between David and the bull. The cowboy reached down for David and hauled him up on the saddle and to safety. Tornado's flank strap was released, and he was herded to another pen.

"Well, that was sure sumthin'," Finley said. "We're givin' thirty points to the rider and forty-five to the bull. Thought we might also give ten points to the barrel man," Finley said, waving at David. "That was some nice work for a greenhorn."

Cheers, laughing, and pistol firing.

* * *

Finley sniffed the air. "Smells like them beef haunches're 'bout done. Let's break for chow then we'll have the bull doggin' and bronc bustin' after that." He and Doc Worley climbed out of the stands, mounted up, and headed for the picnic tables under the big cottonwood.

199

This time Rebecca and Izabella sat with the other women, and David and Josif sat with the men. The kids were in small scattered groups.

* * *

Over the sound of talking and laughing, the picnickers gradually became aware of a distant buzzing, which abruptly became the unmistakable sound of an airplane. Cowboys rode into the open to get a look.

"By golly, that looks like a Lockheed Vega," Doc Worley said.

"Ain't the Winnie Mae a Lockheed Vega?" Finley asked.

"She shore is," Doc replied.

"Looks like that plane's circlin'," Finley observed.

"Looks like that plane's gonna land on yer road," Doc said. "If that's Will Rogers and Wylie Post, we oughta grab a coupla horses and go meet 'em!"

CHAPTER NINETEEN
Out of the Blue

Half the rodeo guests rode out to meet the visitors who were disembarking the plane. The plane was Wylie Post's Winnie Mae, and he and Will Rogers were visiting.

Finley dismounted and stuck out his hand. "By golly, It's Will Rogers and Wylie Post! It sure is an honor to meet you and have you visit the Lucky D. What brings you up here?"

WILL ROGERS   WYLIE POST

Will shook hands with Finley and grinned. "A couple things. One is they're dedicating the carving of George Washington on Mt. Rushmore today. Thought I should see that firsthand.

"The second is a friend a mine from New York said he was gonna be at a weddin' an' rodeo on the Fourth of July up near Devils Tower. Sounded like somethin' not to be missed. Since Mt. Rushmore and Devils Tower are so close, we thought we'd stop by after the dedication for a few hours, say howdy."

David and Josif joined the crowd. "Looks like you're fittin' in okay," Will said. "You look like an average cowboy."

"You're right. I do, but that's a long story," David replied.

"You showed up just in time fer lunch," Finley said. "Let's head over to the BBQ and get ya a couple plates."

Will reached inside the Winnie Mae and pulled out two large burlap bags of oranges. He handed them up to two willing cowboys. "I was in Los Angeles last week workin' on a movie. Thought you folks might enjoy some fresh Valencia oranges to round out your Fourth of July picnic and weddin' feast," he said.

"That's real thoughtful of ya, Will. Ain't too many oranges show up around here." Finley said.

Will and Wylie mounted the two extra horses and the group rode back to the picnic tables. Ladies handed the guests heaping plates and cleared spots for them at the table with Finley. Another table was pulled over and Frank, Fred, David, Rebecca, Flora, Fritz, Slim, Josif, Izabella, and Doc Worley sat down.

Will smiled as he looked around at the gathered crowd. "I see most everybody but the women and children've got black eyes. Was it a group event or a buncha skirmishes?"

"Group event," Finley said. "We seem to have one every year."

"Looks like you got to join in," Will said, looking at David.

"In a manner of speaking," David replied. "I played defense."

David, Slim, and the Doyles filled Will in on the events of the last few days.

"That should make pretty good copy for the *Times*," Will said. You sure packed a lot into a few days!"

"And we're still not done with the rodeo. Then there's the wedding, feasting, and dancing; a newspaperman's dream," David said.

"Speakin' of that. When the *Times* heard I was comin' out here to make sure you lived through your Wyoming welcome, they asked me to bring you more film from L.A. I gotta big box a slides fer your Speed Graphic still in the Winnie Mae."

"That's great, Will. I can sure use them."

* * *

David got his camera and took several group photos with Will and Wylie. He also got one of just Will and Finley.

Pete handed Will a rope and asked if he'd do a few tricks. Will asked for a second rope and did two overlapping horizontal flat spins, which he jumped back and forth between. He did one spin to the side and another up and down over his head at the same time.

Then he handed a rope to David and they each jumped in and out of the other's loop at the same time.

The crowd cheered.

They each made a vertical loop to the side and rolled it from one side of their bodies across the back of their necks to the other side and back again. They did several more matching spins with Will announcing them.

Daniel got several photos with his Brownie.

* * *

"We got bulldoggin' next if you'd like to join us." Finley said.

"One a my favorite events," Will replied.

Will and Wylie joined Finley and Doc Worley at the judging box.

In this event, a mounted cowboy gives a steer a head start. Another cowboy is on the steer's opposite side to keep it from veering. The mounted cowboy reaches over and grabs the steer by the horns. He brings his feet to the ground and braces them, twisting the steer's neck at the same time and throwing him. An average time was four seconds.

BULLDOGGIN'

Fritz decided to give this event a try and due to his height and good leverage, threw his steer in three seconds.

Whoops and gunshots.

Moose was up next and also managed three seconds. More whooping.

At the end of the competition, Fritz and Moose were tied with the best times. It was decided to award the win to the longest and highest hay bale throws between them. Although others liked to participate in the hay bale throwing contest, it was clear this was between Fritz and Moose.

The entry to the ring was topped by a twelve-foot-high log. Moose grabbed a bale, swung it backwards, then up with a great heave. It cleared the log and flew apart upon hitting the ground. Moose smiled and stepped back.

Fritz grabbed a bale as though it weighed only a few pounds. He swung it back and heaved it upward. It also easily cleared the log and exploded on the ground.

"Well, we got no clear winner and nothin' higher to throw a bale over, 'cept the windmill. Let's see how these fellas do with distance. If you both start at the same place along the fence, we'll be able to measure by countin' the posts, which are eight feet apart."

Fritz and Moose stood about three feet apart. They grabbed a bale, swung back and then forward with a grunting effort that lifted them off the ground. The bales landed next to each other at forty feet, a Lucky D record.

"I guess this is meant to be a tie," Finley said. "Although if it weren't Fritz's weddin' day, we'd probably be decidin' with fisticuffs."

Cheers and hoots. Will guffawed. "That'd be a good fight," he said.

* * *

Saddle bronc riding was next. This and bareback bronc riding were the two most popular events. Scoring was the same as in bull riding with the animal and rider each eligible to receive fifty points.

The rider must follow specific guidelines during his ride. He must not touch the horse or himself with his free hand and must mark the horse out when exiting the bucking chute. This required having their spurs touch the horse above its shoulders before and until the horse's front legs touched the ground on its first leap.

Then on free-swinging stirrups and in coordination with the horse's moves, the rider must swing his heels back and forth to touch his spurs to the horse's flank, then shoulder. The rider must stay on for eight seconds. A horse with good moves and a strong buck could earn a cowboy winning points. The cowboy matching the horse's rhythm with his spurring and movements would score well.

There is no saddle horn on a bronc riding saddle. The rider holds onto a thick braided strap attached to a leather halter on the horse. This was a contest of skill, control, and quick reactions.

* * *

Bronc riding was the last event of the rodeo. Josif, David, and Fritz all wanted to try. David figured saddle bronc riding would be easier than bareback. The first few contestants showed him otherwise.

Fred Doyle did saddle bronc riding; his brother, Frank, rode bareback, as did Slim.

Fred drew a horse named Sore Loser who earned his name with stiff- legged, jarring landings. He exited the bucking chute with a tremendous leap and hard landing. Fred marked him out and lasted eight seconds of twisting, bucking, and bone-jolting punishment. His footwork's rhythm was several times interrupted by Sore Loser's erratic movements. When he heard the bell, Fred jumped off the horse, landing in a crouch.

Cheers and gunshots from the crowd.

Finley asked Will to judge Fred for him to avoid accusations of favoritism. Between Will and Doc Worley, Fred received a score of eighty-five, the highest so far.

Many cowboys entered the bronc riding events, as breaking wild horses was a skill of great pride. Most of the horses were broke for ranch work. The hardheaded ones became rough stock, rank animals guaranteed to put up a worthy fight.

SADDLE BRONC RIDER

* * *

Bareback bronc riding was the last event. The rider had no saddle and hung onto the horse with a thick handle attached to a strap around the horse behind its front legs. His free hand must not touch himself or the horse.

The cowboy must spur the horse rapidly and in rhythm with the horse from shoulder to girth strap for eight long seconds.

Josif was first up. He had drawn a horse named Hard Times. As he lowered himself onto the horse's back, he could feel the contained power that would soon be unleashed. The horse was restless and kicked the chute.

A cowboy showed Josif where to hold on, and where to have his spurs touch the horse. "Nod when you're ready," the cowboy said. "I wouldn't wait too long."

Josif nodded. The chute opened and Hard Times dove into the ring. Josif marked him out just before the horse put his head down and bucked, heels high and spinning. Josif became airborne. He landed on his butt next to Hard Times who kicked at him and continued bucking until roped and led back to the horse pen.

Josif got up, and dusting himself off, headed for the fence. The crowd laughed and cheered. Izabella sighed with relief.

David drew Cyclone. He suspected this horse would give a ride similar to that of Tornado, the spinning bull. He was right. David was on the ground with his feet in front of him trying to mark out Cyclone just as the horse bucked and twisted out of the chute.

Laughter and applause. "Nice try, David," Will said over the microphone. "Looks like you got about one-eighth of a full ride." More applause.

When Fritz's turn arrived, he'd drawn Strawberry, a horse named both for his red roan color and similarity to the horse in the song, *The Strawberry Roan*.

Strawberry was rangy, not handsome. As in the song,

> "*His legs are all spavined, he's got pigeon toes*
> *Little pig eyes and a big roman nose*
> *Little pin ears that touched at the tip*
> *A big 44 brand was on his left hip*
> *U-necked and old, with a long, lower jaw*
> *I could see with one eye, he's a regular outlaw.*"

Fritz grabbed the handle, raised his left hand, and nodded. The chute sprung open. Strawberry bucked into the ring. Fritz managed to mark him out. Strawberry leapt high in the air and sun-fished, turning his hind legs to the side and his belly up. Fritz leaned to maintain his center of gravity and stayed on the horse but had stopped his footwork.

Strawberry bucked, spun, and kicked high. Fritz managed to last the eight seconds, but it was not a controlled ride. He got twenty points from the judges and Strawberry got thirty-five.

Applause and a few gunshots for lasting eight seconds from the crowd. Another sigh of relief, this time from Flora.

Frank Doyle earned eighty points on a feisty Quarter Horse named Trouble, again judged by Will and Doc Worley.

* * *

Slim drew a powerful bay brute named Loco. Loco was unpredictable. He would buck high, spin fast, sun-fish, then spin in the other direction with his head down, inviting the cowboy to slide down his neck. His moves were strong and angry.

It was the heat of the day now and sweat trickled down Slim's neck as he braced himself over Loco before mounting. A startlingly cold stream of liquid poured from above, hitting Slim's back without warning. It was accompanied by a cry of dismay. Slim glanced at the bleachers overhead. He caught a glimpse of a mortified Deborah sinking down out of sight, an open pop bottle in her hand. Caroline, Rose, and Billy Cooper were looking at her in horror.

Slim settled onto Loco, adjusted his grip on the handle, and gave the nod. Loco bucked out of the chute. Slim marked him out and kept his toes out, moving his rondelled spurs from shoulder to girth through all of Loco's moves. He didn't miss a move or fly off Loco's back, although he did spend time above it.

The visitors watched in wonder. This is how it was done. Slim was focused and responding instantly to Loco's moves. He had clearly met these challenges before.

Slim and Loco both scored forty-five points for a total of ninety, high score for the day.

Two more riders performed, ending the rodeo.

"Well, that's the end of the events," Finley announced. "We shore had some rank rough stock and cowboys!"

Cheers and gunshots.

"Everone did their best and we had some fine performances!"

Cheers and applause.

"The cowboys did perty good too."

Laughter and gunshots.

"Now it's time for the awards. Since we got a celebrity cowboy here, I'm gonna ask Will Rogers to present them to the winners."

Cheers.

Finley read a list of winners and gave Will the appropriate ribbons. High scorers in each event received a corona saddle pad: a homemade colorful thick saddle blanket with a thick, striped wool edging

The winner of the rodeo was Bill Olson of the Double O Ranch, brother of Jim Olson, the father of Tim and Tom. He had received high points for both himself and his rough stock.

Bill received a new beautifully worked tan saddle made by Louise LaVoi and her family, the local tanners and leatherworkers.

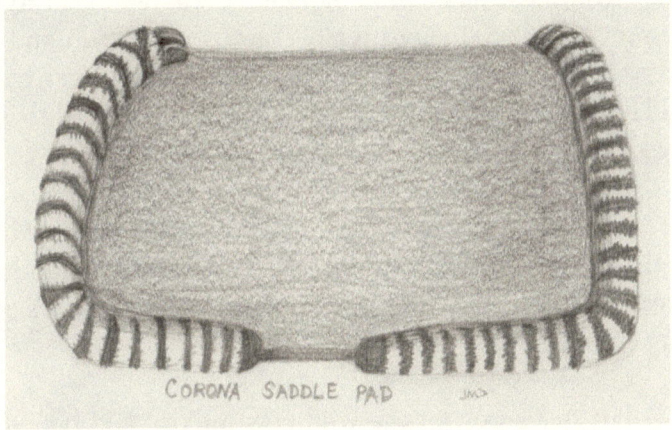

CORONA SADDLE PAD

A huge round of applause, gunshots, and cheers for Bill, the saddle, and the rodeo.

Finley got the crowd's attention again. "There's one more award to be given, and I'm gonna hand the mike over to our Lucky D foreman, Slim Stanton, to give it."

Slim took the mike. He looked around at the crowd. "You can all imagine just how much I enjoy standin' up here talkin' into this mike," he said.

Laughter from the crowd.

"You know I don't like it, but I got somethin' needs to be said and done."

The crowd went silent, intent on Slim's words.

Slim looked around at the crowd. His expression was serious, and he looked uncomfortable, but determined. "I got somethin' to say about that New Yorker over there, David Epstein."

The crowd seemed to hold its breath. "I have to admit I was one of the first to label David Epstein before I even met him. I was pretty fixed on the idea he'd be lazy, cowardly, and afraid to get his hands dirty, never mind a callous."

Quiet laughter.

"Well, you may have noticed I was wrong. David Epstein has done everything a cowboy should do and is everything I respect in a cowboy. Will Rogers over here told him he better learn to ride and rope if he hoped to get out of Wyoming alive."

Laughter and applause.

"Well, he learned to rope well enough to save my life in the fire. He tried to learn to ride in New York but didn't learn Western ridin' 'til he got to South Dakota. He's got that licked now."

Cheers.

His team won in the wild cow milkin' and he even got ten points as a barrel man. He hasn't racked up a lotta points, but he's in there tryin'. He refuses to fight, but he pays for that right. He's no coward."

Cheers and gunshots.

"He's clearly gotten dirty and has a good start on callouses."

Cheers and laughter.

"And let's not forget he taught us *Don't Fence Me In.*

Cheers and whistles.

"I have to say if David Epstein isn't a cowboy, it's only in the area of not having learned all the tricks a the trade. Not growin' up around it. He's got the heart and soul of a cowboy. The honor, courage, and grit."

Cheers.

"I taught David how to splice and tie a honda knot. I told him he could always tell a true cowboy if a fella could do those things besides ridin', ropin', and shootin', a course.

Chuckling.

"Well, I thought it was also important for any cowboy who meets David to know he's talkin' to a cowboy, even though he might not look like it at the time. For that reason, and as a token of my friendship, I'm givin' you my Bronc Riding Championship belt buckle, David."

There was a gasp from the crowd, then quiet. Slim pulled his championship buckle from his pocket, giving it to David with a look forbidding him to cry.

David took it and shook hands with Slim.

Will Rogers pushed his hat back with a happy grin.

The crowd erupted in cheers and gunshots.

When the crowd quieted down, David took the mike. He smiled at Slim and held the buckle to his heart. "Dear friends, I can't tell you how happy I am right now. It has been a true honor to be part of your lives for the last four days. I have never lived so much in such a short time. I've learned a little of all there is to know about cowboyin', and have great respect for the amount of skill, courage, and honor you show every day. You are all strong and as wild as the wind. I will be happy if some of that has rubbed off on me, as it has on my wife." David gestured to Rebecca in the stands and there was an immediate standing ovation.

David laughed to keep from crying and Rebecca wept openly. Izabella put her arm around Rebecca's waist.

David handed the mike to Finley. "Well, folks," he said, blowing his nose into a hanky, "this is one heck of a dramatic day. And we're not done yet. Not by a long shot! We're gonna have a weddin' in about two hours. We'll ring the triangle when we're ready. There'll be feastin' an' dancin' after that, so get your dishes ready and get cleaned up.

"Finally, I'd like to thank Will Rogers and Wylie Post for honoring us with their presence. We'll never forgit it."

Cheering.

Will took the mike. "I hafta admit I was a little worried about a New Yorker in Wyoming. I had no idea he'd make out so good."

Laughter.

"I guess it goes to show it's the man, not the place, that's important."

Sounds of agreement from the crowd.

Wylie and I've had a great time visitin' and eatin' your fine food. Thank you all for your hospitality and a fine rodeo."

Applause and cheering.

* * *

A crowd accompanied Will and Wylie back to the Winnie Mae. David got his film. Good byes were said, Wylie started the Lockheed Vega and turned it around on the road. He revved its engines and the plane picked up speed until it lifted into the air; circling the ranch, it headed west/southwest. Everyone watched in reverence until the plane disappeared.

* * *

The next event of the day was Flora and Fritz's wedding. This was a total change of pace with many details to be attended to.

Moose met with Michael-Joseph, Daniel, and the group they were riding with. He gave them detailed instructions.

Izabella met with Rose, Caroline, Deborah, and their friends and gave them instructions.

Slim met with a cowboy with a large truck, making arrangements for the delivery of a wedding present.

Pete was making more beans, and Hank, Fred, and Frank were hanging garlands on the fence where the wedding would take place.

Fritz was cleaning himself up from the rodeo before putting on his wedding suit.

Josif and David were also cleaning up.

Rebecca was decorating the cake.

Izabella and Louise fussed over Flora, making sure she had something old, new, borrowed, and blue.

Finley got a drink, rolled a smoke, and sat down for a while, letting the day sink in.

CHAPTER TWENTY
The Wedding

In several hours, ringing of the triangle announced it was time for the wedding. Guests rushed to the stands. The boys and their friends lined up on horseback, facing each other to make an aisle to the preacher. The aisle had been raked and was smooth and clear of unpleasant things to step in. Moose made sure the groom was buttoned up.

David had picked up Rebecca, Izabella, Louise, and the three-tiered cake in his car. He slowly drove them to the large picnic table under the cottonwood, which was crowded with food. He parked and Rebecca and Izabella went to the bleachers. Louise, as Flora's Maid of Honor, took her position at the gate to follow Flora and Finley up the aisle. David got his camera.

David, Daniel, Josif, and Pete got in position with their instruments in the judge's box.

Fritz and Moose stood next to each other, a formidable presence. Moose was in his washed and pressed best clothes. His russet hair was clean and slicked down; he was freshly shaven. He had just been given the ring box and put it in his pocket.

Fritz was also freshly washed and shaven. Moose had brought his grandfather's traveling preacher's outfit for Fritz, who wore it well. He was in a high-necked white shirt and long, black riding coat with tall black boots over his black moleskin pants. He stood out in the crowd, a larger-than-life image of a former time, rugged and elegant. He was receiving admiring looks from the women.

Fred arrived in the Doyle car with Flora and Finley. Finley was also cleaned up, looking fatherly in his best plaid Western shirt, boots, and a brass bucking horse bolo tie.

Flora was wearing her mother's wedding dress, a full-length gown of white linen and Irish lace. It had long sleeves with pearl buttons up the wrist, a fitted bodice, and Florentine neckline. Her mother's pearls graced her neck, and she wore her mother's satin shoes on her feet.

Her golden hair was gathered at the back of her head in an ornate silver barrette and fell to her shoulders in ringlets. A beautiful lace veil covered her face and fell halfway down her back.

At the instructions of Moose and Izabella, the children had gathered small pine boughs and spread them along Flora's path. Rose, Caroline, and Deborah were carrying baskets filled with flower blossoms, which they would scatter over the pine boughs in front of Flora and Finley. The girls waited by Louise at the corral gate. Caroline was holding a bridal bouquet of wildflowers for Flora.

When Josif saw Flora and Finley get out of the car and into position, he nodded to his fellow musicians. Violin, guitar, and clarinet began the processional song, the *Bridal Chorus* by Richard Wagner, also known as *Here Comes the Bride*.

The boys on horseback forming the aisle raised pine boughs and held them out to form an archway over the path to the altar.

Caroline handed Flora her bouquet. The girls preceded Flora and her father, scattering the colorful blossoms all the way to the minister, then stepped to the side. Louise held the bouquet as Flora took her place beside Fritz. Finley moved to the side next to his sons.

The preacher prayed and said the words. Fritz and Flora made their vows, and Moose held out the open ring box. Fritz took the ring and slid it onto Flora's finger. Then he gently lifted the veil and folded it back over her head. Flora smiled up at him. Fritz put an

BLACK HILLS GOLD

arm behind her back and cupped her cheek with his hand. Her arms were around his waist.

He leaned down and kissed her with a slow, soft kiss, tender and loving. Flora's knees almost buckled.

Sighs from the women.

"I'm pleased to introduce Mr. and Mrs. Fritz Wagner," the preacher said.

Guns fired, people cheered, and Fritz and Flora left the corral to the lively strains of *Happy Days Are Here Again*.

People left the stands and crowded around the couple, laughing, congratulating, and slapping Fritz on the back.

Flora turned her back to the crowd; unmarried girls and women crowded behind her. She flung her bouquet back over her head. A blushing Phoebe Greco caught it and looked for Fred Doyle in the crowd. She blushed even more when she saw he was looking at her.

* * *

As soon as the vows were ended, Slim had ridden to the barn. He returned with a blue roan horse trailing behind Diablo on a lead. It had a black mane and tail, was low-slung at the hips, angular and long. Slim rode up to Flora, dismounted, and handed her the reins.

"Here's that Nokota you've always wanted," he said.

Flora was stunned. "You actually did it! You got a Nokota!"

"Well, your pa an' I did," Slim said. "It pays to have friends in North Dakota."

The Nokota was a native wild horse which had bred with Spanish horses over the years. They had a shuffling gait known as the *Indian shuffle* and were famous for their endurance. There had been a movement to remove them from the more controlled horse gene pool, and many had been slaughtered. The only remaining herds had been isolated in the North Dakota Badlands when the Theodore Roosevelt National Park was formed, thus saving the breed. An unsubstantiated rumor had it that the remaining horses were from Sitting Bull's herd.

Flora stroked the horse's neck, looking at it fondly. "Meet Chief," she said.

CHIEF ~ A NOKOTA HORSE

* * *

To preserve Flora's satin shoes, Fred drove her to the picnic table. It was crowded with casseroles, breads, canned fruits, and vegetables, platters of slow-cooked beef, mounds of fried chicken, sausages, fried potatoes, and beans.

The three-tier wedding cake took center stage. It had pink rosebuds spaced around the bottom two layers and a beautiful open rose on the top. Delicate green leaves framed each flower and silver dew drops were lightly scattered over all.

David took a picture with the wedding couple behind it. Then another of the wedding couple feeding each other a first bite of cake. Flora sliced the cake and the women passed plates around.

Bottles of whiskey appeared, along with glasses and cups for toasting and were also circulated. Finley raised his glass, silencing the crowd. "Let's have some toasts," he said. "I'll start." Finley turned to face Flora and Fritz.

"Flora, honey, I couldn't be prouder of ya, and I know your mama felt the same way. You've grown into a fine woman and you're marryin' a fine man. We're gonna miss you terrible around here, but know you'll be comin' back to visit, bringin' my grandchildren to show 'em their roots. Fritz, I can see you'll take good care a Flora and give her a good life. I wish you both a long and happy marriage."

The crowd cheered and each took a drink.

Moose next raised his glass and made the toast Fritz had suggested: "I wish the bride and groom many long years of wedded bliss and happiness, as many children as they want, and the money to raise them."

Moose's toast was met with cheers and laughter, followed by many more toasts and drinks for good luck and happiness.

* * *

The wedding feast was a relaxed, happy affair. The rodeo was over and had been its usual success. Bottles were being passed, sustaining the happy mood. As shadows lengthened, women packed up their food and stowed it in their vehicles.

On an outer table were wedding presents. Lines of jewel-toned jams and jellies, jars of special pickles, and chunky preserves were at one end. The rest of the table was stacked with towels, bedding, braided rag rugs, crocheted afghans, and other homemade things a new couple would need to get started out.

Frank gathered up Flora's wedding gifts and took them to the ranch house. Josif, Pete, and the boys collected their instruments and headed to the barn loft. Happy couples were already walking up the ramp to the loft where the dancing would happen. Bales of hay and straw were stacked around the edges of the floor for seating. A table near the musicians held a punch bowl and cups. The punch was of canned juices and a bottled carbonated lemon drink. Finley had put out two bottles of whiskey and Josif contributed a jar of *tuica* for addition to the punch or for straight sipping.

Finley joined the musicians and quieted the crowd. "We're gonna start with some square dancin', then we'll have some waltzin' and two-steppin'. Ev-erone grab a partner and git out on the floor." Josif began the melody on his violin and Pete sang the words. Pete played his guitar and Daniel his clarinet.

"*Grab your partner and circle round,*" Finley called out. "*Now all stop, and right and left grand, when you meet your partner, do-si-do, then all join hands and circle all the way round.*"

The dancers laughed and the spectators clapped and tapped their feet in time. The children who'd been riding together formed into their own squares and danced, the locals instructing the newcomers.

Several square dances later, the musicians changed to

waltzes. All the children were dancing but Deborah. She sat in a dark area with her head down, still mortified at spilling her drink on Slim. She felt stupid and an outsider.

As she stared at the floor, a pair of black men's boots approached and stopped in front of her. She looked up. It was Slim. Deborah blushed and blurted out her apology. "I'm so sorry I spilled on you, Mr. Slim. I didn't mean to do that. I hope it didn't make your ride harder." Tears were in her eyes.

Slim looked down at the little girl who reminded him of a younger Flora. "You didn't hurt my ride any. I was so blame hot, it helped me cool down and focus. I may have to get someone to pour something down my back for my future rides. It'll be my secret trick."

They both laughed, and Deborah fell more deeply in love.

"And you can call me Slim. Finley Doyle's the only *mister* around here."

Deborah smiled, "Okay, Slim," she said.

"They're playin' *The Tennessee Waltz*, one a my favorites. May I have the pleasure of this dance with you?" Slim asked.

Deborah was beyond thrilled as well as scared. Slim was so tall, how could she possibly dance with him and not look ridiculous? Plus, she didn't know how to dance.

"I would like to dance with you," Deborah said, "but I don't know how, and you're so tall."

"Well, there's an easy fix for that," Slim said. "I'll dance with you like I did with Flora when she was your size. You just get up on my boots and I'll take you for a ride. You get extra points if you stay on for the whole dance."

They laughed again and got Deborah positioned on Slim's boots. He took her left hand in his right and put his left hand on her shoulder. Deborah hung onto Slim's right thumb and left forearm. The two moved smoothly onto the floor.

Couples moved aside for Slim and Deborah. Eyes softened and smiled. Rebecca realized that her daughter had also been changed by this Wyoming trip. She was having her first crush and it would not soon be forgotten.

* * *

The dancing continued for several more hours. Around 11:00PM, Flora and Fritz said their good byes and headed for Flora's hidden cabin. They planned to leave early in the morning for their trip to Yellowstone Park, a distance of about four hundred miles.

The Epsteins and Dacias would also be leaving in the morning. Their trip back to the farm would be about five hundred miles. They'd be spending a night on the road.

No one was eager to go home. Their four-day trip had flown by. It had been a non-stop adventure full of new experiences and personal growth. They were just getting used to it, and now it was time to leave.

* * *

During the good byes the next morning, sincere invitations were given by both groups to return to the ranch and to come visit South Dakota and even New York. Slim assured them that if he ever found himself in New York, he'd visit the Epsteins first thing.

Finley and his sons agreed. Finley also assured them that Flora and Fritz would be returning to the ranch fairly regularly to visit and maybe even help with the horse racing circuit later in the summer. Any of the others were always welcome. And they shouldn't forget that the Lucky D had a rodeo every Fourth of July.

David reminded Slim and the Doyles that'd he'd be writing articles for the *Times* about his trip to Wyoming. Remembering his assurances to Slim that he wouldn't write anything the ranchers didn't approve of, David suggested that he call the ranch and read his articles before publishing them. Any objections would be discussed, and a compromise found.

Slim and Finley agreed, although they felt sure David wouldn't disappoint them. David also informed them they'd be receiving a lifetime subscription to the Sunday edition of *The New York Times*. David's articles and photos would be in the paper.

Finley made a point of saying a special good bye to Rebecca. "We hate to see you go," he said. "We can always use a good hand around here."

Rebecca smiled, trying not to cry again.

"You did good, gal," Finley said, speaking to her like a father. "You grew up in about two seconds flat. You've got good instincts. We shore hope you'll come back again."

Rebecca lost her battle with self-control. Tears welled up and she dabbed her eyes with her hankie. "Thank you so much for everything. This time at your ranch and with your friends and family has been a highlight of my life. I'll never forget it, or any of you."

Finley blew his nose and he and Rebecca hugged good bye.

With clenched jaws and fixed eyes, David and Slim shook hands and nodded to each other. David knew if he said anything, he'd cry and Slim would leave. They held the handshake a little long and their eyes softened. "Don't be a stranger," Slim said.

"You either," David said. "You'll always be welcome."

Deborah had been staring at Slim during the good byes. He was the most handsome and manly man she had ever seen. And so kind. She wanted to remember him forever.

Slim was aware of Deborah's fascination with him. He had frequently seen her staring at him She so much reminded him of Flora as a girl, the closest to having a daughter he'd ever come. If anyone would make him lose his cowboy self-control, it was her. But Slim had prepared for his awkwardness. He pulled his hand from behind his back with a cold bottle of pop in it. He smiled at Deborah as he handed it to her, then winked.

Deborah winked back and kept herself from running to him and hugging him. They shook hands.

The cars were already packed. They had been told to take their borrowed outfits with them, as they had no other clothing. Rebecca was thrilled to take the fringed jacket.

The Dacias and Epsteins got in their cars and slowly headed out the Doyle road. The children had said good bye to their friends at breakfast. Some cowboys would stay to help clean up, but most were also heading home today. Rose had said good bye to Billy Cooper during the dancing the night before. They had both had their first kiss behind a pile of hay bales.

* * *

So much in four days. The travelers' minds and emotions were overwhelmed. Each sank into a private reverie as the cars headed east, back to the farms in South Dakota and beyond.

This trip had turned out so much differently than any had anticipated. They had all changed, some profoundly. Now they needed to get used to their new selves, to feel comfortable in their new skins.

Izabella's mind moved to her concerns about August and Marie. They were in trouble. Hopefully it would work out, but there were no guarantees.

Trixie and Floyd Delaney were *strigoi* in the making. Evil beings who tried to steal the life and vitality of others.

She would see about that.

CHAPTER TWENTY-ONE
The Reckoning

The travelers made good time and spent Thursday night in a hotel in White Lake. They would be back to the farm Friday afternoon. The race was scheduled for sometime Saturday.

August said he'd been drugged and framed. Izabella believed him, but that didn't change the possible tragic consequences if Marie and Sky lost the race. Izabella had seen Trixie and Floyd in action at the Corn Palace. They were immoral. Even if Marie won the race, these people should be stopped. Izabella began work on a plan involving David Epstein.

* * *

After going to their farm upon arrival Friday mid-afternoon, Izabella called Marie. They spoke in Romanian, their assurance of privacy on a party line. There had been no further contact from the Delaneys. As far as she knew, the race was still on for sometime Saturday.

Grandma Wagner was expecting everyone for dinner, but they should come over whenever they were ready so they could all talk about it.

Daniel and Deborah would be staying at the Dacias again and David and Rebecca at the Wagners with Mrs. Epstein. The children greeted Uncle Jon and Aunt Magda, then went to see Peter and Paul.

"We will save stories for Wagners," Josif said to his aunt and uncle. "Is too much to tell more than once."

"This should be good," Uncle Jon said, grabbing a jar

of *tuica* to take along.

"Yes, I am curious about your trip," Aunt Magda said. "You all look different. Especially you, Rebecca. You are a different woman."

"It shows so easily?" Rebecca asked. "I haven't even said a word."

"It shines from you. You have become confident and strong and something else." Magda smiled at her. "I look forward to this story."

The Dacias took care of the animals and their afternoon chores. Then all piled in the two cars and headed for the Wagners.

* * *

Mrs. Epstein also immediately saw the change in Rebecca. Her son, David, was changed as well. In fact, all the Wyoming travelers appeared more confident. She noted the fading black eyes on David, Josif, and the boys. Also, the different clothing. That was a big part of the change. They looked different, more natural. Their clothes weren't pristine, they were lived in. This was a very different look for David and Rebecca. Rebecca especially.

Gina, her mother Evalina, and Arnold were also present. A clearly pregnant Gina was happily managing several pots bubbling on the stove while aromas of roasting chicken filled the house. Mrs. Wagner poured coffee and lemonade, also setting out glasses for *tuica*.

* * *

August and Marie came in, having just ridden up on Bill and Sky. The children greeted them, then ran out to see the horses.

"Yes, you can ride' em," August called out the door.

Arnold and August brought more chairs to the large kitchen table.

"Why don't you tell us about yer adventures first, then we'll talk about the Delaneys," August said.

"Get comfortable," Josif said. "Many things happen. We can all tell the stories."

For the next hour the tale of the Wyoming adventure was told. Those who stayed home were amazed and overwhelmed by its intensity. The flood, the fire, David saving Slim, Rebecca shooting the steer, the rodeo, and everyone's participation, Slim teaching David to splice and tie the cowboy knot, Wade Dixon and the snake, Fritz's fight with Moose, the group fight and drunken cowboys, Will Rogers, the wedding and cake were all described. Tears filled Mrs. Epstein's eyes when she saw the Championship Belt Buckle and heard about Slim's tribute to her son.

"You will certainly have rich stories to write about in your articles for the *Times*," she said.

* * *

Gina announced dinner was ready and the group moved to the dining table, which Evalina had already set. David described the typical cowboy fare and how one steer had provided all the meat for the two-day rodeo. This led to discussions of life in a bunkhouse and on a ranch. Everyone described the horse they'd been assigned and its special attributes. This led to discussion of Flora's skill with horses, and that led to the Delaneys.

"We ain't heard anythin' from 'em since they came to the house last Sunday," August said. "The race is supposed to happen tomorrow. We don't know when."

"Where will you have it?" Josif asked. "Flora said by wide, deep ditch would be best. Floyd and Buster will think they have advantage, but when Sky slows, they will be in ditch. Is good plan."

"We have a road like that goes behind our east fields," August said. "We'll say there's too many cars that might go by if we use the north or west roads. Floyd shouldn't mind cuz when he sees it, he'll think it's perfect for his con.

"Marie and I can ride back there, but the rest of you should drive over."

"I hate to think the unthinkable," Mrs. Epstein said. "But what if somehow Marie and Sky don't win? Do you have a backup plan?"

"Not right off," August said. "He's not takin' Sky, I know that. But I may get a bad reputation, or even in trouble with the law stoppin' 'im. Plus, he'll prob'ly have his three lyin', cheatin', con artist *witnesses* with him. And his tramp of a wife, Trixie."

Arnold was the only person at the table unfamiliar with the Delaneys. The body language of everyone else told him all he needed to know. Eyes were narrowed, jaws and fists clenched. Even among the women. Even Evalina.

"We will all help you, August. You will not stop them alone," Josif said. "The blame will not only be on you."

"No, we will all will be happy to help," Aunt Magda agreed.

"I have another idea," Izabella said.

"What is it?" Josif asked.

"We can prove the Delaneys drug August."

All eyes were on Izabella.

"Trixie will be the one to carry the drops in her purse. If we can show she has them, we can prove August's story. David can take photograph of drops in purse. Plus, we are all witnesses."

"How will David get Trixie's purse to take picture?" Josif asked.

"I will snatch from her hand when she's not expecting it," Izabella said.

"It's a drawstring purse, Mama," Marie said. "But I'll snatch it, not you."

"No, Marie. I will do it," Izabella said in a tone Marie knew not to argue with. "I was also thinking if David take pictures of Floyd, his friends, and the cars they come in, maybe the police will know them. Maybe even him taking pictures of them will be enough to make them leave."

"That's a very good plan, Izabella," Mrs. Epstein said. "Photographic proof is hard to argue with. Just be very careful."

"Is too dangerous," Josif said. "I will do it."

"A man grabbing a woman's purse will get you arrested. A woman grabbing it will get attention, especially if I am not running away with it." Izabella was unflinching. "I will grab the purse."

"I'll be close by with my camera," David said.

"Then there's the part about gettin' my money back," August said. "I had a hunderd dollars pay and fifty dollars winnin's that disappeared while I was drugged."

"It will already be gone," Josif said.

"The only way seems to be placin' bets on the race," August said. "I heard from Mr. Bowman, Floyd's really been talkin' it up around town. 'Bout how *kind* he's bein' puttin' his old nag, Buddy, up against Sky. Sayin' he feels sorry for me cuz I got drunk and gambled away all my pay and Sky. Says he's tryin' to give me a way to get my money back by bettin' on Sky. No one knows about his brother, Buster. Got a lotta folks already puttin' money on Sky. Mr. Bowman's holdin' the bets."

"Maybe it's time to put the party line to use," Gina said. "I never saw a private conversation get around so fast as on a party line. Maybe word could get out about the bait-and-switch Floyd's got planned. I bet there'd be a lot of interest in any calls coming to August. Maybe if he got an anonymous tip about the Buddy/Buster switch. That news would fly around faster than a bug on a windmill."

Everyone laughed.

"Who should be the anonymous tipster?" Gina asked.

The diners thought and looked at each other.

"It should be a voice no one recognizes," Marie said.

"That would be me," David said. "I can try to sound like Finley."

"That would be perfect," Rebecca said. "Who wouldn't believe Finley?"

"When should you make the call?" Marie asked.

"The sooner the better to get the word around," David replied. "I could call you tonight."

"That'll be perfect." August said. "Everybody should be home then, sittin' around lookin' for somethin' to do. We'll know by how many calls we hear bein' made after the tip how well its goin'.

* * *

August and Marie left shortly after dinner. They were restless, wanting to get the betting going in their favor. When their ring of three shorts happened, August let it ring several times to get everyone's attention. Then he answered the phone.

"Hello," he said casually. August could hear breathing on the phone, and a sound like a hand moving over the phone's mouthpiece. There was a distant sound of a baby crying.

"Got a tip for ya," the voice said.

"Who's this?" August asked suspiciously.

"Not sayin'," the voice replied.

"What's the tip?"

"That horse Buddy's no nag."

"Whaddaya mean?"

"There is no *Buddy*. Real name's Buster. Real strong horse. Likes to push another horse off the track. Usually wins."

"Why're you tellin' me this? Do I know you?"

"Nope. Just hate Floyd Delaney is all. He's tryin' ta convince everbody your horse is gonna win. I wouldn't bet on that. Thought you should know what's goin' on."

"Thanks."

"Good luck."

August hung up and sat at the table with Marie, holding hands. "People were listening," he said. "I could hear 'em." They both stared at the phone. Within five seconds the phone began ringing with local numbers. August and Marie laughed, finally feeling a little hope in this awful situation.

* * *

The next day was Saturday, the supposed day of the race. When the Delaneys hadn't shown up by noon, August and Marie were hopeful they wouldn't show at all.

A stream of cars arriving at one-thirty dashed that hope. "Floyd said the race's happening at two o'clock. Where's it gonna be?" one driver August didn't recognize asked.

"Along the east road. Keep a quarter mile clear. Everybody park on the north or south road," August told him.

Marie called her family, who would call the Wagers and the Ariostos. She and August saddled up. They had only been able to scrape up fifty dollars to bet. Loss of that money as well would be disastrous.

Most of the cars parked along the road perpendicular to the part of the road where the race would end. The Dacias, Epsteins, and Ariostos also parked there.

David had his camera ready and was standing next to a determined Izabella.

As predicted, when Floyd showed up in a new dually, there was no *Buddy* inside. He'd banged up a foot on a rock while out runnin' in the field. He was unfit to race, but his brother, Buster, was available.

Buster was a brown Quarter Horse, large and muscular. He had a small, white blaze and an arrogant look.

Floyd's three accomplices were there. Chance Conroy, the smallest, mounted Buster. A line had been drawn across the road, and Sky and Buster lined up behind it. Mr. Bowman, acting as officiator, announced the race.

"This is a claim race," he said. "Whoever wins rides away with two horses. The two contestants are Sky owned by the August Wagner family, and Buster, owned by Floyd Delaney. The owner of the winning horse gets both horses. The loser gets nothing.

"Before Tor Sorgenstrom drops his hat to start the race, I'm gonna drive to the end of the track to be there to judge the winner. There's a line across the road at the finish and I'll be there. We'll settle up the bets soon's we get a winner. You can all follow the racers to the end of the course but give them plenty of room. Don't crowd 'em."

Sky was calm, waiting for the go signal. Buster was fidgeting and restless. The road was smooth, the ground hard-packed. Deep, wide ditches ran along either side of the road. Marie thought Sky was strongest on his right side, positioning him with Buster there.

Tor kept his eye on Mr. Bowman. When he saw him exit his car and take his position at the finish line, he checked the riders. When they were both looking at him, he held his arm straight out from his body, hat level to the ground. Then he dropped it.

Sky and Buster shot across the starting line. Buster immediately pushed into Sky and kept up the pressure. As long as Buster was engaged with Sky, he wasn't taking the lead. He seemed to be waiting to knock Sky into the ditch near the end of the track.

Marie was counting on that. She let Sky take the pressure and inch toward the ditch. When his feet were within inches of the drop-off and the finish was in sight, Marie gave Sky the slightest pressure with her knees. Sky slowed a bit, and Buster, now exerting his greatest pressure on Sky, flew across Sky's path and into the ditch.

Marie kicked Sky's sides with her heels and urged him on with more urgency than ever before.

Buster had lost time by being diverted into the ditch, but he hadn't lost his balance. He quickly regained his footing, chasing after Sky. But he was a few seconds too late. Sky had crossed the finish line, the winner by a head.

August rode up on Bill and dismounted. He approached Floyd. "Looks like Sky won," he said. "Looks like I gotta new horse." Chance had dismounted, and August took Buster's reins from him. He handed them to Josif.

Mr. Bowman approached, writing numbers on a pad and handing out money to those who'd bet on Sky. August and Marie's desperate fifty-dollar bet earned them the money August had lost at the Corn Palace poker game. Mr. Bowman handed August a hundred and fifty dollars.

Floyd was furious. Trixie was as well. "You lost all our money, Floyd," she accused him loudly. "You said this was a sure thing," she whined, shaking her purse at him.

Izabella took this opportunity to grab Trixie's purse. She snatched it and moved away from Trixie, pulling the purse open. As she had suspected, a bottle of chloral hydrate was one of the contents. Before Trixie could grab the purse back, David took a picture of the open purse. Besides the chloral hydrate bottle, there was a two-inch, snub-nosed revolver.

Trixie seized her open purse, knocking the contents on the ground. Izabella smashed her shoe into the bottle and ground the broken glass into the dirt. Jon kicked the revolver away.

"Why you bohunk bit...", Floyd began to say to Izabella. His insult was cut short by August's fist slamming into his mouth. Floyd was thrown backward into Trey and Lefty; his mouth bleeding, and his lip fat and red. The three charged August, and Chance joined in too. A look of sublime joy radiated from August's face.

The Dacias had never seen August fight professionally, except for Jon, Magda, and Marie on the road show the year before. As with Slim riding a bronc bareback, with August they were seeing a professional fighter who also knew his job. None of the men felt a need to help him, although Josif dearly wanted to.

Evalina and Magda pinned Trixie in place with commanding looks to prevent any mischief from her.

August handed out powerful jabs, uppercuts, hooks, and right and left crosses. If one of the attackers fell down, he'd haul him up and knock him down again. Finally, they gave up and staggered to their cars. Spectators talked about the fight and race as the defeated grifters drove off.

"I got good shots of all their faces, their licenses, and the vehicles," David said. "That truck Floyd was driving looked a bit beyond his means. One of them saw me taking the photos, so they know they can be identified."

* * *

Mrs. Wagner invited everyone over for leftovers and to discuss the day's events. The mood was much lighter now that the race was over. August had made his money back; Marie and Sky had won the race. The Delaneys were gone. Izabella had accomplished her mission, as had David.

* * *

Flora and Fritz were due back from their honeymoon in three or four days, and David and Rebecca were easily persuaded to stay at least until then. The plan was for Deborah and Daniel to spend the rest of the summer with the Dacias. Mrs. Epstein would stay with the Wagners, bringing the children home in time for school. David was due back at work and Rebecca back to managing their home.

While everyone had been in Wyoming, Mrs. Epstein and Mrs. Wagner had moved Mrs. Wagner's belongings out of the master bedroom. They had set everything up for the new heads of the farm, Fritz and Flora. The women were in the smaller bedrooms at the end of the hall. They had decided to keep out of Flora's way as she made the farmhouse hers, giving her and Fritz plenty of privacy by doing things together.

A fourth small bedroom was assigned to David and Rebecca.

What to do with Buster was discussed over dinner. He was not popular with Sky and Bill and had to be placed in a smaller pen by himself. He was a beautiful, powerful horse, but probably not a good saddle horse. He was strong-willed and had been encouraged to bully other horses.

August and Marie hoped Flora would have a solution.

* * *

No one lasted very long after dinner. All seemed drained of energy. Josif drove his and the Epstein children, and Arnold brought Jon and Magda to the Dacias. August and Marie rode home in a lighthearted mood. August had not ruined everything. In fact, he'd ended up with more than he expected.

Marie forgave him for being conned. "I don't know how you could have prevented it," she said. "They were all out to get you. I'm glad you weren't hurt and that we haven't lost Sky."

"I'm glad about that, too, and I haven't lost you," August said. "That worried me the most."

"I won't ever leave you, August," Marie said. "It may not always be easy, and there're a lot of bad people out there, but we're in this together. Forever."

August hugged Marie and kissed her. Later that night in a joyous mood of love and celebration they made a baby.

CHAPTER TWENTY-TWO
Coming and Going Home

David and Rebecca decided to remain at the Wagners until Fritz and Flora came home from their honeymoon, probably Thursday. This way they would have more time with their children. The Dacias, Epsteins, and Wagners would eat most meals together with Rebecca helping Mrs. Wagner with the cooking. They would have a real chance to slow down.

Being Sunday, thoughts of a picnic came to mind. A leisurely day at Goose Lake fit the bill. Phone calls between the Dacias, Wagners, and Ariostos set the time for around noon. Josif would drive Mrs. Wagner and Mrs. Epstein, Arnold would bring Gina and Evalina in his car, August and Marie would ride, and the rest would come in the wagon pulled by Peter and Paul. This time Rebecca gladly climbed into the wagon. She marveled at her previous reluctance.

The group had decided to have fish for their meal and only brought bread, eggs, cheese, and a sheet cake to go with them. The girls collected wood and started a fire, and the men got out their fishing equipment. The boys got a shovel and can and went into the grove for worms. Rebeca prepared a pot of coffee and set it on the edge of the grill.

The women gathered by the picnic tables while the men prepared the lines. Magda and Evalina stood next to each other with arms crossed, studying Rebecca and Marie. They had twinkles in their eyes and were smiling.

"What?" Marie asked.

"You are pregnant, Marie," Aunt Magda said quietly. "So are you, Rebecca."

Rebecca put her hand on her abdomen. "I knew it the

moment it happened," she said. "It was in Wyoming after I shot the steer. On a hillside with a view of the Tower under a shady tree. I just told David last night." She had a smile of private memories on her face.

Marie also laid her hand on her abdomen with a look of wonder. "I thought so but wasn't sure. I guess I am!"

Like cowboys to a fight, women sense and are drawn to all revelations of pregnancy. Izabella, Gina, Evalina, Mrs. Epstein, Mrs. Wagner, and the girls hurried over, and confirming the news began hugging, congratulating, praising God, and laughing.

The men joined them. August picked Marie up and swung her around, then gently set her down and kissed her. "You're gonna be a mama an' I'm gonna be a papa! I'll have to write a song about that," he said beaming.

Josif and Uncle Jon kissed Marie on the cheek. "You will give us a grandchild and make our roots here strong," Josif said proudly. He slapped August on the back. "Good boy."

Deborah and Daniel were speechless. "Really? Another one of us? Are you sure?" Daniel asked.

"Oh, Mama," Deborah said, hugging her mother, "It will be wonderful to have a baby. When will it come?"

"In about nine months, so in April sometime."

"If it's a girl, you could call her April," Deborah said.

"If it's a boy, you could call him Finley," Daniel said. "I bet he'd be real easy-going."

Rebecca and David laughed. "We have plenty of time to decide," David said.

"So you'll be due about the same time," August said to Marie. "In the spring."

"Yes, it will be a beautiful time for a baby to be born."

* * *

"I'm getting hungry," Uncle Jon said. "I think is time to catch fish."

David took a pole and a worm. He held the hook firmly and with a steady motion, heartfelt apology and thanks, slid the hook through the worm.

He dropped the baited hook in the water. Sooner than he wanted, he pulled up a catfish. David braced the slippery fish against his chest with one hand, gently working the hook out of its mouth with the other. He was pleased he didn't cause any bleeding. He slid the whiskered fish into the bucket of lake water with the others.

Soon enough fish had been caught for a meal for all. The men took the buckets of fish and lake water to the shore by the grove. David had decided he had to kill his fish. He couldn't sit back and ask others to do what was necessary to feed him. He had to kill this fish and eat it, offer it to others.

"What's the kindest way to kill a fish?" he asked Jon.

"Quickly," was the response. "With hard blow between eyes. If you are soft, you only hurt it. Must be hard and fast. Like breaking walnut with hammer. Use a rock."

David watched Jon dispatch a crappie and did the same to his fish. The open mouth closed and the gills ceased their frantic straining for water. It had been quick; the fish was dead.

Next he watched Jon clean the fish and did the same. He produced two beautiful fillets, which he added to a growing pile on a platter. These would be breaded, seasoned, and fried. Gina was already melting lard in the giant frying pan.

David didn't know which fried fillet was his, but he felt emotional responsibility for all of them. Humans ate everything. They killed whatever they wanted, wherever they lived. But did that make them bad, or just hungry? Hungry, David decided. But compassion should be part of the process. Respect for the life being taken and eaten. He gave thanks to all the fish for their lives.

Looking around at the large group eating together, David experienced a tribal feeling. A group of people whose lives were intertwined sharing in an act of survival, eating food they had caught and prepared together. Everyone with a job and role in the process. Their lives continuing on the backs of others who were their food source. And their food source also ate others, etc. It was the way of things. It could not be otherwise. He felt a peacefulness and self-forgiveness. It was life.

* * *

Three days passed gently but quickly. There was no schedule except around meals and chores; with the added help they were done quickly.

Marie invited the Epsteins to her new home only a few miles away from her family. August and Marie's house had been a gift from the Wagners. A quarter section with house, barn, tools, horses, a car, and everything to run a farm.

The Gliddens had lived there and recently sold out to move to an old folks' home. They couldn't keep up with farming anymore and wanted to sell the whole outfit. August and Marie had planned their wedding date based on when the Gliddens would move, so there could be a smooth transition between owners and care of the animals and crops.

They had allowed two extra weeks for August to live there alone, painting and making other repairs. Josif and Fritz had helped.

The house consisted of the original two-story structure

on a river rock foundation and an addition of two rooms and an enclosed front porch built ten years later. There were two bedrooms, kitchen, sitting room, laundry room, large pantry, and even an indoor bathroom on a septic system.

August and Marie Wagner's Home

There was a small cold storage room in the basement under the old house. The rest was storage for spare canning jars and other supplies. Two benches, jugs of water, and a stack of blankets outfitted it as a storm cellar. In case of a tornado, this was the place to go.

They also had a barn, hen house, other outbuildings, and a 1927 Ford Model A car. A windmill and water tank stood by the barn. There was a corral and pasture off the south end of the barn. An old cottonwood tree stood behind the house. There were tall red hollyhocks and pink peonies along the front.

The farm also came with a few pigs, cows, and chickens. There was an adjoining quarter section also for sale, which August hoped to be able to buy. It was perfect for August and Marie and located near babysitting family.

Marie served iced tea and cookies to her guests. Deborah and Daniel soon finished and asked to go visit Sky and Bill. David accompanied them.

When alone, Rebecca smiled fondly at Marie. "You and I will be going through our pregnancies at the same time," she said. "You will have your mother for help and advice, but we will also share the growth of our babies through their adulthood. I feel that is a special connection."

"Yes," Marie said. "They'll be like twins from different mothers."

Rebecca laughed. "That will be fun. Please know that you and August are always welcome in our home in New York. Although, I also think the Epstein family will be traveling west to South Dakota and maybe even Wyoming again."

"It looks that way," Marie said, smiling at her new friend.

* * *

Fritz and Flora arrived at the farm late Thursday afternoon. They'd had a wonderful honeymoon at Yellowstone Park and were pleased to see the Epsteins were still at the farm. They arrived in two trucks, the Wagners', and a dually from the Lucky D. Inside the dually were Aces High, Sundance, Honey, and Chief. They hadn't enjoyed the close ride and were happy to be let into the pasture, running and kicking up their heels.

Grandma Wagner called the other families, telling them of Fritz and Flora's return and inviting them to dinner. The men helped unload the truck and carry Flora's belongings inside. Grandma Wagner hugged her, welcoming Flora to her new home.

When dinner was served, she showed Flora to the seat which had been hers at one end of the table. Fritz was at the other.

August and Marie described the horse race and Sky's victory. "We kept Sky and got our money back, but now we got Buster. Bill and Sky don't like him, and I don't think he'll make much of a ridin' horse. Any ideas what we should do with 'im?" August asked.

"Let me ride 'im a little. If he doesn't act right, we'll take 'im back to Wyoming. See if Slim can't put some manners on 'im. He won't be good around Aces High," Flora warned. "Two big stubborn horses like that are bound to fight. At the Lucky D, there'll be enough others just like him that he won't be able to push around."

"You're welcome to him," August said. "He's all yours."

Marie told of Izabella's brilliant plan and the discovery of the knockout drops, and snub-nosed revolver in Trixie's purse.

The boys related August's four against one fight, copying some of his moves.

"I wrote a song about it this morning," August said. "It's called *Get Away from My Door*. "I'll sing it for ya after dessert."

"It'll be interesting to see if those photos I took turn up anything with the police," David said. "They sure were a shifty bunch."

"Floyd Delaney and the crowd he runs with are nothin' but trouble," Flora said. "You're lucky to be rid of them."

"Don't we know it," Marie said.

* * *

After a blackberry crisp with cream and a fresh pot of coffee, August got out his guitar. "This is a happy song," he said. "After my first dealings with Floyd, I wasn't happy. I'd been conned, drugged, and robbed. Him, Trixie, and his three buddies really did a number on me. Thought they'd steal my money and Sky. This is how it turned out. "I call this song, *Get Away From my Door*.

"I just sent four men flyin',
And I'm happy as can be.
They needed a good whippin',
And I sent it C.O.D,

They thought they were really sumthin',
But they got turned around.
I beat 'em up and knocked 'em down.
They're done in this here town.

They tried to con and cheat me.
They tried to do me harm.
Now they're kinda broken,
And far away from my farm.

Be gone you connivin' bloodsuckers,
Get far away from my door.
Don't never invite me to nothin'
Don't talk to me no more.

Slither back under the rocks you came from.
Keep your cheatin' selves outta my sight.
You'll be too broke to pawn
You'll wish you weren't born
If I see you 'round here anymore.

You'll be too broke to pawn,
You'll wish you were gone
If you come 'round here anymore."

The group cheered and clapped for August and his song.

"I'm gonna see if Herman H. Henty'll play it on his show," August said. Maybe record it."

"That's a good idea," David said. "Keep new material out there all the time."

* * *

With Fritz and Flora's arrival, David and Rebecca decided to return to New York the next day. It had been an amazing and life-changing trip, but it was time to return to their normal lives. Deborah and Daniel would be staying for another month, then returning to New York with Mrs. Epstein for school.

Rebecca envied their continued opportunities to ride the horses. She was very fond of Honey.

* * *

It was hard for Deborah and Daniel to say good bye to their parents. They had never felt closer to them. They had all been tested and come out stronger. They now understood each other on a deeper level.

"We will see you both soon," Rebecca said. "You will both be bigger and stronger and full of new stories when you get back. We love you very much and hope you have a great time. Call us whenever you want, and we'll call you when we get home."

David said good bye to his friends and family and he and Rebecca drove away in their Ford.

"Is hard to see them go," Izabella lamented. "We all did so much together."

"It just means we have to do more together in future," Josif said.

CHAPTER TWENTY-THREE
"Well, All I Know is Just..."

When David got home, he went to work on his assignment: articles about Wyoming and South Dakota. These would be on a personal level, focusing on the Black Hills around Devils Tower and Custer State Park. Highlights in his articles would be the Fourth of July Rodeo and Fritz's and Flora's wedding. The flood, fire, and death of Wade Wilcox were unexpected golden copy.

* * *

David told a humorous account of camping in the Badlands, while also praising its stark beauty and wind-sculpted loneliness.

* * *

He wrote another about his face-to-face photo shoot with a bison, including the closeup with the flashbulb.

* * *

A before-photo and after-description of their campsite on the Belle Fourche River attested to the power of nature. It was not to be taken for granted. Those who lived intimately with raw nature respected her and learned her ways. Those who didn't could get washed away in a flood.

* * *

The hidden trouble with soft grasses for bedding and the unexpected benefits of white clay was another humorous submission.

* * *

The truth of the saying *Clothes Make the Man (or Woman)* was a confession and article of ironic good luck.

* * *

Fire and Good Fortune was a modest account of David's role in the fire. It also gave mention and praise to the work of the CCC boys and their fire-fighting courage and dedication.

* * *

What's a Mother to Do? told of Rebecca's courage and decisive action. *In fact, the owner of the Lucky D said Rebecca would be the only one of us he'd be willing to hire,* David wrote. *The incident with the steer was a very immediate example of how things can go wrong in an instant. One cannot take life for granted in the wild, or even on a ranch. One must be vigilant and ready to do the necessary without hesitation.*

* * *

Evening in the Bunkhouse told of storytelling, singing, poker, drinking, and spending an amiable evening with the men of the ranch.

* * *

Articles on each of the rodeo events were very popular, especially since Madison Square Garden hosted

252

some of the biggest rodeos in the country. David's photos were up close and personal and wildly popular. David sent extra copies of the edition with the rodeo photos to the Doyles, and many of the pictures ended up in frames on mantles in the area.

* * *

A *Cowgirl Gets Married* described Flora's wedding in a most respectful and romantic fashion. Fritz in his preacher coat next to Flora in her Irish lace wedding dress behind the three-tier wedding cake had readers' imaginations in full swing. Mention that Fritz was a *Dakota Six* member made him irresistible.

* * *

The *Dance in the Barn Loft* recounting marked a spike in inquiries about square dancing in dance studios around the city.

* * *

The story of Wade Wilcox was told without naming names or mentioning his previous attack on Flora. The story of a cowboy who'd done wrong and got caught in his own trap was told in terms of the reflectiveness and religious response of the rodeo-goers. He'd attempted murder but had died himself. God's hand was present. It was just.

* * *

Finally, David got to cowboy truths. His last article was titled, *A Great American Cowboy*. It was another very personal story:

253

"When given this assignment to go to Wyoming and mingle with cowboys, attend a rodeo, and get to know them, I have to admit I felt apprehensive. How was a New Yorker with city clothes and ways, and a pacifist to boot, ever going to fit in? How would I be able to talk to cowboys when we had so little in common in our daily lives? I feared I'd be a ridiculed outsider, never accepted as a contributor of anything worthwhile in a cowboy's world.

A fortunate string of misfortunes helped enormously. Losing our clothes in the flash flood and the kindness and generosity of the local ranchers put my family and myself in ranch clothing. We didn't stand out in the crowd like cardinals amongst blue jays.

A friend of mine at the Times, Will Rogers, also helped with absolutely true advice: 'if you want to get out of Wyoming alive, you'd better know how to rope and ride.' These two skills, along with being a good shot, are essential for a cowboy to master. Without them one is of no use in the business of a ranch.

With Will's instruction and hours of roping practice on the roof, I became proficient. Not cowboy good, as in being able to rope a moving animal of whatever size and distance, but good enough. That skill allowed me to rope the burning snag and open an escape for a trapped bull, horse, and rider.

I didn't do anything especially heroic. I was only able to do what any average cowboy must be prepared to do, use his skills to ensure his life and the life of his fellows in dangerous situations.

* * *

That is the first cowboy truth I understood. Survival is serious business in Wyoming. If you can't pull your own weight, you're weighing someone else down. If you make an effort and give it your all, you gain respect. And respect from a cowboy is not given lightly; it is a thing to work for and treasure.

Learning to ride western style was a challenge in New York, and I mostly just accomplished being around horses. Instruction from our South Dakotan friends on their horses helped a lot and being assigned a horse to care for while on the ranch made us all eager riders.

* * *

Another cowboy truth is the partnership between cowboy and horse. The two work together as a unit. Horses are broke and trained to do their jobs. A cowboy trains his horse and gains a partner who knows what's expected of him and performs consistently.

Cowboy and horse take care of each other. Horses are ridden hard, putting in long days, but the cowboy knows his horse like himself, and cares for it religiously.

The easy union of cowboy and horse acting as one make a being of formidable ability. Fast and powerful, predictable and inventive, skilled with rope, pistol and rifle, both at one with their work. The two together, a thing of beauty, efficiency, and awe.

* * *

Rodeos were a real learning experience. They are not purely entertainment. They showcase the skill and courage needed in cowboying. Wild horses must be broke, steers and calves roped, castrated, and branded, angry and aggressive bulls controlled, roping and riding perfected to precision.

In case you think a cowboy might weary of such tasks, think again. Cowboys love to pit themselves against the strength and orneriness of the animals they work with. They willingly *lower themselves onto a one-ton bull, intending to ride him for eight seconds, holding on with only one hand while the bull bucks high and snorts, trying to throw the rider to the ground for trampling.*

They endure bone-shaking rides on wild-eyed horses because that is part of their job, and they take great pride in their skill. You aren't considered a man in Wyoming if you can't cowboy, and that is another truth.

Rodeoing shows what a man's made of: his skill, courage, grit, strength, and understanding of animals. Nothing is hidden when out in the ring, from how you pick yourself up after being thrown, to how fast and to what lengths you'll go to save another cowboy in trouble. You wear your integrity on your skin in every action.

And like the rock-hard, determined, and proud men they are, they walk their talk. Rodeos let them go full out and are another of their truths.

* * *

Now I'll tell you about a man I consider a great cowboy and a true friend. His name is Slim Stanton, the foreman of the Lucky D Ranch. Slim and I shared prejudgements of each other. Basically, he had no use for me, and I was intimidated by him.

We could have easily avoided each other for the entire event, but the fire threw us together. I roped a burning snag, clearing an escape route for him and the bull he was herding.

He never forgot that. Not my heroism, as there was none; nor my roping expertise, which was quite basic. It was that I'd made an effort to learn basic cowboying and was there when needed. I'd shown a part of myself he respected.

And with that respect he took me under his wing. He taught me to splice a rope and tie a cowboy or honda knot.

These skills allow a man to turn a rope into a lasso. A rope that can now catch and restrain an animal and many other useful things. A man has a better chance of survival with a working rope. He offered this priceless gift only because I'd done something he respected.

He said he wanted me to be able to identify a real cowboy. If a fella can't splice a rope and tie a cowboy knot, he's a pretend cowboy. Nothing.

Slim will not appreciate me sharing this, but he and other cowboys have tender hearts.

There is a quote by Frances de Sales which I think applies:

'Nothing is so strong as gentleness; Nothing is so gentle as real strength.'

It can take some doing to get to that gentle spot. There's a lot of grit and hardness to find your way through. But once you find it, you find the strength of a cowboy, and it is gentle and from the heart.

Perhaps they need their gentle hearts to sooth their spirits against the hard deeds they must do as ranchers. A job handling matters from birth to death. Castrating and branding, breaking horses, culling, and dealing with wounded or sick animals. They do it all and know life and death intimately. There are times when tenderness has no place; hard reality must prevail, and the cowboy is the one who deals it out.

Slim would never be a pacifist, but he respected my determination to be one. He judged my qualities, not labels associated with prejudicial slurs. He had the integrity to admit he was wrong and look me in the eye to do it. A rare quality anywhere.

But this man of honor did more. After the rodeo and presentation of prizes, he made a speech and a sacrifice. Slim admitted his unflattering expectations of me and declared me a cowboy at heart. He said he also wanted any cowboys lost in New York to know that I could be trusted as a cowboy, even if wearing a suit. To ensure that and as a token of our friendship, he gave me his Championship Bronc Riding belt buckle, which I will always wear and treasure.

What Slim appreciated most in me was standing up for who I was and my effort to fit in. Wyoming was the first state to enforce equality by allowing women the vote, and that defines the cowboy spirit. The only thing that matters is that you show the world what you're made of. The rest is window dressing.

CHAPTER TWENTY-FOUR
Splicing Ends

With twinkling eyes, Magda and Evalina agreed that Flora was also pregnant.

"I thought so," Flora said. "The night we spent near Old Faithful." The room erupted in laughter.

"We're gonna have cousins!" August said, slapping Fritz on the back.

"That will make four babies in same year," Izabella said. "Three in this neighborhood. Will be a happy time."

Josif and Jon got out *tuica* for toasting.

* * *

Fritz and Flora drove Buster back to the Lucky D for training. He would soon be earning an honest living.

It was hard to say who was happier about Flora's pregnancy, Finley or Slim. They got out whiskey for toasting.

Old Faithful became an addition to Fritz and Flora's wedding story. Flora thought she'd start a scrapbook and put her Old Faithful postcard in it. It would always make her laugh.

Moose had a new nickname for Fritz.

* * *

David had developed all his photos from the trip. The ones of the Delaneys and friends had been submitted to the police around Sioux Falls, Rapid City, and Cheyenne. Floyd's dually truck was stolen. Chance, Trey, and Lefty's cars were wearing stolen plates. All of them, including Trixie, had a record.

They'd be out of business for a while.

* * *

Louise La Voi sent Rebecca a fringed jacket made from the hide of the steer she'd shot. It was yellow, soft, and supple, smelling nostalgically of leather. Finley had traded a calf for it.

Louise also told Rebecca to keep the jacket she'd worn at the ranch. It was old and worn, no need to return it. Rebecca thought she might keep the old jacket and give Deborah the new one to grow into. The old one had been part of her identity when she changed.

* * *

As promised, David had consulted with Finley and Slim about the articles he wrote. He had called on Tuesday nights and read the articles over the phone. They had consistently given their approval, although Slim objected to the tender-hearted part. Finley overrode him. They toasted David several times for every article.

* * *

Slim had a new rattlesnake hat band.

* * *

Fred and Frank Doyle were engaged to Phoebe and Penelope Greco. A double wedding was being planned for August. More babies were predicted.

* * *

The Dacia and Epstein children rode horses and played happily the rest of the summer.

* * *

Marie and Flora rode Sky and Sundance over to Gina's daily. They would bring Honey, and the three would take long rides, which would settle their stomachs and babies down.

* * *

Get Away from My Door was recorded, and with publicity getting out about the Delaney con, there was a jump in sales. Agent Bert Hanson was finding August frequent work and appearing trustworthy.

* * *

Rebecca couldn't explain the changes in herself to her friends. Most times she didn't try. They had no frame of reference to even begin to understand.

She kept her thoughts to herself and remembered Wyoming. She knew she would have to go back.

Be sure to check www.DannWorks.com
for links to music and articles related to
the *Good Neighbors Series*.

Biography

Janet Dann . is the author of *Debts and Vengeance*, the third volume in the *The Good Neighbors series*. Janet was born in upstate New York, and spent many summer vacations with her family visiting their relatives back on the farm in southeastern South Dakota. She also spent a year in VISTA in north central South Dakota, on the Standing Rock Sioux Reservation. She has a BA in Anthropology from NYU, and a BS in Nursing from Alaska Methodist University. She is currently retired and with her husband, traveled the country for nine years in an RV. They are now living on San Juan Island in Washington. Her current interests are Astrology, writing and drawing.

Be sure to check www.DannWorks.com
for links to music and articles related to
the *Good Neighbors Series*.